Gothic Heat

'You have beautiful hands,' she purred, 'very skilful.' Still holding him, she sat up, letting the sheet fall to reveal her breasts and belly. 'Would you like to touch me now?' She drew his hand to her breast, closing it around the soft resilient orb and pressing his fingers down over a nipple that was erect and puckered. As his grip tightened reflexively, a man's natural response to a lush breast against his hand, she made a low sound in her throat and tipped her head back, closing her eyes and moaning and pressing herself more closely into his hold.

By the same author:

Continuum
Entertaining Mr Stone
Gemini Heat
Gothic Blue
Hotbed
Lust Bites
Magic and Desire
Shadowplay
Suite Seventeen
The Devil Inside
The Stranger
The Tutor

Gothic Heat
Portia Da Costa

BL

Black Lace books contain sexual fantasies.
In real life, always practise safe sex.

First published in 2008 by
Black Lace
Thames Wharf Studios
Rainville Rd
London W6 9HA

A catalogue record for this book is available from the British Library.

www.black-lace-books.com

Typeset by SetSystems, Saffron Walden, Essex
Printed and bound in Great Britain by CPI Bookmarque, Croydon, CR0 4TD

Distributed in the USA by Macmillan, 175 Fifth Avenue, New York, NY 10010, USA

ISBN 978 0 352 34170 9

The Random House Group Limited supports The Forest Stewardship Council (FSC),
the leading international forest certification organisation. All our titles that are
printed on Greenpeace approved FSC certified paper carry the FSC logo.
Our paper procurement policy can be found at www.rbooks.co.uk/environment

1 3 5 7 9 10 8 6 4 2

This one is for 'himself'

Contents

Introduction

Previously, in *Gothic Blue* ...

At an archduke's reception, a handsome young nobleman falls under the spell of a malevolent but irresistible sorceress. Two hundred years later, Belinda Seward also falls prey to sensual forces she can neither understand nor control.

Stranded by a thunderstorm at a remote Gothic priory, Belinda and her boyfriend are drawn into an enclosed world of luxurious decadence and sexual alchemy. Their host is the courteous but melancholic André Von Kastel, a beautiful aristocrat who mourns his lost love. André has plans for Belinda, plans which take her into the realms of obsessive love and the erotic paranormal.

Paula Beckett is Belinda's friend. A chance encounter with evil, in the garden of a sleepy English pub, has dangerous and unforeseen consequences. Allying herself with an enigmatic lover who may or may not be her friend, Paula too is drawn to the mysterious Sedgewick Priory and the web of dark, sensual magic that surrounds it.

Gothic Heat is her story ...

1 Whose Dream Is It Anyway?

Am I dreaming?

Yes, you are, said the low, seductive voice inside her head. *But it's my dream, bitch, so just enjoy it and don't you dare try to wake up or you'll regret it.*

Adrift on the edge of sleep, Paula Beckett surrendered. What would it be tonight? Heaven? Or hell? Or just a whole lot of sex, like the last time?

The night was sultry. A high, yellow moon rode above the park at Sedgewick Priory and the scent of lush summer roses hung in the muggy heat.

The sorceress smiled as she stood naked at the open window of her boudoir, the moisture of her recent bath still glistening on her skin like tiny jewels.

All was well. She had everything she wanted. At last.

Somewhere out in the fragrant green shadows, a night bird called, and a moment later came the sharp cry of a fox or some hunting animal signalling for its pack. The sorceress felt a deep bond with these predators that roamed the copses and the hedgerows, seeking prey. She too was a hunter to the bone.

Somewhere in the great priory, a clock chimed, reminding her that the time of her tryst was approaching. Turning from the window, she continued with her toilette.

The bedroom itself was just as luxurious as she'd imagined, and the tall pier glass presented a more than satisfactory reflection. Her borrowed body was somewhat different to the one she'd been born with all those years ago, but even so it pleased her. The breasts were full, the waist narrow and the hips generously flaring. She shook her head, and her hair, already black again, rippled in a silky tumble to her shoulders. At her crotch, it was thick and flossy too, a moist grove to tempt even the most resistant of lovers.

Turning this way and that, she perused her belly, admiring the glowing sigil of her power, the ultimate symbol of her triumph over those who would vanquish her, including the very man she awaited. Visible now, the iridescent black design was almost three dimensional on her belly. It hugged the soft, rounded curve like a tattoo, just beneath the insolent dink of her navel. Touching it fondly, she savoured the heat that emanated from the intricate motif, then idly moved on, anticipating the night ahead. She slipped her hand between her legs, seeking her clit and the valley of her sex. She was wet and slippery, the fluid abundant on her fingers as she delicately teased herself.

Mmmm, that was so good. And soon other fingers would be playing there. Should she pre-empt the pleasures ahead, or stave them off to increase their intensity? She chose the latter, knowing her lover would soon put in an appearance.

Selecting a vial of oil from several on the dressing table, she slowly and thoroughly began to anoint her body. The golden viscous fluid was laced with a heady blend of aphrodisiac spices of her own concoction, designed to sensitise her skin and increase her sexual pleasure. The ingredients were rich yet subtle and devilishly effective, inducing a delicious glow of heat without causing irritation. Her red mouth curled cruelly as she remembered, centuries ago, testing the quantities on her maids. There had been tears and moans. Weeping at the fire of too much spice. Wails of unquenchable lust as their bodies burnt with a different heat, twisting and writhing with the need to be pleasured. It had amused her to watch them jiggle and twist their thighs as they knelt down to lick her sex, one after the other, satisfying her while their own desires went unanswered. Afterwards, she'd permitted the girl who'd given her the most orgasms to run naked to the stables, where she'd been serviced repeatedly by a dozen grooms in a wild orgy.

But tonight's oil had precisely the right proportions. And the sorceress's low moans were of delight as she smoothed it lightly across her skin.

Flickers of heat drifted over her limbs, her belly, her thighs, sinking in below the surface and gently glowing. Tipping a generous quantity of the oil into her hands, she parted her thighs and assumed a lewd, splay-legged stance, then sluiced the golden fluid over her vulva.

'Ah! Ah! Ah!'

Oh, the delicious, warming surge of sensitivity. Her hips swirled of their own accord as the spice stimulated the reactive tissues of her sex. Even as she slicked on the oil, her fingertips went back on her previous decision and began the inevitable dance of masturbation.

Her thighs shook, her belly clenched, and she closed her dark eyes, imagining her lover standing before her, watching, watching.

'Soon you will enjoy this body, my lord,' she purred, flexing her thighs, dipping lower, and thrusting her pelvis to and fro.

Her pleasure mounted, the rush of blood in her veins firing the heat of the spice even higher. Her hips jerked and her sex grabbed at air, clenching in a swift, intense orgasm. Filling herself with her own fingers, she gurgled uncouthly, her voice low and animal.

Oh, but the rapture was magnificent. Every time, every climax, was unique. But soon there would be finer pleasures. And those were redolent with other deep, darker emotions than that of simple physical satisfaction. As she withdrew her fingers from her crotch, the sorceress's smile was triumphant with anticipation.

A firm, forceful tread in the corridor announced the arrival she'd awaited for so long.

Her fingers still fragrant with the oil and her own heavy musk, she snatched up a richly embroidered wrap from the bed and flung it around her. Clutched low against her breasts, it enhanced their creamy curves, the jewel-dark reds and purples of the sensuous fabric contrasting dramatically with the creamy pallor of her skin. The edges of the luxurious robe barely met at the front, offering shadowed hints of her thighs and crotch.

There was barely time to strike a pose before the bedroom door was flung open, only the sheer weight of the great slab of oak preventing it from crashing off its hinges. She'd been expecting a knock, but clearly he was in no mood for the niceties of polite behaviour. Once upon a time he'd been a courteous young man, beautiful, respectful, almost scared of her. But now he was confident with the experience of years. So many, many years.

In the doorway stood a lean masculine figure, a sight so splendid her mouth almost watered. As it was, her oiled and still trembling body lurched with subtle pleasure on seeing the man she'd wanted for so long.

'Madam.' His curt nod made his long hair swing. It was dark, with light strands of silver striating the silky fall.

So handsome. But then, he always had been. The sorceress sank momentarily in a mocking curtsey, aware that the action exhibited the midnight patch of her pubic hair for just a second.

Let him see it, she thought, feeling the curls moisten as he noted the display.

His eyes were blue. The bluest of blue, like sapphires, like a summer sky, a dazzling blend of many shades of one colour. They burnt with heat – surely desire but also hate and emotions far more complex.

He strode towards her, his blue star-strewn silk robe swishing lightly as he walked.

They stood eye to eye. He was tall but barefoot, and so was she. The fire in his eyes seemed to reach out and stroke her sex like a hand, and his nostrils flared as if taking in the odours of the oil and her arousal.

Without warning, his hand whipped out and grabbed the back of her neck, drawing her to him. Their mouths crashed together, hard, unforgiving, combative, and, though the sorceress admitted him, it wasn't a capitulation. As his tongue probed, she fought back, nipping him wickedly with her sharp teeth. He made a rough, raw sound in his throat, his hand tightening on her neck, crushing their lips even tighter together. Her jaw aching from the pressure, she laughed inside and let her tongue soften, giving ground temporarily.

The grinding kiss went on and on, primal communication flashing back and forth between their battling mouths. It was a war, a delicious mêlée, sending the heat of lust around her body, centring in her breasts and in her sex. When he suddenly released her, she could hear the thudding pulse of gathered blood.

'My lord.' She lowered her eyes but her tone was sardonic.

Long, elegant hands snatched at her robe, whirled it from around her and flung it across the room. His brilliant eyes narrowed at the sight of the sigil, his mouth pursing in a tight, bitter line. Its presence clearly angered him, and though his scrutiny darted from her lush breasts, to her glistening pubis, it returned, as if against his will, to the marker.

'You look well, my lady Isidora.' His red tongue circled his lips as if savouring the magnificent dish that was her body.

'As do you, my lord André.' Her eyes dropped pertly below the belt of his blue robe to where the fabric was visibly tented by the mighty pole beneath. Unable to stop herself, she reached for him, longing to flip aside the silk and expose him as he'd exposed her.

A grip like iron clamped on her wrist and held it away from both their bodies. 'Not yet,' he hissed, twisting away from her as she tried to get to him with her free hand. Within the blink of an eye, he had both her hands secured and he'd manhandled her down onto the Persian rug.

The sense of being dominated was as delicious as it was novel, filling her veins like heated honey. Of their own accord, her thighs gaped wide apart as she knelt before him, her head bowed.

With his free hand, he cupped her breast, squeezing it hard, lifting and moving the heavy orb like a horse-breeder examining the flesh of a prized mare. The sorceress groaned, her juices welling up and sliding down her leg. The pressure hurt but she rocked her hips involuntarily as he fondled her. The urge to demand that he caress her sex was overpowering, but the blue ferocity in his eyes compelled her silence.

He squeezed and palpated. First one breast, then the other, flicking at her nipples and goading them to intense sensitivity and stiffness. He was tormenting her, overpowering her, amusing himself by denying her satisfaction.

Eventually, she let out a groan. 'My lord ... my lord ... I ... please touch me.' Flaunting forwards her hips, she tried to entice him with her odour.

'All in good time, madam.' His voice cold, he released her breast and her hands with a disdainful flourish, as if her skin repulsed him. The dramatic force of it sent her hurtling onto her back, on the rug, legs akimbo. She lay sprawled, her thighs open, mute and compliant.

Turning away from her, he rose to his feet and, with a languid elegance, shed his robe. Almost in slow motion the light silk slid down over his body, revealing his broad back and hard sculpted bottom. Between his thighs she could see the dark rounds of his balls.

He was magnificent. Splendid. A prime, awesome male. He more than made up for all the long decades of waiting. Walking away, he was a poem of pale gilded skin and working muscle, and she watched avidly, her flesh heating anew as he snatched up the flask of oil from the sideboard. Plucking out the stopper, he sniffed its contents then shook his head as if to clear it. His hair shimmered and rippled, sliding and slipping across his shoulders.

Then he turned. And the sorceress gasped.

Had he always been this big? She had seen so many men over the years that it was hard to remember. But surely he was mightier now than when she'd last bedded him, when he was young and callow. He was a man now, not a befuddled boy, and his shaft thrust out before him, high and proud and ruddy, his rounded glans distended with raw arousal.

His eyes seemed dismissive as he stared at her. Dismissive of her nakedness, and also of his own. For a moment, she thought that he was about to reach for his robe and just leave her there, burning with lust – but then he shook his head again, pursed his lips and, after pausing only to fondle his erection, he returned to the circle of the rug, carrying the flask.

The sorceress reached for him, but again he dashed her hand away, pushing her back onto the floor and the soft weave of the precious carpeting. She subsided, loving his dominance and yearning for his sex. Reclining like a houri, she draped her arms backwards, exhibiting her body as he knelt beside her and raised the glass vessel.

She closed her eyes, still seeing him with her perfect inner vision.

Slowly, with precision, he poured the spiced oil onto her belly in a gleaming ribbon. She felt it slide over her skin, coating the hot sigil and pooling in her navel. When it overflowed, the streams of fluid spread like the points of a star across the curve of her abdomen, and one line of it flowed into her pubis, between her labia.

The heat in her sex grew, calling out to the man who

was overwhelming her. She writhed against the rug, creating yet more heat in the cheeks of her bottom.

The crash of glass against the sideboard made her eyes fly open. Her lover had flung away the flask and was glaring down upon her, his beautiful chiselled face a complex mask.

He hated her.

He admired her.

He wanted her.

In the centuries ahead, against his will, he would love her.

His rampant penis loomed over her like an alchemist's staff, as rigid as mahogany and just as mysterious and powerful. She wanted to reach for it, but his eyes, almost black with lust, forbade her movement.

In a swift, vulpine lunge, he bent over her, his face close to her body as his flattened hand settled on her belly and the oil-covered sigil. Slowly, oh so slowly, he began to circle with the heel of his hand and his palm, all the time watching the expression on her face as he pressed and swirled.

'I see you have tricked us, as ever,' he hissed, momentarily clawing at the stark design of the Thousand Hour Marker, the magical sheet anchor that had kept her from being swept away irrevocably into eternal darkness and thus enabled her return from the banishment he'd effected. His nails gouged at her, as if he wanted to rip it from her skin, but then his hand relaxed and returned to its caressing action.

The compulsion to writhe like the lowest slut consumed her senses. She could feel the burn of the rug against her bottom as she wriggled in time to his circling hand, her movements only exacerbating the tension in her belly and her sex. Despite the oil, the constant slight tugging and jerking on her clitoris drove her to distraction. She wanted him to reach between her labia and pinch and pull on it. Trying to entice him, she spread her legs even wider, flexing the cords of her thighs in an extreme effort.

Without warning, he swooped down, replacing his hand with his pale sculpted face and the touch of his reddened lips. He rubbed his cheek against the oil, then his mouth and, parting his lips, he drew his teeth along the Marker beneath her navel. A second later, he nipped hard, biting the lush curve of her belly and inflicting real pain.

A sensation like the ignition of two precious chemicals fired in the very quick of her sex, making it shimmer and ache on the very edge of orgasm. He bit again and her hands flew to her cleft, but before she could masturbate he slapped away her hands with an angry snarl.

'No, madam! Not yet! Your pleasure is mine, and mine alone ... after all this time.'

After reaching for her leg and snatching it by the calf, he doubled up the limb, bringing it against her chest, creating tension. Then, with no further ado, he thrust his fingers into her.

One. Two. Three. Then his whole hand bar the thumb, stretching her entrance cruelly, yet inducing crude excitement.

'Whore!' he hissed, beginning to pump his flexed fingers in and out, the action rough, yet with an infernal, magical rhythm that made her head toss and her throat constrict around unearthly feral cries.

As his thumb flattened her clitoris, her flesh clenched, every bit of it contracting around the intrusion of his fingers, every cell, every molecule pulsating. She shouted and raged as her body roiled with pleasure so intense it was painful. She grabbed at him, her fingers and nails gouging at his alabaster flesh as her free leg kicked and flailed, her heel thumping again and again at the floorboards. His cock was like a rod of hot metal against her, a branding iron that knocked against her as she struggled.

The orgasm went on and on, yet seemed not to resolve itself. If anything her lust was growing, not waning. As he reared back, wrenching his fingers out of her with a rude sucking sound and flinging her from him, the fire in the pit of her belly raged and rose.

'Be done with it! Satisfy me, my lord,' she growled at him, catching his eyes with hers, trying to overpower him as she once had, that first time.

But he was too strong for her. His own eyes were like glittering blue stones, their radiance exquisite and hypnotic. She wanted to move, but suddenly she could not.

Between her legs, her sex thudded, heavy with renewed frustration, yet her arms were weighted and unable to direct her fingers to her burning clitoris.

'Never!' he said, so soft and low it was barely audible. On his feet now, he stood over her, nude and magnificent like some classical colossus, his body perfect, his rearing cock hugely red and rampant.

Tossing his hair out of his eyes, he glowered down upon her and, as his mouth curved in a wicked line, he grasped his penis. He gave it four slow, deep pumps, then bit down on his lip, suppressing a gasp as he climaxed.

Pearly semen flew and splattered on the sorceress. It

tasted bitter on her lips as she groaned and burned for him and, as the room fell away from her, all she could see were his ice-blue eyes.

Instantly awake, Paula Beckett shot up in bed, as sick and disorientated as if she'd just been on a roller coaster. Licking her lips, she half expected to taste the angry blue-eyed man's semen. But the only moisture on her face was sweat and a few tears she rubbed at angrily.

There was plenty of moisture between her legs though. A river, goddamnit! She was swimming, oozing, and so hot and frustrated that she could almost imagine her sex sizzling. She'd been rubbing herself in her sleep again but, like the evil thing beneath her skin, she'd been denied. She hadn't come.

I can't go on like this much longer, she thought. I'll go off my head.

Swiftly, and without much joy at first, she began to play with herself. Circling her middle finger over her clit, she soon found her rhythm and the familiar rise of pleasure cleared her mind. No mad, vindictive sorceresses, no blue-eyed lovers who hated her. Just herself, and her own body, and the simple love of it.

She felt almost calm again. Sex was good. Sex could help her.

She could do it. Do it for herself. Just for herself.

As her climax bloomed, its sweet white glow blunted her fears and brought a calming boost of strength.

Gasping on the bed, she lay waiting for the whispers, preparing to fight them. But nothing happened. The intruder in her mind was temporarily banished. No passenger murmuring filth and words of madness. But if she lay here alone in this bed for any length of time, it would all come back again. She touched the curve of her abdomen. It was cold and smooth, but soon enough the peculiar pattern of heat would appear again, the slight raised welts, like nettle stings, that almost felt like letters and numbers. The invisible marker that told her the bitch was in residence. And with it would come the words, inside her head.

Give in to me ... Give in to me ...

'Fuck you, Isidora, whoever you are!' Paula shouted and snapped on the bedside light. It was only ten fifteen.

The sex dreams were OK in a bent sort of way but the other stuff, the falling through blackness and visions of boiling in eternal torment, were unbearable. And watching the telly or reading didn't make a scrap of difference. Only company could stave off the night terrors.

Flinging back the covers, she let out a fruity curse – profane stuff, Isidora-talk that she'd never have used until a month or so ago. Clenching her teeth on the foul language, she reflected on just how much she'd changed in such a short time, and how much she longed to go back to the days before ... before this stupid, unbelievable thing that she didn't really understand had happened to her. The temptation to cry like a baby rose up like an enveloping wave, threatening to capsize her.

No way! Don't give in to it! she told herself. What the hell good would tears do? They'd just make that bitch laugh.

Taking deep breaths, Paula prowled around the room. Affirmative action was required, some kind of distraction. She'd bloody well go out. There were pubs and clubs open. Maybe she'd meet someone she knew. Although that probably wasn't a good idea, seeing as how she was supposed to be on sick leave. But there were other venues, ones her work colleagues didn't go to. Maybe she'd look for some real, human, quantifiable trouble. Something external, something explicable, something that would fill her mind and push out her intruder.

Her jaw set, she strode for the bathroom and set the shower running while she gathered clothes and make-up.

If she was going out, she needed to be clean and smart – and sexy.

You need a man, the inner voice said low and cajolingly. *You need a fuck. A big cock between your legs.*

'Yes, maybe I do, you unholy cow,' she growled at her tormentor, 'but when I get one, it's for me. *Just* me. So bugger off!'

2 Smoke and Mirrors

Three-quarters of an hour later, Paula's eyes were smarting from dry-ice vapour. It was being pumped out onto the Raven's dance floor in some kind of pathetic attempt at spectacle in the shabby suburban club. Unfortunately, all it succeeded in doing was pissing people off and making them bitch and complain and rub their eyes.

'What the hell am I doing here?' Talking to herself, or anyone inside her, wasn't a problem here. Nobody could hear anything over the cacophony of badly mixed drum and bass that boomed out of the poor-quality speakers. She could have had a full-on slanging match with Isidora and nobody would have been any the wiser.

The Raven Club was dark, loud and grimy – and reeked of cheap, mismatched perfumes, overpriced beer and a lot of sweat. Paula wrinkled her nose. It wasn't really her scene, but she'd found herself outside, in the queue, before she'd really realised what was going on.

Since when had she ever been a clubber or a party girl? Had her passenger brought her here or just suggested it? The lines were getting worryingly blurred but she didn't think the bitch had complete control of her. She was getting pretty damn good at persuading though.

The Raven's saving grace was that it was full of *real* people as opposed to figments of her imagination or characters that stalked her dreams. Since that frightening event five weeks ago, Paula hadn't been able to rest much at home, day or night. She'd lie awake, wondering what had happened to her during her 'lost hours'. The time between setting off to meet her friends, Belinda and Jonathan, for a reunion holiday full of booze and laughs, and the black moment when she'd woken up in a hotel room, stark naked and with a yawning gap in her memory and no idea where her car was. And even if she did doze or sleep, it was worse. Losing a firm grip on her consciousness allowed the thing under her skin to wake and taunt her.

Her flat simply wasn't the haven it should have been any more but, unfortunately, this crappy dive didn't seem to be much better. It seemed to suit Isidora to the bone, and Paula could just imagine the bitch's disembodied smile of glee and that pair of brilliant-green eyes drinking it all in, the darkness, the perversity and the thuggish sin.

As Paula scanned the insalubrious man-made cavern, she wished she'd chosen a different venue. What did it matter if someone shopped her to the management for being out while she was on the sick? There was nothing worse that could happen to her than what had already happened, and she could feel the inner presence laughing and taunting her. Watching through her eyes and making them feel as if they were too big for their sockets. Sliding around inside her, caressing her skin and making it prickle and heat up, both on the surface and beneath. Her breasts suddenly tightened, the areolas crinkling and rising as if fluffed by an unseen lover's hand. Between her legs, her sex rippled, growing moist and plump and sticky again.

'Here we go again.'

Sighing, she took a large gulp of industrial-grade Chardonnay from her plastic glass. And nearly choked. The wine was more akin to vinegar than anything that ever came from an Australian vineyard, but its main virtue was an unexpected strength. Maybe if she drank enough of this cheeky blend of acetic acid and paint stripper, she wouldn't care about Isidora. Maybe she could even poison the vicious cow. Or maybe she'd stop feeling guilty and scared and confused and just embrace this inner dark side she'd had forced on her.

The constant fighting was wearing her down, making her crazy. How could she run from what was inescapable? Seeking professional help had been useless. Her GP had just told her she was tired and given her Valium and the sick note.

Overboosted bass lines thudded on and on. Banging so hard, they made her feet and the muscles in her thighs tremble. Coloured spots flashed and mini searchlights raked the tiny dance floor and the crowd of shifting, scoping, drunkenly horny bodies that surrounded it. Clubbers lurched and gyrated across the handkerchief of space and the thought of joining them in bass-driven oblivion was suddenly tempting.

Maybe I can shake her out of me like some kind of fundamentalist repentant.

But there were no answers among the sweaty and probably drugged-up throng. Dabbing surreptitiously at her mascara, she blinked hard again, blaming the dry ice for her teary eyes as she grappled with self-pity. When the chaos of the club swam back into focus, she saw something she hadn't noticed before. Somebody. A tall figure leaning against the polished steel railing at the other side of the dance floor.

For a few seconds, one of the wheeling, manic search-lights hovered caressingly upon him, giving Paula a perfect view. Her glass almost slipped from her fingers but she managed to hang onto it, her heart bashing so hard against her chest that she thought it must be visible.

For a moment, she seemed to see 'Lord André' from her dream. 'How the hell are you here? It's not possible.' Shock and a surprise made her gulp down the rest of her wine, unable to understand how she could be seeing a character from her erotic dreams. In living flesh.

Inside her, where Isidora dwelt, there was a howl of glee and triumph that made her shake her head, imagin-ing it ringing out over the sound of pumping house anthems. A deep dark satisfaction, or maybe just the anticipation of it, made her sex throb.

Paula swayed, dropped her empty plastic glass and grabbed onto the rail, the colliding intersection of two worlds making her giddy. A woman beside her looked at her aggressively and mouthed something like 'stupid, drunken cunt'.

Fired by a sudden rush of intense energy, Paula surged forwards, glaring. The sigil on her belly seared her for a moment, and she had the most extraordinary sense of being bigger than herself, and stronger. Exhilaration gey-sered through her like an orgasm without sex, and she laughed out loud as her erstwhile combatant shrank back with fear in her eyes and an open mouth.

A heartbeat later, Paula was clutching the rail again, her knuckles white in the gloom.

Was that you, Isidora? she demanded silently.

To her surprise, there was no answer. Not even that familiar chuckle of glee.

Winding her way along the balcony, Paula headed for the exit. This sudden Jekyll and Hyde thing was new and she wasn't sure she was safe to be out. The next drunken slag she faced off against might not be so easily intimidated or might simply have a lot more booze in her.

But, by the steps, she paused, her eyes drawn downwards. The man by the dance floor was still there, and the sight of him made her catch her breath and wonder. Now he seemed to look entirely different. What she'd seen before must have been an hallucination.

Raven Club man didn't have the aristocratic glamour of Count André and he didn't even have the long exotic locks. His dark hair was cropped quite short and it made him look earthy and dangerous. He had the aura of a conscious outsider about him, a rebel, and a bit of stud maybe, but in a raw, maverick way. In contrast to the boring but colourful designer-outlet finery around him, he was wearing a battered black leather biker jacket, narrow black jeans and some kind of heavy, buckled work boots.

A pair of dark, narrowed eyes scanned the room just as hers had, their hooded lids predatory and jaded-looking. His mouth was rather hard and thinned a little, as if the club inspired just the same sense of distaste and disappointment in him that it did in her.

Yeah, I know, it's a dingy old sump, isn't it? thought Paula. So what the hell are we doing here? We should be elsewhere. Together.

She watched his hands. They moved quickly and edgily,

even though his large body was still and poised. First he tapped his fingertips against the smudged railing in time to the music, and then went through the motions of patting his pockets, reaching into them, digging about. Only to be snatched smartly back out again.

Ah, hah! A smoker – or an ex-smoker – searching for his ciggies. Having done hard time giving up herself, Paula recognised the tell-tales. Maybe the tall, hard-looking and vaguely bikerish man wasn't quite as calm and self-assured as he looked. The urge to smoke was a natural reflex when ill at ease.

The large hands appeared again, and suddenly he cracked his knuckles. The sound of it shouldn't have been audible over the cacophony of the music, but even so it echoed across the room as if they were the only two people in it.

Hands still clasped, the tall stranger looked straight up at Paula.

Connection hit her like a thump in the solar plexus. Lines of force zipped between the two of them, and the man down below cocked his head as if listening to their hum.

A powerful urge to run gripped Paula, but then died again.

Take him, he's yours, the voice of Isidora purred beneath her skin. And Paula's eyes and limbs obeyed it. After holding the tall man's gaze, she glanced towards the club's emergency exit, and then, not looking back, she began to walk quickly towards the steps to the lower level.

Rafe Hathaway was fed up of the Raven Club, and fed up with himself because he couldn't stay away from it.

Why did he keep coming back to this crappy little sinkhole again and again? It smelt, the music was appalling and the clientele worse, and yet it had a kind of obnoxious energy that he found disturbingly reassuring. It was a low, disreputable dive, but then again he was a low, disreputable person, so he fitted right in. And it was distracting, which was something he needed more and more with every day that passed. The way time flew, it was becoming more and more necessary to flirt with danger, to stay on the edge, to do any damn, stupid, immoral or amoral thing to keep the dark thoughts at bay.

A bitter smile twisted his lips. What use were all his meditation and relaxation and self-hypnosis techniques now when he most needed them himself? Fuck it, he was supposed to be an expert. But it was a case of physician, or whatever, try to cure yourself, man.

Once a fraud, always a fraud.

The words were as savage as his nicotine craving. More crap he should have been able to deal with. What would his adoring harem from Inner Light think if they saw him in this repulsive dive, burnt out and fed up and dying for a cigarette? Christ, he was so full of toxins tonight, he was a walking advert for self-abuse!

For the dozenth time, he reached into his pocket for his cigarettes, and for the dozenth time he dragged his hand back out again. He wished he could claim it was strength of character, but no such luck. The Raven was as subject to the national smoking ban as anywhere else, and there was always some small-minded busybody who'd rat on you just for the sheer pleasure of it.

But it wasn't really a cigarette he wanted anyway. His

entire body was edgy and hungry. A strange energy flowed over his skin tonight, making it tingle and his clothes feel tighter than normal. He was horny, but it was more than that. Much more.

Chi? Natural galvanic electricity? What the fuck ... His jeans clung to his crotch and his buttocks, embracing his cock like a stern yet dismissive hand. The feel of the rough denim – without the ameliorating effect of under-wear – made him hard.

He needed sex as well as a ciggie. Real sex. Not the fabricated, supposedly mind-expanding little encounters with the overtanned, over-made-up matrons who frequented Inner Light for some of his special, under-the-counter 'hands on healing'.

No, he wanted a proper fuck. A hard fuck. A wild meeting of equal bodies and minds with a woman who'd give at least as good as she got.

Cracking his knuckles involuntarily, he suddenly felt an overpowering urge to look upwards. There, on the mezzanine, stood what could be just that woman. She was watching him, her eyes bright and focused, even in the gloom.

Are you the answer to my prayers, lady? he wondered.

Probably not. She didn't look as if she was anything to do with prayers. And nothing to do with faith, goodness or enlightenment either.

Oh fuck, lady, I want you!

The ever-changing lighting was a mess, but suddenly he could see her with preternatural clarity. She wasn't a fabulous beauty, but there was a power about her that called to him, an intensity of eye and of the way she held herself. A dark fire that spoke loud to his unsettled mood.

She didn't move at first, or even acknowledge him, but she kept on staring. Then, a few moments later, her bright eyes twinkled and she nodded in the direction of the emergency exit.

Not bothering to look at him further, she began to move towards the stairs.

And so did he.

What am I doing here?

The cold moist air in the alley behind the club cleared Paula's head. It had rained on and off for days, and the dew-laden freshness of the atmosphere was as reviving as an icy downpour. Her eyes stopped itching and aching and her limbs felt lighter and less wracked by nervous tension.

I could just walk away now, and nothing would happen, she thought.

That was it. All she had to do was just get out of the alley, walk, run or get a taxi back home. Then continue her search and her battle to understand herself another day.

She'd find Belinda and Jonathan, and this Sedgewick Priory place that they'd kept banging on about when they'd visited her in hospital. Sighing, she wished she'd listened properly, but they'd just gone on and on about their adventures at what sounded like a haunted mansion. And this man they'd met there, its owner, Count André Von Kastel or whatever his name was, who they'd claimed was over two hundred years old – and a sorcerer into the bargain – but who had now disappeared off this earthly plane after some kind of ritual. It'd all sounded stupid and far-fetched, like something out of a very cheap horror movie, and her head had been hurting so much that she'd just lost her temper with them, especially when they'd kept bugging her, and asking her if she remembered meeting anybody. Eventually, she'd told them to 'just fuck off'. And unfortunately they had. Her missing car had turned up in a Tesco's car park a week later but her friends seemed to have disappeared off the face of the earth, and now she couldn't find them or their miraculous priory.

But it *had* to exist, there *had* to be a way to locate it. Presumably Belinda and Jonathan had returned there and they knew more than they'd been letting on about what might have happened to her. She'd hit the library and local reference sources. She couldn't just keep drifting around and letting herself be driven mad, day after day, by a voice in her head.

Tomorrow she'd get online and start checking. Or just get in her car, drive north to Belinda and Jonathan's hometown and try to track them from there. No more unanswered phone calls and emails. She'd do something active instead of just faffing around and letting things happen.

A smile curved her lips. Suddenly she felt lighter and happier. She began to walk. Swiftly and with energy, she headed for the main drag and a nearby taxi rank. She was back in control again. She could do this. She could get back her peace of mind, and her mind itself.

Fool!

The hated inner voice chimed in her head and she faltered. Gritting her teeth, she kept on walking, but it was as if she were wading through dark mud or treacle and between her legs she felt so heavy and slippery and sexy that it made her gasp.

You feel horny, little bitch, why deny it?

And God, it was true, her body wanted sex. But who was in the driving seat? Was it *she* who wanted the familiar yet unfamiliar man with the leather jacket and the dangerous eyes inside her? Or was it the thing, Isidora, who fancied a shag with him?

Paula stopped dead. Thought hard. Examined her senses. Goddamnit, *she* was the one who wanted him! She, Paula Beckett!

And there was nothing wrong with that.

The realisation was a jolt. But reassuring. For all these weeks, she'd been hating herself more and more for giving in to this volcanic sex drive, and for actually enjoying it. But no more. If she wanted sex, she would have it, and she would glory in it!

Good girl, purred the hateful inner voice.

'Oh, fuck you,' muttered Paula, turning on her heel. Shut up. I just want him, nothing more than that. You go to hell.

Swift steps brought her back to the shadowed, litter-strewn alley behind the club. As she'd half expected, the tall man from the dance floor was there, leaning against the stained wall, dragging hard on a long cigarette.

'Ah ha, another smoker. I guessed as much,' he said as he spotted her. Blowing out his smoke, he gave her a thin, almost weary smile as if they really did already know each other. As she approached him, he fished in his pockets, pulling out a packet of unfamiliar-looking ciga-rettes, his own ciggie still dangling louchely from his lips.

'No thanks, I've given up, sort of.' Paula hesitated, watching him cock his head on one side, making light from a window above glint on his short dark hair. At close quarters, she could see it had a slight curl where it clung to the strong shape of his head, and just a touch of silvery grey among the near-black at his temples. 'I'll have a drag of yours though,' she conceded. 'I don't know that brand.'

'They're special. A Turkish mix. An indulgence from the days when I had a bit of cash.'

After snagging the cig from his mouth, he put it to her lips, his fingertip brushing her mouth for a fraction of a second. The contact was brief, almost non-existent, and yet it jolted her, making her sex clench between her legs, deep and hard. For a moment, she seemed to see him not in a murky alley, but a luxurious bedroom, wearing a beautiful robe of star-strewn blue silk, not an old leather jacket.

'OK?' His eyes narrowed in the shadows, his brow puckering. Up close, she got the impression that he was maybe not as young as he'd first appeared. His forehead was quite smooth and his lightly tanned skin was relatively unmarked by time but, to go with his touch of grey hair, he had a few character lines around his dark eyes and in them there was a strange and haunted aura. He was definitely older than her dream lover, André, but the chief difference between them was that this man was far from patrician. He was wilder, coarser and more muscular, but just as attractive in a down-to-earth, gutsy way.

And his eyes were brown. Dark brown, like antique mahogany – troubled and deeply, deeply beautiful.

'Yeah, fine, thanks.' She took the cigarette between two fingers and dragged on it. Rather harder than she should have. The foreign tobacco was fiercely strong and scoured at the lining of her throat like a sand-blast. Coughing furiously, she almost threw the thing back at him, doubling over. The exotic cigarette went flying, arcing upwards then plummeting down again to plop in a puddle, fracturing the water's reflective surface.

The tall man gripped her by the shoulder, slapping her back until the wheezing subsided. 'There . . .' His smile was warm as he looked down into her face. 'Nothing like a bit of rough shag to drive out the inner demons.' Touching her delicately, he smoothed away the moisture from beneath her eyes.

Paula laughed, almost starting to cough again. Inner demons? My God, she thought, if only you knew!

'OK now?' His eyes wide with concern, he looked younger and kinder. His features were strong and masculine, but there was a quirk of sympathy there too. And the mouth that had looked hard now seemed full and soft and passionate.

'I'm fine . . . thanks. Sorry about your special cigarette.'

Big shoulders shrugged, and that rather special mouth curved into a smile. 'No, I should thank you. I shouldn't smoke. In fact I'm giving up.' He laughed, a soft rough sound, and the way he shook his head suggested the return of his cynicism. 'I'm supposed to be on the side of light and purity, not abusing my body with the demon tobacco. You've done me a favour.'

Light and purity? Now there was an odd turn of phrase. Paula's eyes narrowed as she scrutinised him. If she'd been forced to assess him, she'd have classified him as 'dark'. Disreputable. Dark of clothing and eye and hair. Everything.

He laughed again. 'Yeah, I know. I don't come across as a devotee of peace and inner harmony, do I?' He reached out, touched her again, his fingers smoothing her hair.

'I really don't have the slightest idea what you're talking about,' Paula answered, laughing too. 'Are you some sort of guru or something?' She looked up at him, trying to figure him out.

'Nah.' He shrugged his solid shoulders in their leather carapace. 'But I am a therapist of sorts – massage, hypnotherapy, that kind of thing. I work at Inner Light, in the marketplace. Every been there?'

The idea of him as a masseur shook her. Her sex fluttered again and for an instant she seemed to feel thick fingers inside her, flexing and stretching her. Oil on her skin, slowly sliding as he fondled her. Perfume and spices filling her head as she climaxed.

Can you heal me? she asked him silently. Can you irradiate me with pleasure, the way he did? And drive *her* out?

She wondered if he'd heard her. It seemed he might have, because his dark eyebrows lifted. Or maybe he'd heard the laughter of the evil presence inside her, the thing, Isidora, now so mightily disdainful of the possibility of ever being ousted.

'I've not heard that one before. Is it a line? Does it work?'

Real laughter rang out, not the imaginary psychic kind.

'Well, I have used it as a pulling strategy. Far too often, in fact.' He was grinning, showing unexpectedly white teeth for a smoker, but there was still that pall of darkness in his eyes. She smiled crookedly back at him, experiencing a piercing sense of affinity, of fellow feeling. 'But the therapist angle is true. Cross my heart. I can give you my card if you don't believe me.'

'It's OK. I believe you.' Her voice shook as she spoke, the images intensifying. Her skin rippled as if those long, elegant hands of his really were sliding over her body, skin on skin, riding on a veil of exotic oil, and alternating between cruelty and exquisite beneficence. Just like in her dream. 'It's not what I would have pegged you as. But then, appearances can be deceptive.'

His hand cupped her face, the fingertips just resting against her skin. Could he sense what lay beneath it and within her? His eyes – intense, dark, yet strangely glittering – gave nothing away. What she did feel though was energy, five little points of it where his fingers and thumb hovered.

Was it her? Was it him? Impossible to tell. Where the contact was, it felt as if they were one.

'Indeed,' he whispered, edging a little closer. 'But you, what about you? Do *you* have inner demons?' His eyes flicked downwards as if commenting on her unwise clothing.

Paula blushed. Why on earth had she put on this outfit? It must have been Isidora's doing. An impulse that had got the better of her at the critical moment.

'I've got dozens,' her companion continued, his eyes puckish despite their strange sorrow. 'But you look like a good girl masquerading as a bad girl in that skirt.' His free hand dropped to her hip, curving and gripping. Instead of dressing safe, she'd ended up in her sexiest outfit – a leather mini skirt and a thin cotton camisole. Thank God that underneath she'd managed to exercise a degree of caution. The thought of the strange mark on her belly had made her change her knickers at the last minute.

If only she could tell him. If only she *knew* what all this was. Belinda and Jonathan could probably tell her, but, because she'd alienated them, they were going to take some finding.

'Yes, I *have* got one, actually ... an inner demon, that is.' She smiled, hoping she wasn't going to sound like a complete fruitcake. 'There's the spirit of an evil woman, some kind of disembodied sorceress or something, inside me. And she keeps goading me and making me do bad things.' Which was the truth. As far as she understood it.

She waited for the laughter. The backing off. Or worse, a look of humouring and 'she's drunk, but I'll go along with her to get a shag'.

But his strong, sculpted face remained calm, more curious than anything. And he didn't back off. 'What kind of bad things?' His hand slid over the leather of her skirt, smoothing it across the surface of her hip and thigh beneath.

'Things like following a man I don't know from Adam out into an alley as if I want to have sex with him.'

He laughed again. Not mocking. Not hard. It was almost a happy sound.

'Now that *is* a bit mad.'

Take him! Take him! chattered Isidora, rampant.

'OK! I will!'

Her companion's eyes narrowed, but Paula was beyond caring what he thought. Lifting herself on her toes – this close, she realised, he was very, very tall – she reached up and grabbed the nape of his neck, pulling his face down to hers.

The taste of the dark tobacco was like a potent drug on his tongue and, hungry for oblivion, she sucked on it. His body was solid and muscular beneath his leather jacket and, as she slid inside it, she encountered the heat of his skin, burning through the thin cotton of his black T-shirt.

Savouring his fragrance, she breathed in deep through her nose as she took advantage of his mouth. He smelt of herbs and cinnamon, like a health-food store or an apothecary's shop, pungent and invigorating. The flesh and bone beneath her fingertips was hard and fine, and so was his cock when she let her hand drift to his jeans.

'Hey, are you sure about this?' he gasped, pulling back, 'I mean ... I'm not complaining. I mostly get propositioned by middle-aged ravers during massage sessions, and you make a refreshing change from wrinkles and a sunbed tan.' He touched her face, a puzzled expression in his eyes. 'But I'm not sure this is really you, is it?'

Paula crumbled. Was it just Isidora driving her lust? Would she ever be able to have sex just for herself again? Before she knew what was happening, tears were pouring down her face, making a streaky mess of her mascara.

Big powerful arms, clad in leather, encircled her, and drew her into a warm stronghold. He felt like home, mad as that seemed, far more so than her own flat or any place she'd ever lived. She slumped against him, sliding her arms around his big, muscular torso and pressing her lightly clad body against his. Holding on to him, she felt safer than she had in weeks and yet, at the same time, subject to the low pull of sweet desire. She felt it more powerfully than she'd ever done before because his body was such a refuge. But it felt natural. It felt right. It felt clean.

'Look, do you want me to take you back inside? Or get you a taxi?' He paused and seemed to sway, as if he too was affected by this mutual care-taking. Was he just as lost and confused as she was? And grasping, however briefly, at the same sense of rightness? 'What about a coffee? There's an all-night place just a short walk away, and I think you need to talk rather than fuck.'

He was trying to be the chivalrous knight, bless him, but the iron thrust of his cock against her belly told another story.

'No! Please ... I want to fuck. I want to fuck now.'

And she did. She wanted sex, but she wanted it for herself, not the dark bitch inside her. There was no manipulation here. This strange tall man was a therapist, and she needed therapy right now, from his cock.

His brows shot up, but he smiled, tilting his head on one side again as if he didn't quite know what to make of her. 'Well ... er ... yes then. No problem. I just wanted you to be sure.' He reached behind her and pulled out the couple of pins that held her hair in a sexy knot, then ran his fingers through it as the tiny bits of metal hit the ground. After pausing only to sniff the scent of her shampoo, he cradled her cheeks between his hands and then leant right in to take a first kiss.

This time he was in control, thrusting with his tongue in a way that was teasing yet gentle. Paula teased back, wanting to smile beneath his lips. Their tongues were duelling but it was nothing like the dream.

For several long moments, they let their mouths enjoy

each other. Lips, tongues, dancing and licking and darting. Nothing too rough, nothing too harsh, just playful hunger.

But, eventually, the wild imperative of lust ramped up a notch.

Then another, then another, then another.

Her companion spun her round and placed her against the wall. Paula almost sagged into the stone when he launched himself into kissing her again. This time they were deep, deep kisses that stretched her lips and jaw in a way that exhilarated her senses. This was the fuck-kiss, raw and primitive. It made her sex weep slippery fluid in sumptuous readiness.

When he pulled back, she whimpered aloud in thwarted frustration.

'Don't worry.' He darted forwards, kissed the corner of her mouth quickly, then pulled away again, reaching for the strap of her shoulder bag which lay diagonally across her body. 'Just getting things out of the way.' He flipped the bag clear of her and let it drop at her side.

Then he set to opening the little buttons down the front of her flimsy cotton camisole. Isidora's choice, Paula accepted, but now she was glad of it. Her tall lover was able to bare her without wasting time.

'No bra?' he purred. 'I like that. I like it very much.' His long hands cupped her breasts as if they'd been fashioned just for that purpose.

Paula groaned, her knees weakening at his touch, the wall solid and reassuring at her back. She felt as if her breasts had been aching to be held ever since she'd woken up, sweating in her bed. The way he fondled her and manipulated her was such a relief, such a gift. As he strummed her bright, aching nipples, the moisture between her legs welled and overflowed, escaping the crotch of her knickers and slipping down her legs.

'Good?' he whispered, thumbs moving. Flicking . . .

Paula felt like a doll pinned to the wall. Her arms dangled at her sides, she was too caught up in the delicious sensations even to reach for him in return. Thudding pleasure beat in her body like a triangle. Breast, breast, sex. She rolled her head involuntarily against the stonework, her mouth lolling open, her eyes closed.

For a moment, whispers of darkness flittered through her mind, but with a cry, almost a shout, she banished them. Her eyes flew open and she found her companion watching her closely again, his hands stilling, ready to withdraw. His lips opened as if to question her, but she forestalled him, reaching up to touch them, to run her fingertips across their velvety surface as she pressed her body into his hold.

'No questions,' she said firmly, rolling her shoulders against the wall, loving that he was quick to resume pleasuring her despite this unwanted hiatus in her concentration. With her free hand, she foraged beneath his jacket again, cupping one tight buttock and bringing his crotch close to hers.

'Not even one?' he persisted, then sucked impishly on her fingers, circling his hips so she could feel his tense erection.

Paula shimmied in a syncopated movement. He was big, so very big, oh goody!

'All right, just one. Because I like you.' She cast a quick look downwards, lowering her lashes, and he laughed, instantly getting her meaning.

'What's your name?'

It was the question she'd expected, but what she hadn't expected was the power of that other name, springing involuntarily to her lips as if it were her own.

Isidora.

The second it had dashed through her mind, she fought to banish it but the ease with which it had almost escaped was terrifying. Shaking, she clung more tightly to the hard muscled round of her lover's backside.

'Paula! My name is Paula!' It was an evocation. An affirmation. A shout of defiance, though spoken softly and huskily.

'Paula what?' he whispered, one hand still at her breast while another slid over her ribs, her waist, her hips.

'No, no, that's another question. It's my turn to ask now.'

'Ask away.' His voice was husky, teasing. His hand was beneath her brief leather skirt now, searching and seeking. The gliding contact of his fingertips was pleasantly cool against her burning hot skin.

'What's *your* name?'

She felt vaguely disappointed with her own mundane question, yet had no idea what other thing she might have wanted to ask. Tossing her head and rocking her buttocks against the dirty stone wall, she almost growled at any goddamn impediment to having sex with this unknown man.

'Rafe. My name is Rafe.' He mocked her with a smile as his exploration reached her panties. 'Good God, what are these?' He flicked at the edges, plucking at the firm elastic texture of the Lycra. 'I thought only Bridget Jones wore these big reinforced jobs?' He smoothed his hand around and gripped her bottom cheek through the clinging fabric, letting his fingers press the crotch piece from behind.

Paula grunted with frustration. She'd exerted herself with these knickers, pulled them on at the last minute, fighting the darker compulsion to go commando. The mark on her belly was invisible but it could be felt, she was sure of it. She wanted it hidden, out of sight, out of mind. It just showed the depths of confusion she was mired in. She'd come out to get a man, but she'd trussed herself up in a chastity belt.

His other hand slid down, tweaking up her skirt to her waist. He held her bottom tight, pressing her against him, as she pressed him against herself in return. Unspeaking, they began to circle their hips in silently co-ordinated tango, caressing each other through denim and Lycra like two teenagers sneaking a stolen frottage behind the bike sheds.

The sensations were delicious, but she wanted him inside her. She wanted this 'Rafe' inside *her*, Paula. Not Isidora. Not Count André from the dream. Not any figment of her stupid fragmented imagination. She wanted to feel, really feel. And celebrate life.

'You're going to have to take these off, love,' said Rafe, more gently. When she looked up at him, so close, she could see concern for her in his eyes, a sense of her troubles.

'No! Please ... let me pull them to one side.'

Reaching down, she dragged at the damp crotch of the control panties. They were tight, and it was awkward, but she made an entrance for him. Her clit throbbed at the proximity of her fingers, burning and aching.

He was perplexed, she could tell, but he shrugged, released her momentarily, and slid his hand into his back pocket for a condom.

'Just a second,' he whispered, then surprised her with a kiss at the corner of her mouth. It was soft as thistledown, almost platonic, but strangely sweet. Moments later, he was tearing open the tiny package and then wrapping his cock in the silky latex.

Paula glanced down, eager to see him, and caught her breath at the raw size and girth of his flesh. He was fiercely and angrily red beneath the sheer film of rubber, the big head bulbous and flared, and the tiny eye open. She seemed to have special vision to see every detail in the dark.

He was beautiful, huge and animal, a totem of sex. Her own sex wept and shimmered, silently calling to him.

Still holding aside the gusset of her knickers, she reached for him with her free hand, folding her fingers around him and cradling him gently. He felt like life, the very essence of it. He almost hummed with it. She could feel blood slowly pulsating in his veins.

With care, with trepidation, she began to caress him, even as she felt the lush slide of her juices down her inner thigh, released as they were now by the exposure of her sex. The night air was warm, but it was cooler than her cleft, and a naughty breeze played and teased her moist, pouched flesh.

There was pleasure just in standing here, against a wall, holding a man's cock in her hand while exposure to the night kissed her intimate nakedness. She moaned softly, still stroking Rafe as she bent her knees and wafted her hips to and fro. There was pleasure revelling in her own rudeness and wantonness and knowing that it was her own will that had brought her to this state.

'Let me touch you, love,' whispered Rafe, but before she could give her assent he was already making moves.

His fingers jostled hers as they moved into her sex, coasting up and down and side to side in her tropical lubrication, but never actually settling on her clit. Behind her back, his other hand slipped slyly beneath the edge of the Lycra and snuck unerringly into the groove of her bottom. One fingertip began delicately playing with her anus, catching the rhythm of the ones that taunted her clitoris.

'Oh . . . oh . . . oh . . .'

The sounds were involuntary, as were her movements. She rocked harder against the wall, her hips swivelling and moving, seeking that perfect contact while Rafe almost cruelly denied it. He played ruthlessly with her bottom, but the knot of nerves that screamed for attention he still avoided.

'You want it, don't you?'

His voice was velvet, wicked. It reminded her momentarily of her dream again. Arousal. Denial. The battle of the sexes.

'You want me to finger your clit, don't you?'

His mouth was at the side of her face and his tongue slowly slid the whole length of her cheek. At the same time, the pad of his finger pressed against the tight pucker of her arse.

Without thinking, she squeezed his cock and he hissed through his teeth.

'Don't worry, baby, I like it rough. You won't make me come before I'm ready to.'

His teasing fingers left her sex and settled over her own fingers where they held aside the fierce knickers. He stroked her hand and the rosette of her bottom in a leisurely counterpoint.

'Please ... please ... please ...'

The frustration was agonising and intense. It was almost as if her clit was shouting even if she was only groaning softly. She knew she could have abandoned his cock and just rubbed herself and brought about her own completion, but she felt compelled to maintain her hold on his exquisite flesh. The feel of his hardness was everything that was light in the midst of dark and anguish.

'Just ask for what you want and I'll give it to you.'

He sounded so reasonable. So normal. Paula laughed suddenly, her heart lifting at the absurdity of finding herself standing in an alley with her fingers wrapped around a man's big cock and his finger beginning to push inside her bottom.

'I want you to rub my clit and bring me off. And then I want you to fuck me.' She smiled at him in the gloom and saw his white teeth gleam in answer. 'There, is that plain enough for you?'

'Perfection!' He laughed too, a happy triumphant sound as his fingers slid from the back of her hand to her clit.

The touch, when it came, was nothing like she'd anticipated. He caressed her lightly, almost delicately, and with a strange respect for the tenderness of her flesh. The feel of it was peculiarly nurturing and loving.

And it was this that made her cry aloud and come. As her sex lurched and clenched, she felt as if she'd been waiting to come like this for a long, long time. Since before she'd set eyes on him, since before she'd entered the Raven, since before she'd begun her determined attempt to wrest her mind back to be solely her own.

She'd been waiting for this orgasm since she'd woken in a strange hotel room with over two days missing from her life and a ghostly, disquieting memory of utter evil.

For a moment, as she clung to Rafe, both hands around him to hold herself up, she felt the brush of that darkness now. But embracing the pleasure of his long hands, she gritted her teeth, drew on his strength and managed to vanquish it.

Seconds later, he was manhandling her. In a good way. Pressing her against the wall, he lifted her leg a little, to give himself a better angle, then, taking the head of his own cock, he fitted it neatly between her labia.

'Help me,' he whispered, adjusting their bodies, manoeuvring his loins and her loins for perfect alignment. Paula pulled at her knickers, wrenching them furiously aside, allowing more access, and Rafe jerked his hips, plunging upwards with a hard thrust, right inside her.

Paula groaned long and brokenly as he filled her, savouring the sensation of stretching, and being lifted by his smooth, rhythmic lunges. Her body clamped down on him in another intense orgasm, yet in the calm part of her mind she experienced that unexpected feeling of safety again.

In a grimy alley, amongst the litter and smells, she was sheltered from harm. And as it began to rain, sudden and hard, she barely noticed it.

For the first time since that dreadful, disoriented awakening, she wasn't afraid.

3 Inner Light, Inner Dark

It was raining again.

Jonathan Sumner glowered at the damp landscape outside. Why had it suddenly started raining all the time? There'd been barely a drop since that fateful night when they'd got lost on their way to meet Paula, but in the last day or so there'd been some truly torrential showers.

Not for the first time since they'd returned to Sedgewick Priory, he wondered what was happening with their friend. They'd rowed and parted on bad terms, and he'd sensed there was something deeply amiss with her. He felt enormous guilt that they'd not hung around to enlighten her, but it was probably best that Paula never remembered running into Isidora anyway. His anxiety over Belinda's welfare, and the need to get back here for her sake, had taken priority.

Sighing, he turned from the window and the perpetual rain, and back towards his lover. Belinda was restless today, moving against the pillow as if plagued by a nightmare, even though it was mid-afternoon when she normally slept quite soundly.

He padded over to the bed and, almost on a reflex, looked up at the portrait that hung icon-like above it.

'Bloody André Von Kastel, what have you done to us?'

The man who had been Belinda's lover – and his own – looked down on them, his blue eyes mild. Not long ago,

Jonathan would have imagined that the mysterious European nobleman was watching them, monitoring their every move from within the portrait, but now it was just paint, a fine likeness but nothing more.

Count André had gone, to wherever he and his beloved Arabelle had intended to go, but they'd left an indefinable void and a sense of dislocation in their wake. Not to mention an unforeseen side effect.

'Fuck you!' muttered Jonathan, glancing from the painting to his darling Belinda, twisting and turning, her new norm since she'd helped the count perform the exotic ritual that had set him free.

He slid into bed beside her and cuddled up. The pretty Victorian nightdress she'd been wearing was bunched and crumpled, and she had one hand nestled firmly between her legs. Well, that was one side effect he hoped wouldn't go away, her increased libido. Their friend Michiko reckoned Belinda's bizarre sleep patterns – and her newly blue eyes – would normalise eventually, but Jonathan quite fancied a girlfriend who was always up for sex. Or even a fiancée. Once things settled down, he'd decided to pop the question.

In the meantime, they were here, back at Sedgewick Priory. The Japanese sorceress said they'd done exactly the right thing. Only here could the magic dissipate correctly and be reabsorbed into the old house's mysterious structure. According to the saying, time would heal all wounds. But how much time? He'd somehow lost track of it. Had they been here a week? A month? Longer? The days passed as if in a dream . . .

With a sigh, Belinda reached for him. She was still drowsing, but her body seemed constantly tuned to his, always ready and wanting to pleasure them both. With her eyes still closed, she took his hand, drew it to her sex, and folded her own hand over it, encouraging him to play with her.

Oh, baby, thought Jonathan. Caressing the woman he loved was never a hardship and, still touching her, he manoeuvred their bodies until they were lying like spoons and he could fondle her breasts beneath her soft night-gown while he dabbled his fingers in her cleft and strummed her clitoris.

God, she was so wet! So pliant and slick. He could feel her juiciness coating his fingers and running so copiously it oozed out over the inside of her thighs. While he pressed against her bottom his cock was as rigid as a bone. Shimmying against her, he stimulated himself, rocking and rubbing.

Slowly and leisurely, they moved against each other. Belinda still hadn't spoken and he wasn't sure quite how conscious she was. Was she thinking of him or was she still dreaming of André? He supposed it was possible. After all, her brief acquaintance with the enchanted count had been intense.

But as she began to murmur, his fears melted, and he smiled and pushed himself harder against her.

'Oh, Johnny,' she sighed, rotating her bottom while still holding onto his hand and making sure it didn't stray from between her legs, 'you know just what a sleepy girl needs.' As he flicked her harder, she grunted with pleasure, the sound uncouth, yet at the same time strangely lyrical. The wild cries excited him and made his cock throb and judder.

Suddenly, his own need to come was urgent. Belinda

was climaxing, her body arching and jerking beneath his hand as she muttered his name and a litany of husky swearwords. But the covers around them were twisted, and so was the voluminous nightgown. He kicked his legs a bit, but the tangle only seemed to get worse.

Moaning with impatience, he managed to wrench down his boxers and push his cock against the soft curve of Belinda's bottom. The smooth yet cuddly fabric of her nightdress was unexpectedly delicious against his penis, and shoving and pumping against it was exquisite, as good as a real fuck, but piquantly sweet and different. Within moments, as Belinda groaned again, he joined her in pleasure, shooting his semen against her cotton-covered buttocks.

Replete, Jonathan found he too wanted to drift away and slumber. He wasn't on Belinda's schedule, but sleep began to envelop him. The bed was warm and the frowsty, foxy smell of sex was soporific.

And yet just as his consciousness frayed at the edges, his beloved seemed to wake up. She tossed her head a little, her body momentarily tensing.

'I'm worried about Paula, Johnny, aren't you?' she whispered, patting his hand where it still rested on her belly. 'We shouldn't have just left her like that. Even if she did tell us to fuck off. She wasn't thinking straight. We should have helped her more.' There was raw anguish in her voice, and Jonathan felt it too. The nagging guilt resurfaced and he wondered whether to express it or try to calm Belinda's fears.

He decided on a compromise. The Priory was in 'protection' mode, magic rendering it hard to find, and almost as difficult to get out of – but they could still try.

'Try not to worry, love. We'll do something. Tomorrow, I'll see if I can get a signal on my mobile or find out how Oren contacts the outside world.' Lord André's faithful servant was the epitome of helpfulness about everything except that, and it was difficult to argue with a person who couldn't speak. 'Failing that, if you feel a bit more normal, we can see if the car will start so we can visit her.' He laced his fingers with his lover's to reassure her and comfort her fears. 'I mean, we can always come back here again, if we need to. We've almost certainly lost our jobs now, anyway, so what's the difference if we play hooky a bit longer?'

'I love you, Johnny. You're the best.' Belinda's voice was barely a breath, and yet her sweet words managed to make him smile.

But as he slipped into sleep, he couldn't stop brooding about their friend.

The smell of sandalwood filled Rafe's nostrils.

Mostly he liked it. It was a smell that normally meant sex to him, and he liked that too. But today, the pungent scent was strangely dispiriting. He wanted to sneeze but he managed to suppress it.

'Mmmm, that's so nice,' murmured the woman on the massage table in front of him. Shifting her thighs against the white towel beneath her, she rubbed them against each other in a blatant attempt to excite him. Normally, this would have made him smile, and his penis leap automatically. But today, like the sandalwood, it just depressed him.

What the hell's wrong with me? he thought, gritting his teeth.

He dug his thumbs into the woman's meaty buttocks. Harder than he should, and than was necessary. But instead of protesting, she purred and pressed her crotch suggestively against the table.

'You're a naughty boy, Rafe. You know I like it hard, don't you?'

Her name was Mrs Butcher and she was one of Rafe's 'specials', the women for whom he sometimes provided extra services. Ones that weren't listed on the pages of Inner Light's brochure amongst the usual raft of aromatherapy, massage, Reiki and hypnotherapy. Services that were off the record, under the counter, strictly hush-hush.

It had been so easy to start slipping a bit of sex on the side to these needy female clients. When he'd done it once, he hadn't felt so bad about the next time. Or the next. Or the next. And it'd been the same with the gifts. Given his past history, he'd felt horribly uncomfortable at first, but before long he'd become used to generous financial tips and gifts of clothing and expensive toiletries.

You're a whore, Rafe. A male whore.

When he thought about it, it bothered him. So he mostly tried not to. After all, he'd put his talents to worse purposes in years gone by – until the consequences had caught up with him. Mostly he was able to rationalise that, in his case, a bit of supernumerary sex was always a good thing. It was life. And making the most of it. While he could.

But today the prospect of climbing aboard Mrs Butcher on the massage table made him shudder. And it was himself, not her, that he felt distaste with. When she reached out unexpectedly and cupped his cock through his yoga pants, he flinched like a reverend mother instead of pushing himself into her grasp, as he usually did.

'What's wrong?'

Barbara Butcher rolled over, gifting him with the sight of a pair of breasts that weren't bad at all for a fifty-plus grandmother. She was a handsome woman and, under normal circumstances, sex with her was delightful. And slightly kinky. She had a sense of humour too, and she was kind and fun. He'd started to toy with the idea of taking things further. Barbara Butcher had been left nicely off by her late husband, and he could think of a lot worse people to spend the rest of his days with.

Not that there might be many, a bitter voice reminded him. He was almost forty, and his father had been gone by forty-two.

Shaking off dark thoughts, he focused again on his client. He could see fear of rejection in her eyes, and his heart lurched in sympathy. But he didn't think even his acting skills would allow him to fake it this time and he wasn't in the mood for touching either.

Something had changed last night and he didn't know why. He'd had knee tremblers around the back of the Raven before too, but today he couldn't remember anything about them.

Not the build-up, not the orgasm, and certainly not the women. They'd all disappeared, supplanted by a vivid, full-sensory recollection of the mysterious and wary Cinderella figure he'd so fleetingly fucked last night.

'I'm sorry, Barbara.' He smiled reassuringly and took her gently by the shoulders, rolling her back to the face-down position. 'I didn't sleep well last night. Insomnia.' Which was the truth, he realised. 'I don't feel that great today. You don't mind, do you?'

Barbara's answer was forestalled by the bell chiming in

Reception. Rafe frowned and lifted his hands clear of her shoulders, not wanting to transfer his tension and negativity to her. Bloody Lynn, the new receptionist, was taking one of her marathon lunch breaks again.

'Sorry again,' he muttered. 'I'd better check on that.' Wiping his hands on a towel, he strolled to the small CCTV out on the landing, where he could check on Reception and ring down to speak to whoever was there.

The tiny black and white image made his heart thud.

Dear God, you came!

Last night, after their coupling, he'd asked Paula to come back to his place to spend the night. It was the first time in a long while he'd done that, but he'd really wanted to hold her. When she'd refused, it'd twisted his gut in a sense of disappointment that had been out of all proportion. He'd only just resisted the embarrassing urge to beg. It had seemed that she wanted no more to do with him and, even when he'd pressed his business card on her and asked her to ring him sometime, he'd confidently expected it to be in the trash somewhere by now.

But here she was.

Displayed by the small screen, a shockingly different Paula stood in the airy sunlit reception area, twisting and flipping that very card between her fingers. Gone were the leather micro skirt, the skimpy top and the sexy heels. Today's Paula was fully covered, uptight and every button fastened. Her skirt was long and flowing, a pretty thing made of yards of unrevealing fabric. Her lightweight cardigan was closed right up to her throat. The silky dark hair that he'd let down last night was caught back in a prim ponytail. He'd never seen a woman more wary and ill at ease, and he had the most peculiar flash of insight. The most powerful in ages.

Why are you so scared of yourself, love? he wondered, stabbing at the intercom button.

'Hi, Paula! Can you wait just a little while. I'm with a client at the moment but I'll be down as soon as I can. Our receptionist should be back soon. I don't know where the fuck she is!'

He watched her look around, her eyes darting and then settling on the 'press to speak' unit on the desk.

'Rafe? Is that you?' Her voice sounded as tinny as his probably did.

'Yes, it's me. I'll be down in a little bit. Please don't go!'

You sad fuck! Don't grovel! he told himself, watching her twizzle the card around, folding it in a kind of nervous origami. Dear God, he was holding his breath. And not only that, his cock had suddenly heaved itself to a full, lively stand with painful speed. He could still feel the brush of those fingers against his flesh as the two of them had grappled with her stretchy knickers in the dark.

'No, it's all right. This was a bad idea.' Frowning, her eyes flashed around the room again, crushing his card in her hand and dropping it on the counter, then running her free hand up and down her wool-clad upper arm. 'Look . . . leave it. Forget it. I'm going. Sorry . . .'

'No!'

The sound of his own voice horrified him. It rang with all the neediness he'd only just managed to quash last night. A quality she'd be able to hear, crappy speakers or otherwise.

'No, please don't go. Stay!'

There was a long pause, during which Paula's mouth moved as if she were talking to herself. She was twisting at the top button of her cardigan now, pulling it so hard it was in danger of coming off.

'OK. I'll wait. But don't rush with your client. I'll read a magazine.' Abruptly cutting off the speaker, she strode to one of the low chairs, threw herself down in it and picked up an old copy of *Spirit and Destiny*.

Ridiculously shaken, Rafe turned away from the tiny monitor and headed back to the treatment room, where Barbara had slid off the table and was shrugging into one of the centre's fluffy white towelling robes.

'Don't worry, kiddo. You can make it up to me another time.' Her eyes dropped to his groin and she gave him a heavily mascara-laden wink. 'I guess she's the cause of your sleepless nights, isn't she, eh? Better get downstairs, lad, and sort out that little problem.'

Rafe stared down at his own body, rampant where before it'd been indifferent, his erect cock clearly defined beneath his thin jersey yoga trousers.

'I'm sorry, Barbara,' he said quietly and, when she continued to smile at him in a way that was more maternal than frisky, he shrugged.

'No problem, love. Catch you later. Enjoy your friend.' She winked again, just as she was leaving in the direction of the changing rooms. 'Because it certainly looks like she's going to enjoy you.'

I'm not so sure of that, thought Rafe.

His nerves pinging with a strange foreboding, he pulled on a loose shirt to hide his condition and walked swiftly to the stairs.

* * *

What am I doing here, thought Paula, slapping her foot against the polished wood floor in a nervous, compulsive movement. This is mad. He can't help me. Nobody can help me.

The energy was building in her again and it had to have an outlet. Tapping her feet. Tugging and mangling at her cardigan buttons. Suddenly the one she'd been worrying broke free and skittered away across the floor and under one of the other beige leather-covered couches.

'Fuck!'

Something stirred in Paula's gut and in the back of her mind. Isidora, come to life as if roused by the word she was so fond of. *That's what you want*, she seemed to say, *isn't it? You want to fuck him. He's coming now ... And here you are, dressed like a frigid spinster librarian.*

Blood surged in Paula's veins, frothing with hormones. She wasn't sure whether it was Isidora driving her or just her own memory of last night, and an experience of sex that was both raw and strangely exquisite. Whatever it was, her fingers flickered at speed over the buttons of her cardigan, revealing her breasts, so barely concealed by a light cotton camisole. Her nipples were hard, dark and plummy, roused instantaneously by the prospect of seeing her sleazy alley lover again.

Faint footsteps padded down the corridor behind a door marked 'Treatments This Way' and, as an unseen hand manipulated the lock, she tugged out the covered band that secured her hair, then fluffed at it haphazardly.

It probably just looked untidy, not tousled-sexy, but who cared as the door was swinging open.

And suddenly Rafe was standing there, watching her. He frowned slightly, his head cocked on one side.

Paula pursed her lips. What to say? What had she been expecting of him in the warm light of day? More jeans and leather? A retread of last night's dangerous erotic bad-boy image?

Certainly not this look, that surprised her almost as much as her appearance clearly surprised him.

Today's Rafe was Mr New Age, all peace and light and hippy-man in his loose white trousers and a white linen shirt, only partially buttoned. His large feet were bare and a pungent smell of sandalwood wafted into the room as he stepped forwards.

'Hello again, Paula.' He smiled, then momentarily snagged his lip with his white upper teeth. 'I didn't expect to see you again. I hoped, obviously, but somehow I didn't think you'd actually turn up.'

Paula's heart thumped as she stepped forwards too. What was the protocol when meeting a one-night stand? He'd almost been right. When she'd set out this morning, she hadn't had the slightest intention of seeking him out.

What do I do? she thought, taking another step. Kiss him? Hug him? Just look at him like a dork? The only compensation was that Rafe seemed as unsure as she did.

Or maybe they should shake hands?

'Hello, Rafe.' Her voice was small as she reached out.

Rafe's smile blossomed, lighting up his whole rather stern face. With a shrug, he wiped his hand on the side of his trousers, then held it out and, when their fingers touched, she felt the very faintest kiss of slippery oil upon his skin.

Caught unawares, she swayed so hard that she thought she might fall backwards through some invisible barrier and into the dream of Isidora and Count André.

Instantly Rafe's arms shot around her, as strong in the light as they had been in the dark. Just as quickly, Paula righted herself and shrugged free of him, not knowing how she could possibly explain about the oil and the dream. And yet if he *were* to help her she'd have to, sometime soon.

'Sorry about that. I've been giving a massage.' For a moment, his tongue – which was teasingly pink – slipped out and flicked against his lip. He hesitated and, if she hadn't known better, she would almost have thought he was bashful. 'Do you want one? I've got a free slot.'

Delicious heat pumped through her veins at the thought of his hands on her. Last night, he'd proved that his fingers were nothing short of magical and at least the match of Isidora's blue-eyed dream lover. Her body was already screaming for more of what she'd had in the alley. Her breasts ached. Lust roiled low in her belly, surging like the heart of a volcano. The invisible tattoo prickled and dark urges propelled her towards saying, 'Yes, yes, yes . . .'

And yet.

It was imperative she *not* give into every single wayward surge of lust, either hers or Isidora's. She was *not* the bitch's puppet and, if she could actually resist sex sometimes, it might give her a fingernail grip on control.

'Why not?' she heard herself say, to the sound of inner gleeful laughter.

He'd always had smooth lines with women. He'd always been able to sweet talk and find exactly the right note, the right approach, to get his quarry into bed.

So why was he suddenly as tongue-tied as a spotty

teenager faced with his first sight of a real naked woman?

Rafe watched from across the treatment room, shrugging off his shirt, then fidgeting with his towels and his vials of oils while Paula pulled off her very few clothes without hesitation or modesty.

Again, he sensed raw sexual determination in her. It glinted in her eyes as she looked at him. She had very lovely eyes. They were large and liquid and a soft shade of hazel, and yet, when she slanted a glance at him, there was a breathtaking flash of green now.

Underneath her long skirt, she wore a pair of strangely serviceable black cotton knickers. They were cut full and made from opaque, thick-looking material, and the very incongruousness of them being worn by a woman so keen to strip off put him in mind of the support pants of last night. He waited for her to slip her thumbs into the waistband and peel them off but, even though she plucked at the elastic, she left the garment on, her lips pursing tightly.

Watching Paula climb gracefully onto the massage table, Rafe tried to centre himself and gain control over his body and his senses. He smiled at her, and then turned away to drip a little soothing lavender oil into his massage base, while at the same time attempting to tune into the messages of her emotions.

What was her mood? How did she feel about him?

She seemed a conundrum of conflicting urges and auras. It was a long time since Rafe had tried to use his empathy in anything more than the most general and unfocused way. It was one thing trying to get a sense of the women he worked on here, so he could please them, and quite another to go deep and almost try to read their thoughts. Unsavoury memories of the trouble it'd got him into in the past still left a bitter taste.

But Paula was one woman he had to decipher.

She was chaos. Lust, fear, hope, a genuine honest attraction – and yet roiling under the surface there was something darker and so unexpected he almost recoiled. There was something so powerful in her that his hands shook and lavender oil skittered over the surface of the counter. Tamping down instantly, he cleaned up the spill, feeling the bump, bump of his heart and a sense of panic that threatened to ruin his composure.

Controlling his breathing, he quashed the urge to run from the room and find a still quiet place to meditate and regain his equilibrium. Everything about him wanted to believe Paula was just a sexy, attractive but reasonably ordinary girl who didn't mean harm to anyone. In fact, if he'd never discovered his ESP or whatever it was, he'd be smirking to himself, anticipating a delicious time ahead for them. But he *did* have this strange, fickle ability sometimes, and now it was clanging like a klaxon and flashing red warning signs of danger.

With a less than sure hand, he capped the bottle and shook it thoroughly to mix the oils. When he turned back towards the table, he found Paula lying face up, her legs akimbo and her hands cupping her breasts.

'I suppose you must get lots of sex here on this couch.' Her voice was husky and seductive as she looked at him from beneath her lashes, her fingers flexing. She should have looked ridiculous, like a living burlesque, cheap and crude. But she entranced him. He couldn't speak. His cock was iron.

'It's a very sexy environment. Very conducive to acts of wickedness.' Her green eyes glittered as she slowly licked her lips. 'To getting it on...'

Rafe gripped the oil bottle tightly, fighting for breath. He experienced a disorientating sense of double vision that made him giddy and, for a second, he seemed to see two women on the couch. It was like a drug trip, as if someone had loaded his massage oil with peyote and he'd absorbed it through his skin. Paula's dark hair looked silkier, longer and lusher; and her eyes were slanted and imperious, assessing him as if he were sexual meat for her delectation. Her body was simply sublime, full of breast and sumptuous of hip. Her serviceable black knickers were gone, discarded on the floor to reveal the perfect, fragrant triangle of her bush. She held out her hand to him like a queen, and he walked towards her.

'Mmmm...' Taking the bottle of oil from him, she pulled the stopper and sniffed deeply, smiling to herself. Then, in a sudden violent gesture, she hurled the thing across the room, laughing as the oil arced from it, flying like a pale-yellow ribbon. 'A pretty scent –' she adjusted herself on the table, slithering around until she was perched on the edge '– but artificial, my Rafe, too artificial.' Parting her legs, she offered him something that was both natural and beyond nature instead.

Rafe gasped, dragging in both oxygen and the odour of Paula's genitals. The room was filled with lavender, but it seemed to come from a distance and through a filter. Only the essence of woman had real truth and real meaning.

Staggering slightly, he fell to his knees and pressed his face between her thighs, aware of a great well of tightly focused heat, emanating not from her sex but the white curve of her belly. He tried to lift his head and search for a visible mark or glow, and for a moment he imagined he saw a slight raised pattern on her skin. But before he could get a closer look she pressed down hard on the top of his head, forcing him to pleasure her.

She was hot, fragrant and intoxicatingly delicious. A million impressions crowded his senses, both ordinary and unusual. The taste of Paula was like power itself, infinitely greater than his own puny gifts. Supping at her earthy juices, his mind seemed to expand and a rainbow of colours exploded in his head.

'Yes! Yes! That's marvellous. More of that!' she goaded him as he flicked his tongue over her. Swift, deft hands dug into his scalp, cramming his face against the juncture of her thighs. Rafe felt as if he were drowning, drowning so fast and hard that he'd probably expire just at the moment of her extreme pleasure. His cock was a rod of agony that seemed to belong to another man.

Harder and harder he licked, covering every bit of her sex, licking her clit and her lips, and sipping at her entrance. She writhed against him, sultry and serpentine, groaning and shouting, praising him with a string of lurid profanities, language even fouler and more extreme than even he'd ever comfortably used himself. Her heels bashed against his back and his entire head felt as if it were on fire. His eyes were shut but somehow he seemed to see a burning, setting sun, searing his vision and extinguishing his self-control.

When he sucked hard on her clit, she howled. But instead of falling back and surrendering herself to orgasm and pleasure, she surged off the massage bench and knocked him backwards, so he sprawled on the wooden floor and slid in the spilt oil. As he lay there with the wind knocked out of him, dimly away of shards of glass digging into his shoulders and back, she climbed astride him, and knelt over his pelvis, her dark triangle hovering tauntingly over his loins.

'So, sex-god, do you have a condom in your pocket?' she jeered. Then without waiting for an answer, she inclined over him, feeling around and under him into the pocket of his yoga pants. Her fingers felt hot through the thin cloth and with deadly accuracy they secured and prised out the contraceptive he might have used if he'd been able to bring himself to fuck Barbara Butcher what seemed like a century ago.

In a swift sharp yank that had him bouncing and swinging up to slap his belly, she dragged down his trousers and, handling him ruthlessly, she rolled the latex jacket onto him. Then with no further ado, she sat down hard, taking every bit of him into her with one voracious lunge.

It was like plunging into the heart of a black star, burning hot, yet at the same time utterly dark. He'd never felt anything quite like it, not even with this same woman, last night in the alley.

But was it even the same woman? He no longer knew or cared, the way she moved, the way she rocked, the way she gripped him in a slow, then fast, then slow, devilish rhythm. His spine was melting and running away across the floor, blending with the spilt oil and the remnants of his flawed self-respect.

Pathetically he bucked his hips upwards, trying to make some impact on her, but she slammed down hard, making him feel as if his scalp were lifting off. He tried to hold her hips, but she dashed his hands away, then grabbed them again, bringing them to her breasts.

'Hard. Do it hard.' Her command was low, yet echoing as if it were coming from the vault of a cathedral. He complied and, as he did, she slid a hand to the juncture of their bodies and began masturbating herself as furiously as she was ruthlessly fucking him.

'Yes! Yes!' she screamed. 'Yes, you vile bastard, I've got you now!'

Rafe blinked, trying to focus on her face, and got a jolt of shock. Paula's eyes were rolled up and her grimace was that of another woman who was in another place. She bounced harder, gripped harder, and, with some last faint shreds of conscious thought, he received the distinct impression that she was trying to fuck not him to death but another man entirely.

But then those shreds dissolved, his vision went red and he hollered like a dog, his abused loins erupting in a painful, blissful surge of total orgasm.

His last awareness was her answering snarl of pleasure.

The smell of lavender filled Paula's head, making it whirl and her stomach flutter ominously.

Slowly, she sat up and surveyed the war zone, trying to focus.

Her clothes were everywhere, the floor was shiny with oil and what looked like smears of blood, and Rafe was stretched out to one side of her, gasping like a beached porpoise. His yoga pants were dragged down to his knees, exposing his crotch and his subsiding cock, still clothed in its latex coat.

Was it going to be a habit, this? Waking up, dimly

remembering doing some crazy thing, but not quite knowing how she'd got herself into it?

She dragged in a deep breath, sickly lavender or no, in an attempt to calm her panic and work out what had led to what. There would have been some comfort in being able to blame everything on Isidora. But truth was hard, and she had to face the fact that the bitch hadn't been entirely in control. All she had done was bring out urges that already existed, seething and latent.

Which was the true horror of her possession.

Fighting nausea and unable to look anywhere else, Paula studied Rafe.

He looked like a man who'd just survived a hurricane, but somehow that made him strangely beautiful. Despite his short cropped hair he had the look of a warrior angel, a character flying aloft in a Renaissance fresco. She could almost imagine him on the Sistine Chapel ceiling. His deep chest was still heaving, his reddened lips parted. There was a thin film of sweat lying across the surface of his naked chest and belly, and the blood smears on the floor were obviously his, because a thin trickle or two of it was seeping out from under his back.

She'd never seen a man that looked more shattered, shagged out or debauched, but, deep in her centre, the demon lust reanimated. And this time there wasn't even a whisper of Isidora. The desire was just hers, deep and true.

'Are you OK? I'm not sure I am ... I think I've just been possessed by the devil.' Rafe sat up, flinching and grimacing as he straightened.

'Don't say that!'

The words were out without thinking, and Rafe's eyes

shot open, wide and puzzled. And concerned. Ignoring the glass and the oil, he slid along the floor and put his arms around her, folding her close. There wasn't anything sexual in it, even though she was naked and he was almost the same, but, even so, her libido coiled, wishing it *was* sex.

'Are you OK,' he repeated softly. 'That was pretty wild. I feel shell-shocked. How about you?'

'I . . . I don't know.'

It was the truth. She didn't know what to feel or think. The heat of Rafe's skin against hers was the only thing that was real and, automatically, like a kitten seeking comfort, she snuggled closer.

His arms tightened. 'Now why do I think that what just happened isn't the sort of thing that you'd normally do?'

Paula shook her head. Over the last few weeks, she'd almost forgotten what 'normal' was like, and being reminded of that hit her like a blow.

To her horror, she began to cry. Hard. Her shoulders and her whole body shook with the force of the sobs, and embarrassingly she began to gulp and hiccup like a toddler after a tantrum.

'Hey, hey, don't worry.' Long, lavender-scented hands slowly stroked her hair and her back therapeutically. 'It's all a bit sudden, love. But it's good. No harm done.' He laughed softly against her ear. 'And I still respect you.'

Suddenly, the crying hiccups mutated into giggle hiccups. Paula rocked in his arms but it was with laughter rather than distress. A giant weight seemed to lift off her shoulders and her chest, and darkness, the now familiar darkness, receded away. The light and warmth of the pleasant white room was an embrace as comforting as that of the semi-naked semi-stranger who held her so kindly in his arms.

'There, that's better.' As they drew a little way apart, he brushed her hair away from her face. His brown eyes were warm, but a little curious still, and he was frowning. 'Let's get this lot –' he gestured to the mess of oil and glass and clothing all over the floor '– cleared up, and then I'll make some tea and we can talk. And maybe you can tell me what you really came here for. I've a feeling that it wasn't just to shag me senseless, delicious as that was.'

'OK. And you're right.' Paula allowed him to help her with great care to her feet and lead her with infinite caution out of the glass zone. Suddenly embarrassed, she stared at the narrow white counter where the oil bottles stood.

'What? That you didn't come here to shag me, or that the shag was delicious?'

'Both.' When she turned round, she found Rafe holding open an oversized white fluffy bathrobe for her to slip into.

He laughed softly as she shrugged it on and they set about the cleaning up.

4 Therapy

'So, why did you really come here?'

Rafe was eyeing her over the rim of his teacup and, put on the spot, Paula didn't have the first idea how to even begin telling her story.

How do you tell someone you want help casting out an evil spirit? she mused glumly. Or whatever the hell Isidora is.

They were in a different room now, one she guessed was used for counselling sessions. Paula noticed that Rafe had gently manoeuvred her into lying back on a white leather-covered recliner, while he sat in an easy chair just to one side.

I'm ready for my close-up now, Dr Freud, she thought, and couldn't help but laugh. When Rafe narrowed his eyes, she said, 'I don't know where to start.'

Weariness washed over her, and she reached for her own tea from the side table, hoping for an energy boost. Late nights in alleys and strenuous afternoons on treatment-room floors weren't conducive to mental clarity, and her story was going to sound like the demented delusions of a crazy woman. Or a drunk. Or a junkie.

God, it would have been so much easier if she *could* blame booze or pills!

Sighing, she put aside her cup. 'I came here because I need someone to help me. I don't know ... It's hard to explain...' As she met his look, Rafe cocked his head on one side. His expression was calm and gently encouraging, a therapist's cliché. He was probably good at his job, but all she could think about was the way his short, crisply cut hair just curled a tiny bit at the edges. And his eyes, too. They were utterly beautiful, like gleaming, polished wood, dark and wise and knowing.

Is it an act? the sudden cynic in her asked. Was he wondering how long he had to wait before they could have sex again? She had a horrible suspicion that his wide massage table might see more than therapeutic action now and again.

'Just try.' He abandoned his own teacup and reached for her hand.

Almost immediately, she felt a discreet freeing sensation, a loosening of her thoughts. 'I think I'm possessed. I think there's another mind, another consciousness inside me sometimes.' It *did* sound mad, but how else could she describe it? 'Not all the time, but there's something in me that connects this ... this "thing" to me and it keeps coming back.'

She puffed out a breath. The words had come relatively easily, and seemed to make sense.

'What makes you believe that?' Rafe's grip on her was light and unrestricting, but his thumb circled slowly over the back of her hand. He was soothing her, she realised, in a pleasing, abstracted way.

'I have dreams ... and I hear her voice. She speaks to me and goads me into doing things and saying things. It's not really against my will. They're things I might have done anyway. But she sort of encourages me into actions that I know are stupid and dangerous.'

'She? It's definitely a woman?' Still the thumb circled, delicately and comfortingly. Rafe was closer now and she could smell his freshly showered body beneath the black T-shirt and jeans that he wore.

'Oh yes, and I sort of know who she is. I've heard her name in dreams and I think I met her once, although I don't actually remember anything about it.' Jumbled memories flooded into her mind and the rush of them was so great it made her giddy. She bolted upright on the recliner, her skin as cold as winter in the warm, sunlit room, all her sense of well-being shattered. She wanted to run, but what was the point when her pursuer was inside her? Instinctively, she pressed her hand to her belly, seeking the heat of the invisible tattoo. It was cool there now, but it wouldn't be long before it began to sizzle again.

'And there's ... there's this mark that comes up on my belly when she's around. It's like a pattern. I can't see it but I can feel it. And it's hot.' She clawed at the place through the robe, but there was nothing she could do. It would always come again. 'She's put some kind of brand on me, the bitch, and I can't get rid of it!' Shaking her head, she let out a cry, overwhelmed by the horror of finally voicing what had happened.

Immediately, Rafe leant forwards and wrapped his arms around her. His body was solid and real, like a rock. Paula hugged him in return, gripping on tight to her only anchor against being whirled away to madness.

For a while, he held her in silence. She didn't cry this time. She hadn't the energy. She needed everything to cling on, just cling on.

Eventually she wriggled free, putting him from her with a hand on his broad chest.

'You must think I'm mental.'

'No, I don't.' He placed his hand over hers again, still soothing, still calming, 'There are some strange, strange things in the world, Paula.' For a moment, he seemed to go away from her, as if visiting some private trouble of his own, but then he squeezed her fingers. 'And I don't even think this is the only world either.'

For an instant, cynicism reared up and she glanced around the room at posters advertising sessions with spirit guides, reflexology, angel interviews. Things she'd always dismissed as claptrap.

'Of course, you're into all this New Age stuff, aren't you? It's your business to tell nutters you believe all this nonsense.' She gestured at an image of a smiling Indian swami.

Rafe shrugged. 'I believe some of it.'

'But do you actually believe me? Be honest. No bullshitting because you want to get in my pants again.'

He nodded. 'Well, yes, I do sometimes tell white lies to women and I'm not proud of it. But in this case, I'm telling the truth. I do believe you.'

And she believed him. After being fobbed off by her doctor with pills and vague mutterings about being 'just tired' and 'having had a shock', it was refreshing and reassuring, and something seemed to lift off her, something indefinable. She knew that, if she found Belinda and Jonathan, they'd probably know what was going on – but they were out of reach for the moment. Now, though, there was someone who she could touch and feel and talk to who was prepared to listen and believe without dismissing her as ill or neurotic. The sense of relief was almost blissful.

'Really?' she whispered, her eyes watery.

'Of course.' He drew her hand from his chest and, twisting his wrist, just clasped her fingers loosely. 'Why don't you tell me as much about it as you can. And then maybe we can work out a way to help you.'

Paula heaved another sigh, letting go of some of the tension that had been gathering so long. How to begin? She really didn't know where. Most of it was vague in the extreme.

'Well, about five weeks ago, I was supposed to meet a couple of old college buddies who were on holiday near here. It was just a casual thing. We were going to hang out a bit, maybe motor round a few quaint villages and whatnot. Probably drink lots of beer in between enjoying the local colour.'

When she paused, Rafe said, 'Sounds cool.' He gave her a little nod, encouraging her.

'But I don't remember much of what happened after I set off to meet them.' Shaking her hand free of Rafe's, she wrapped her arms around herself. It was as if she had to or her body would fly apart. 'The next thing I do remember clearly is waking up in a strange hotel room, naked and with a whole chunk of time missing. Someone sent for a ambulance and they took me to hospital. It's all a bit blurred. I suppose they thought I was a druggie but apparently there was nothing obvious in my system. Just a bit of alcohol but not enough to have caused me to black out.' Tremors rippled through her body, icy waves of panic. She gripped herself hard, holding on as best she could, staring into the middle distance and trying to grab at fleeting images and fragments of recollection. 'And I had absolutely no memory of the preceding two or three days. During which I'm now beginning to suspect I met this bitch inside me!'

'And have you remembered anything since? About those lost days?' Rafe's voice was soft and low, subtly leading. If she hadn't been so freaked out, Paula would have laughed at how touchy-feely he sounded. Glancing at him, she discovered he'd crossed his arms and had a knuckle pressed to his chin. The cold spell breaking, she laughed out loud at the sight of him.

'What's the matter?' He grinned back at her, and she sensed that he knew.

'It's the shrink act. The infinitely understanding therapist routine. It's so funny after what just happened on that couch in there.'

Rafe shook his head, then shrugged. 'Yeah, yeah, yeah, I know. I should be struck off, shouldn't I?' For a moment his mouth hardened, but almost as quickly he was smiling again. 'In fact I would be if I was "on" anything to start with.'

As Paula unwound her arms again, he reached for her hand once more, holding it loosely.

'Seriously though, *have* you remembered anything?'

Paula dragged in a breath, centring herself. She felt calmer now, more in control, her nerves settled by the heat in Rafe's fingers.

'Well, not at first, but in the last week or so, some stuff's started to come back.' Stay calm, stay calm. But her equilibrium was tilting as fast as it had settled, sliding sideways into panic. She gripped Rafe's hand harder, nails digging in. When he winced, she shook herself free. 'Sorry about that.'

He shrugged. 'No problem. Go on. What's come back to you?'

Paula breathed deeply. Suddenly she didn't want it to come back. The thing, Isidora, wasn't here now and she was loath to stir her dark presence up again. 'Well, it's just these fragments and dreams. And this sense that ... that ... whatever she is, this woman-thing inside me ... that she's evil ... and she is, or was, very powerful.'

'In what way?'

'I don't know. Black magic or witchcraft or some shit like that.' She shrugged and shook her head. 'But the thing is, I don't even fucking well *believe* in the supernatural! At least I didn't. It's always been just mumbo-jumbo to me.' She sought Rafe's eyes but they were neutral, offering nothing definitive. 'Until now.'

'But now you *do* believe?' He looked at her steadily, his gaze level, but somehow Paula sensed a keen interest under the surface of his placid, therapeutic mask.

'Yes. Yes I do. When Belinda and Jonathan visited me in the hospital afterwards, they started to tell me some insane cock and bull story about this guy they'd been staying with who was two hundred years old, and kind of immortal, and how they and this supposedly friendly Japanese sorceress had helped him move on to the next plane of existence or some cobblers or other like that.'

She remembered the state of total confusion, total incomprehension she'd felt. The inability to take in the wild tale her friends had told her, and the sense of deep, irrational hostility she'd felt when they'd asked her what she remembered. 'I got angry with them. I said it was all stupid bullshit and they'd been boozing too hard and/or smoking too much weed or something ... and they'd dreamt it all up.' She'd felt shame too. A sense of dirtiness, of being used. Had it all been her own fault? Had *what* been her own fault? If she could only remember what that bitch had done to her. 'I told them to fuck off, and that I didn't want to see them again. And I never have done since.'

'Was there anything else they told you? Can you remember?'

Paula's head came up. Rafe's voice was subtly sharper, more insistent somehow. It was obvious that he wanted to know what had happened too, but some kind of inbuilt radar told her that suddenly his interest was slightly less altruistic. Or was she just imagining things? Again.

But a slight frown puckered his brow and he was leaning forwards in his seat, his brown eyes intent. 'What about the immortal man? Did they say how he came to be that way? What was the source of his longevity?'

'How the fuck should I know! They didn't say, and I was too tired and too angry and embarrassed to ask. And now they've disappeared. I can't contact them at their workplaces or their home.' Suddenly, she rubbed at her eyes. They felt gritty, almost as they had done last night from the dry ice. Her mouth opened of its own accord in a massive yawn.

'You're exhausted, aren't you?' He took her hand in both of his, smoothing it, his finger circling in her palm. 'Why don't you rest for a while? There's no one else due in here today. Try to get some sleep. You'll feel better for it.'

Suddenly the idea of sleep was blissful. Would she be safe from the dreams here? Positive vibes and all that.

She shrugged. Inner Light was supposed to be just that, a haven of light and peace, but Isidora had definitely been in the ascendant back in the treatment room, so there was no reason to think she was safe from her here.

But still, she was so damn tired.

Rafe's fingers were subversively sensual. There was a faint sexual edge to his slow circling touch, but it wasn't aggressive. He could be a friend, couldn't he? Not just a fantastic lover. And God knows she needed someone on her team right now. Belinda and Jonathan were probably the only people who could shed any light on her situation, but they seemed to have vanished into thin air, not to be found, or reached by any means. And as for the 'good' sorceress, their Japanese buddy? Who even knew if she actually existed?

Paula tried to look into Rafe's face, but her eyelids were incredibly heavy and she could barely focus. The upholstery beneath her was a cradle and she shuffled down into it.

'Get some rest now.' Rafe gave her hand one last squeeze before he released it and, as she began to drift off, she felt him gently lift her head and slide another pillow beneath it. 'Get some sleep and then, later, we'll get to the bottom of things. We'll find out what's going on, and we'll find those bloody friends of yours and get a straight answer out of them!'

We?

That sounded so nice. She was a part of a 'we' now. She wasn't alone with her demon any more.

Rafe's heart thudded as he looked down at the sleeping Paula.

It would have been so easy to put her under and question her in more detail, but he hadn't and he didn't know why he'd held back. There had been plenty of times in the past when he'd never bothered with such scruples. He'd used his acquired talents and his natural gifts less than ethically without thinking twice. His mouth thinned as he remembered, disliking himself.

Paula looked so innocent, so vulnerable. Not a bit like the hungry seductress who'd literally floored him back in the treatment room. And yet still, she was sweetly desirable. His cock stirred and he imagined waking her and coaxing her into sex again. He could do it, even if she wasn't interested. But something new in him, some dormant shred of decency that both disturbed and cheered him, prevailed.

He threw himself down in the armchair and watched her, his fingers steepled, their tips pressed hard together as if that might keep him from going back on his decision.

God, there was power in her though. It had felt like a thousand volts flowing into him as they'd fucked, a real force that was capable of anything and everything if only it could be channelled. Her story about a possessing 'demon' was pretty far out, but he'd heard of stranger things, and she seemed to believe in it utterly. Maybe it was real, maybe it wasn't. If he was honest with himself, what she really needed was the help of a reputable consultant psychiatrist to help her work through this, and a long course of intensive treatment, not just the self-serving ministrations of a second-rate hypnotist charlatan like himself.

But one word rang in his mind, again and again, and he found himself leaning forwards again, as if getting closer to her could summon its secrets from her sleeping mind.

Immortality.

Her friends had spoken of a two-hundred-year-old man and a Japanese sorceress.

A two-hundred-year-old man? How did that happen? If such a person truly existed, there must be a way to extend life. Could anyone do it, with the right spell or whatever? Or did you need to be a sorcerer or a sorceress to achieve it? Like the Japanese woman, or even the creature inside Paula?

Into the mêlée of his thoughts came the image of his father. Skeletal, dead at 42, having gone out in a hard, hard way. You're nearly forty, man, he thought, and, if you've got what he had, you need some kind of magic mojo – and you need it fast.

Staring hard at Paula's sleeping form, he sat for a long time, turning thoughts and possibilities over in his mind, grappling with inner demons of his own, ones that were real rather than just supernatural notions.

Was there a way to get her secrets, and still not use or hurt her?

It started to rain outside as the same thoughts revolved, repeating endlessly.

Longevity, possession, magic, Japanese sorceresses, again and again and again.

Michiko Asaka stared out of the window of her newly acquired apartment and frowned at the dirty London rain. What had happened to the sun? And to the peace and golden contentment that had settled upon her after André's leaving? She had been happy for him then, and for Arabelle, but now she missed him. Great Amida, how she missed her old friend!

But it was more than just that. All was not right, she sensed, and there were things not quite done, left unresolved. After staying a couple of weeks at Sedgewick, counselling her friends Belinda and Jonathan, she'd become restless again. So, after leaving the Priory protected by magic, she'd returned to the city. But now the metropolis oppressed her and, suddenly, the urge to sling her leg across the back of her motorcycle and just leave for the country again was almost irresistible.

Maybe tomorrow? Yes, tomorrow. At least tonight she had a diversion to alleviate her restlessness.

Looking back into the room, she scanned the stark white walls, so newly washed and painted. There was very little furniture in the apartment, just a few mats, low tables, the necessary futons and the usual electrical appliances of modern living. Everything else had been stripped out and destroyed, burnt to ashes – taking with it all reminders of its previous hated owner.

Maybe that's it, thought Michiko, clutching her quilted man's dressing gown more closely around her. Maybe it's impossible to completely eradicate her after all.

But it had seemed a waste when Isidora Katori had disappeared, presumably into the black pits of hell, not to take advantage of her smart apartment in a prime London location. Ever the pragmatist, Michiko had simply located it, moved in and taken over. It had been effortlessly easy to delicately 'persuade' everyone, through the force of her mind, that she had a right to. Isidora's human employees, apparently unaware of her true nature, had just disappeared to other jobs when there had been no one to pay them.

And still the rain clattered down, rattling a tattoo on the narrow balcony. Michiko drew the long velvet curtains she'd just had hung and, abandoning the sitting room, followed the delicate smell of incense to her bedroom.

The lover she'd left, tied up on the bed, was motionless.

Insolent young pup, thought Michiko fondly, admiring his buttocks.

In the days since André's freeing, she had sampled many men and women. In fact, in between stripping out this flat and making it over, she'd done little else but fuck in one form or another. New friends. Old friends. Friends who she wasn't sure were friends at all. She frowned, thinking of one invitation she hadn't yet answered.

Balthazar Davenheim had often sought her company over the years. He was a physician, trained in many fields of medicine as well as being proficient in magic. Currently a professor of plastic surgery, his accomplishments were many and his charms considerable, but she'd never succumbed to him. They were too alike. They both liked to dominate and take control in the bedroom.

That he should approach her now troubled her. Did he think that with André no longer around she would turn to him? Or had he been in league with Isidora and was now seeking revenge on her behalf? Either way, Michiko had declined his invitations, even though she knew he had a hoard of magical treasures that interested her. Instead, she'd played and fucked with all manner of partners who were not of the craft, sleeping and partying her way across half the city of London and resigning at last from her assumed life in the Takarazuka Revue.

The board had at first been astonished and vexed to lose their principal *otokoyaku*, their top star, right in the middle of the Star Troupe's prestigious world tour, but they had quickly found themselves 'persuaded', without their realising it, that Michiko's exit was mutually agreed and amicable and a great chance for a new star of the all-woman review. An unprecedented and hugely generous resignation bonus had been immediately forthcoming.

With a slow, appreciative gesture, Michiko stroked the padded silk of her luxurious dressing gown. The board had even found themselves gifting her some of her costumes. Most of the suits were too flashy for everyday use, of course, but some items were eminently wearable.

Enjoying the slide of the silk against her body, she walked slowly to the bed.

Hiro was a new prize, one of her countrymen, picked up at the hairdresser's of all places. Michiko stroked her own neatly barbered hair, freshly coal black, thanks to Hiro's skills as a colourist. She supposed she could have done the job herself, by magic or more conventionally, but a whim had driven her out to a salon when her bleached, orange-tinted locks had begun to bore her. And serendipity had handed her Hiro with his nimble fingers, his artistry and his sexy, camp, but still deliciously hetero-sexual style. His large doe eyes had adored her from the very first instant they'd alighted on her. He was no Davenheim, laden with a cluster of degrees and dazzling intelligence, but was cultured in his own way, fond of the art and literature of their homeland, and precociously skilled in drawing and calligraphy. His first gift to her, apart from his body, had been an exquisitely wrought scroll glorifying her name and his regard for her beauty.

Hiro was a gem, and chief amongst his charms was his willingness to be her happy slave without the need for magic or mind control.

As she joined him on the futon, those big dark eyes snapped open and the look of worshipful terror in the depths made her sex moisten and her blackberry nipples pucker hard in a way that was almost painful.

'Where were we?' She slid her hand down his sleek thigh for emphasis. His body was as yet unmarked tonight and, though it seemed a shame to interfere with the caramel crème of his skin, the untouched canvas was intimately tempting. How delicious it was going to be to adorn him with blotches and streaks of pink. That was one of the many things that added to his appeal for her. He both marked up beautifully and healed with remarkable speed.

With a hard shove on the side of his hip, she forced him onto his back, with his bound hands trapped awkwardly behind him. His superb cock, thick and dark, seemed to leap up and reach for her. He squealed like a baby when she slapped it for its insolence.

It was hard to know what to do with him first, he was such a treat, but she took hold of his penis and tugged on it lightly. He moaned, flirting his narrow hips up, following her like a pup on a leash, then shouted out loud when she struck his lean thigh a hard crack with her free hand.

'Your cock is mine, boy. You don't move. You don't make a sound. I play with this –' she pulled on him again, then pressed the sturdy flesh against the flat smooth surface of his belly '– and you stay still and good and quiet.'

His near-black eyes widened, but he held himself magnificently in check, his sweet face and sweeter body as still as she demanded of him.

For several minutes, she amused herself, holding him by the very tip, inclining his fierce erection this way and that, smoothing the delicate under-groove with her thumb, sometimes even leaning forwards to lick at his thickly dripping pre-come. He was salty and ripe with musk, utterly delicious, but she didn't take him fully into her mouth, merely sampling his fluid without giving him any pleasure.

When she looked up at him again, his rosy mouth was working and a silver stream of tears was trickling from his eyes.

Sliding up his body, she licked at those too, before rising to her feet.

Standing over him again, her sense of ennui returned.

His skin was too honeyed, his hair, streaked with electric magenta, too dark. His eyes, though pretty and soft and expressive, simply weren't blue.

Irrational anger surged in her gut. It wasn't supposed to be like this. For a moment, she imagined making him over. Making him appear, at least, to be a simulacrum of her dear departed friend. It was a simple matter to do, and her fingertips twitched, ready to make the necessary passes, but then stilled.

Life must go on, for her at least. And with such a long life ahead, she must adjust.

So now, she had a distraction. Why not enjoy it?

After padding silent and naked across the room, she lifted the lid of a large rosewood chest and looked inside, tapping her chin, deciding, deciding. Finally she smiled, lifting out several items that she held up for Hiro's perusal. When his eyes widened fearfully and his lips trembled, she knew that she'd made an apposite choice.

On her return to the futon, her pet was shuffling towards the edge, cringing away from her. She knew that much of his cowardice was artfully feigned, a ruse to increase her enjoyment and ingratiate himself with her because he'd deduced she was wealthy, but still the sight of him trembling made her sex clench with delightful anticipation.

The surge in her body produced a surge in her spirits. Glands and hormones pumped and pulsed, physical electricity tickled her nerves and her pleasure receptors. It felt like magic, but the kind anyone could wield.

Setting out her toys, she lunged forwards quickly and kissed Hiro on the lips. He'd been drinking sake earlier, and its flavour was pungent yet familiar. She licked the last traces of it from his mouth and then subdued him with the force of her hungry kiss. Gently domineering him, she forced him backwards, reached for his balls and cradled them delicately, stroking his perineum with her thumb as she fucked his mouth with her tongue.

Oh, the game was sweet, and it would pass a little time.

5 Going Under

'Do you live here alone?'

Rafe's voice sounded very close as he followed Paula into the flat, so close that she could almost feel his breath on the back of her neck and the heat of his gaze on her waist and on the curves of her bottom. She'd caught him watching her stuffing her knickers into her bag before they'd left Inner Light, and knowing that he knew she was naked beneath her skirt made her feel doubly bare. Despite her worries, she smiled, feeling naughty.

'Yes, there's just me. I like it that way.'

As she spun round, his eyes flicked up to meet her face, and she just had to grin. Men were so hopelessly transparent.

'Sorry, it's just I saw you put them in your bag. And us men just can't help but dwell on these things.' He paused, his eyes levelling on her. 'Especially as you were so insistent on keeping everything covered up before.'

Paula laughed. It surprised her that she could, but it was good to be out in the open with him. Particularly now, while Isidora was sleeping, or in Hell, or whatever happened to her when she wasn't lurking around whispering and taunting. Pressing her hand lightly to her belly, Paula felt only coolness, not the strange subcutaneous heat of the mysterious mark.

'Well, you know why I wanted to be covered up. It's

this thing on my belly. I didn't want you to feel it.' It was a difficult thing to get her head around. The fact that she wanted to both hide herself and fuck, virtually at the same time, didn't make sense to her so how could she explain it to him. She narrowed her eyes. Who was he to talk about underwear anyway? 'But what about you? You don't seem to bother with underwear at all. What's that all about? Easy access?' Unable to help herself, she glanced at his groin. The denim of his jeans was well worn there, and it was easy to imagine his large and undeniably impressive cock just beneath it.

Broad shoulders shrugged beneath the leather jacket. 'What can I say? I just like the feeling of freedom, of having unfettered equipment.' He gave her a roguish wink, and advanced further into the room, looking around. 'It's nice here. Cosy.' He turned to her, his brown eyes narrowed, assessing. 'No man around to share it?' He shrugged. 'I suppose not, or you wouldn't be seeking help from a reprobate like me.'

'It's a tip,' said Paula, swooping to snatch a pile of magazines and a cardigan from the sofa. 'And there have been men. But there's no one around at the moment, that's all.' She thought briefly of Jonathan, who she'd had a painful crush on at one time. 'Look, I don't think I'm ready for a mind probe or anything just yet. I don't want to stir "her" up. Do you fancy a glass of wine? Or something to eat? Or both?'

'Wine would be nice.' Rafe strode over to the settee she'd just cleared and flung himself down on it. Typical man, he appeared happy to let her wait on him, but, just as she reached to door, he called to her.

'Are you hungry? Shall I order some pizza to go with

that wine?' Reaching into his pocket, he pulled out his mobile.

'Er, yes, OK. Great.'

'Any preferences?' He was already punching in a number.

'Nothing with chilli. I don't like chilli. I don't like too much heat.'

He quirked his brows. 'OK, I get that. Not too much heat.'

'Right, I'll get the wine.' Still clutching her cardigan and magazines, she swept away from him and into the kitchen as he began to speak into his phone.

Was this a relationship of sorts beginning? Or just a random conjunction of two people who'd had casual sex a couple of times, and who could maybe help each other?

'Now why do I think that?' she muttered to herself, grabbing a bottle of white from the fridge and a corkscrew and a couple of glasses from the counter. She was the one who needed help, and then some. Why did she get the impression that Rafe needed something from her in return? He seemed totally self-contained, self-sufficient, a classic loner. Unless, of course, he *had* a wife or a girl-friend – and he simply wasn't letting on?

Back in the sitting room, Rafe was lounging again, looking completely at home, his call finished. As if he owned the place, he'd stretched his long legs out in front of him as he flipped through a copy of *Cosmopolitan*.

'Is this your type?' His eyes glittered as he flourished a nude centrefold at her. The man was lean, young, pretty. Exactly what she'd *thought* was her type.

'I don't have a type.' She waved the bottle and the opener at him as a distraction and, dropping the magazine, he efficiently did the honours. 'So what are we drinking to?' She could feel his eyes on her as she sat down beside him, their thighs interestingly close on the small settee. Taking her glass, she clutched it tight as if her life depended on it.

'I don't know. I don't even know what we're doing here.'

Quite true. She'd picked him up last night just to quell the driving heat inside her, and the fact that something in his bearing reminded her of André, from her dream. Curiosity and the same heat had compelled her to find him again this afternoon. It was just impulse, coincidence, serendipity that had brought them together and, though their bodies seemed to know each other, they were strangers in every meaningful way.

'Well, you need help, and I might be able to give it. Cheers!' He clinked his glass to hers, then drank, still eyeballing her over its rim.

She eyeballed him back. Maybe *he* was her type now? He was quite beautiful in his own way, although not pretty, and certainly not young. He had a face that spoke of life, and not always an easy one, and that peppering of grey at his temples only reinforced that. He'd taken off his jacket now and the solid muscularity of his arms and chest in his close-fitting black T-shirt reminded her of his strength and his raw sexual confidence.

That was what she was doing with him. Sex, and the fact he seemed inclined to help her with her 'problem'.

'Have you changed your mind?' he asked softly, a slow glint in his eyes. Paula shuddered. Could he actually read her mind, maybe? 'Don't you want to find out what's happened to you? And find your friends?'

The urge to trust battled with her natural caution while Rafe eyed her steadily. Still reading her? He took a long swallow of wine and the way his strong throat undulated was both erotic and strangely vulnerable.

'Yeah, I know, you're asking "why"? What's in it for me? Why would I just help you, out of the blue?' His glass clumped softly as he set it down and, for a moment, he looked almost coquettish, flashing surprisingly long and luxuriant lashes at her.

'Out of the goodness of your heart?'

Leaning against the cushions, Rafe spread his arms across the back of the settee, claiming territory. His warm body was very close. He appeared relaxed but ready for anything.

'No, not that really. I'm not sure there is much goodness in my heart. I'm probably worse for you than your inner demon is.'

His eyes were dark, almost black, shining with heat.

'So, what do you want, Rafe? What's your price?' Suddenly her skin began to prickle. Was it Isidora? Surreptitiously, she touched her hand to her belly but it still felt cool and normal through her skirt. There was no burning, invisible marker, just the quieter renewed gathering of desire.

'Sex.' Rafe's matter-of-fact voice belied the foxy, tantalising curve of his mouth. Which made Paula's loins shiver. 'I like sex.' He reached out and laid his hand over hers where it rested, close to her mound. 'And I really like having it with you.'

Paula laughed out loud. Suddenly she felt happier and sillier than she had for a month, entertained and turned on by this outrageous, blatantly horny stud of a man.

There was nothing like the direct approach, and it was infinitely sexier than having him go around the houses, pretending to respect her and be in touch with his sensitive side, just to get her into bed.

As Rafe spread his fingers, lacing them with hers and pressing their twined hands more firmly against her pubis, she smiled back at him, feeling shameless herself and just as horny.

'So you'll help me if I pay you in meaningless sex?'

He pressed more tightly, his long, flexible middle finger probing against the cleft of her sex, pushing the thin cloth of her skirt against her, dividing her labia.

'Not meaningless.' Surging forwards, he leant over her and pressed her back against the cushions. 'Never meaningless. I might be a sex addict, but it's got to mean something. I'm getting too old for quick shags with my massage clients. Or casual pickups against a wall behind the Raven.' His tongue swept over his lips, wetting them in a way that made Paula's sex flutter. 'I want ... I need something more.'

There was intent in his voice, a palpable hunger. They'd been together twice now in the space of less than 24 hours, and Paula wanted him again. But there was something deeper going on too, she sensed, something unconnected with *her* problems.

'OK then. *Meaningful* sex.' She gasped as he pressed harder, rocking his fingertip against her clit. Her skirt was wet now, absorbing her swimming arousal, the cotton growing dark in a small but telling circle. Clutching at the old settee and bunching up the shabby throw covering it, she jerked her hips up to meet the caress of their twined hands. Her eyes were closed but she still seemed to see

Rafe. His spicy herbal fragrance filled her head, making her dizzy as his mouth came down on hers and stifled her groans.

They kissed for a long time, his finger still plaguing her. His skill and intuition were astonishing, but then he was a master with his hands, wasn't he? Massaging a clit required all the same deftness and nuances of pressure that a full body massage did, and it was obvious Rafe was long practised in his craft.

Again and again, he brought her almost to the peak. And again and again, he kept her hovering there, her body pouring with sweat and aching with furious desire. Deep in her belly, a heavy knot was winding, winding, winding, inexorably.

'Please ... please ...' she begged, appalled by the weird, almost mewing note in her own voice.

Rafe's answer was another kiss, a deep probing onslaught. His tongue stabbed at hers in a sweet, dark thrust, quick and ruthless. And as he kissed, he lifted his hand and freed hers.

'No!' she cried into his mouth, the word garbled by his probing tongue.

An instant later, she felt cool air on her thighs and belly as he pulled up her skirt and tucked it in a bunch around her waist. Hooking a hand beneath her knee, he edged her forwards in her seat and nudged her legs further apart.

His fingers and his palm felt cool against the burning warmth of her skin as he drew them slowly and almost at leisure down the outsides and up the insides of her thighs. For a moment, she almost sobbed with relief, thinking he was going straight to her sex, but then he swerved and draped his hand across her belly, as if feeling for the hidden mark of her nemesis.

'Is she here?' he murmured in her ear, his breath scented with the wine they'd shared. 'Is this a threesome?'

Wound up by lust, Paula listened for the voice, the gloating, mocking, salacious voice, expecting any moment to hear its deep but silvery tones say, *Oh yes . . . oh yes . . .* But there was just silence save for the thudding of her heart, and her breathing and Rafe's, heavy and synchronised.

'No, it's just me! Only me! It'll have to be enough,' she gasped. Reaching down, she pushed at his hand, directing it imperiously towards her cleft. Maybe she wasn't as domineering as the spirit that plagued her, but she was a woman and she'd take what she wanted.

Rafe laughed, and spread his fingers, the middle one sliding silkily between her labia. When he found her clit, she shouted, 'Yes!' and jammed her hand down on his, reversing their previous configuration.

He rubbed. He stroked. He teased. He flicked.

She writhed. She whimpered. She wriggled. She came.

Grabbing at him, she twisted, her hips rising up from the couch as her sex fluttered and pulsed. Her arousal, honeyed and viscous, oozed and slithered, coating the inner slopes of her buttocks and dripping down onto her rumpled skirt beneath her. The ripe fragrance of her pleasure rose up and blended with her sweat-scent and Rafe's apothecary cologne.

As she began to descend, her body glowing, the doorbell rang.

'Mmm, pizza,' announced Rafe, straightening up. His hand was still buried between Paula's legs. 'Are you hungry?' He kissed the corner of her mouth, his fingertip still delicately rocking. To her amazement, desire stirred yet again.

But just as it began to gather, Rafe withdrew his fingers and sprang to his feet. 'I'm starving!' Cheerful, he headed for the door, leaving Paula barely able to believe that he was oblivious to the dramatic bulge in his denims. He was mightily erect, his shaft clearly outlined beneath the strategically faded fabric.

Paula began to tweak at her skirt in order to cover herself but, with his hand on the doorknob, Rafe paused and looked straight at her sex.

'No! Leave it. I'll be back there in a minute, so why cover up something so beautiful?'

'But –'

He quelled her with a glance, his eyes near black.

Then he opened the door, but thankfully only a narrow sliver, just enough to see out into the hall.

The conversation with the delivery boy seemed to take an eternity, with much bantering and laughing and slight, but dangerous swinging and creaking of the door. She watched Rafe reach into his back pocket for his wallet and count off a bill. Her essence was on his fingers as he paid the boy. Could he still smell her? Could the boy smell her? Were they speaking to each other in some kind of secret, arcane male semaphore? Sharing the fruity details of her arousal, her writhing and moaning, her shamefully easy climaxes?

But, at last, the transaction was over. Rafe closed the door and turned, the traditional square box balanced on the tips of his fingers.

'Smells fantastic,' he said, sniffing not at the box but at the fingers of his free hand.

'I'll get some plates and cutlery.' Paula made to get up, but Rafe shook his head, and somehow that froze her in place, her skirt still not covering her.

'No need, we have the box. And our fingers.'

Her belly shuddered. How deliciously decadent! The taste of herself and the fragrant pizza in one mouthful. Between her legs, her sex rippled, ready again.

Rafe brought the box to her, then set it on the rug at her feet. Sinking down gracefully, he sat beside it, close to her knees and her rudely spread thighs. With the box flung open, he tore at the pizza, pulling off a slice and offering it to her.

Luckily the base and toppings weren't exceptionally hot, and the moment she took her slice, she realised she was famished. With her life turned upside down by dreams and anxiety and the battle to feel normal, she'd been missing a lot of meals. Suddenly she couldn't remember when she'd last eaten anything substantial. Biting into the savoury crust, she almost moaned again, both from its delicious Mediterranean flavours and the perversity of eating it with her crotch bare and exposed to her lover.

Rafe ate with equal relish, biting lustily at his slices almost like a lion devouring a carcass. He also seemed to be licking his fingers with far greater frequency than was necessary and, as he chewed his pizza, he stared almost constantly at her sex, his brown eyes warm with mischief and a gourmet appreciation that was nothing to do with Italy's national dish.

'I can't eat any more,' said Paula eventually, after three slices. She was full in her belly, but elsewhere she was empty, hungry. Rafe's provocative gaze had banked up her inner fires again.

'But I can,' he growled, kicking aside the box and wiping his mouth and fingers on the paper napkins that had come with it, and swivelling around until he was kneeling between her legs. 'And I'm still hungry.'

His hands were gentle on her skin, skating lightly over her thighs, parting them wider, then diving between to slide underneath her, cupping her bottom. He began to lift, to pull gently, angling her towards his face.

Paula's hands shot out, cradling the strong shape of his head as his mouth oh so slowly approached her sex. His short hair was unexpectedly silky, the scent of a sweet herbal shampoo clinging to it and blending with the sharp smell of woman rising like a wave from her body. He breathed in deeply as if he was inhaling it too.

'Delicious. Far better than pizza,' he breathed, blowing lightly on her moist membranes and making her struggle again. His fingertips dug into her bottom, controlling her.

'Much better,' he growled, diving to sup her honey.

Later, exhausted, they fell into bed.

Paula was drained by pleasure, by the stress of the last days, and by the broken nights and troubled days fighting something she didn't understand and couldn't eradicate. Most of all, though, she was weary with relief. She wasn't alone any more, isolated by her struggle. She finally had an ally who seemed to believe her.

After coaxing her to orgasm with his tongue, Rafe had hauled her onto the rug, stripped off her clothes and his own and taken her there, fucking her fiercely and with a strange desperation. She'd castigated him as he'd ploughed her, laughing and telling him off for taking his 'payment' before he'd actually delivered any goods. Rafe had just laughed back at her, and thrust deeply, again and again.

He'd extracted payment again in the shower, more gently, loving her with lush precision beneath the tumbling water, and now they were in bed, not fucking but lying quietly together, both silent and absorbed in their separate thoughts.

A great drawn-in breath made her turn to him.

'Something wrong?' She wondered if he was afraid he'd made a mistake.

'No, just dying for a cigarette. Post-coital and all that.' He turned to her with a wry smile on his lips that suddenly made him look younger.

'Well, have one then.'

'I never smoke in other people's houses.' He pulled himself up against the headboard, adjusting the pillows behind him as he looked down on her. 'It's a filthy habit. I'm packing it in. It pollutes the body.'

And yeah, it would be a shame to pollute a body like yours, she thought, admiring him. He wasn't a youngster, but he was well set up, well muscled, a prime specimen. There was a fine gleam on his lightly tanned skin, and even a crisp energy to the smattering of wiry dark hair on his chest. She wondered what exercise he did, because it was obvious he did something. Perhaps he was a runner? Or maybe he lifted weights? Or boxed? Up close, it looked as if at one time he might have broken his nose.

'And it'll kill you too,' she remarked idly, glad he'd

chosen not to smoke, remembering the agonies of temptation when she'd given up.

Rafe's harsh bark of laughter made her jump. What had she said to bring such a sudden expression of bitterness? Had he lost someone to lung cancer, was that it?

'If it gets a chance,' he muttered, half under his breath as he gazed into nothingness, clearly not seeing anything of the room and its haphazard furnishings.

'What is it? What's wrong?' She sat up and put her hand tentatively on his arm. How stupid was it to be scared of touching him after what they'd just shared? Yet she was. In the blink of an eye he'd become distant and angry. Was it at her, or at some persistent inner thorn of pain and anguish?

'It's nothing.' His voice was terse, the muscles in his face taut as a mask.

Then he smiled as he turned to her and gently touched her cheek. The gesture was sexless, but the contact of his warm fingers faintly stirred her. She could still feel the echo of them roving across her body. 'Nothing compared to your problems, love.' He gave a little shrug. 'Problems I haven't done anything to help you with yet. Despite being very handsomely paid.' Leaning across, he kissed her mouth, soft and slow.

Passion coiled yet again but for once Paula suppressed it. Now was the time to do something, make some progress in her quest, hopeless as it seemed. She couldn't let herself get sidetracked by sex again, no matter how sensational it was with Rafe. After savouring a few moments of the kiss, she pushed on his chest.

His eyes were very bright, yet narrowed. 'To business then,' he said quietly, then slid his arm behind her, to tip her forwards, while he rearranged the pillows again. Setting her back down again, he slid her body so that she was lying, comfortably propped up. Then, to her surprise, he took both her hands in one of his, lifted her arms, then drew the sheet up over her, and tucked it under her armpits. It was a strangely tender action, almost paternal, and the way he shrugged seemed to suggest that he didn't quite understand it himself. Offering no explanation, he just patted her hand and scooted himself into position beside her.

'What can I do for you?' he asked, folding his legs beneath him in a semi-lotus position. Reaching for her hand again, he cradled it lightly in both of his. 'How can I help you?' He cocked his head on one side. 'Do you want me to try to contact this "Isidora" of yours and see what she wants? Or do you just want to remember what happened to you first?'

Paula slid her free hand to her belly, a habit which was becoming obsessive. She couldn't feel the mark, the heat, so could the evil bitch even *be* contacted? It was a relief, and at the same time frustrating. And as for memories of what had happened? Now it came to it, she was afraid. There might be a nasty shock in store.

'What I want to do first is find that place, Sedgewick Priory. I've a feeling that all the real answers might be there.' She stared at the ceiling, and then scrunched up her eyes as if to wrench the memory out of her grey cells unaided. Despite her growing fondness for Rafe, the idea of hypnotism still made her uneasy.

'I was still pretty out of it when Belinda and Jonathan came to see me. And we didn't talk much before things started getting, well, rather awkward. But I do remember them telling me about the sorcerer, the two-hundred-year-old guy, and his friend, the Japanese sorceress, who's a goodie as far as I understand. They talked about rituals, books of magic, spells ... If there's a way to "exorcise me" or whatever, I think that Sedgewick Priory is the best place to start. What do you think?'

Rafe was silent, his hands warm and motionless around hers. There was a sense of calculation about him. An intentness. Paula wrinkled her brow. What was he thinking?

'Well, I know some people who are into white magic and Wicca and benevolent paganism. But they live out in the Scilly Isles now, and I don't think it's the sort of thing that can be diagnosed over the internet or on a video mobile.' His finger began to move lightly against her palm, circling. 'So finding this Priory of yours probably *is* the best place to start.'

Paula frowned again. She was starting to feel sleepy but her mind was still working. 'Do you *really* believe in all this?' In a detached way, she noticed her voice was slightly slurred. 'Or do you think that I've just freaked out and it's all my imagination and I should go back to the doctor's?'

'I told you that I believed, didn't I?' His voice was even, soft. He was Mr Therapist again. He sounded sage and soothing and trust me, trust me. 'Now you've got to believe that I believe you.' He paused. 'Or this won't work.'

'OK.'

'Now then, when you spoke to your friends, did they say where this Priory was?'

'No, I just think they assumed I knew.' She frowned, snatching at fleeting fragments. 'I got the impression that they'd given me directions. But it must have been during the time I "lost".'

Fingers circled against her palm. Slow, rhythmic ... hypnotic.

He's putting me under, she thought almost dreamily, and suddenly she didn't need to frown. She still couldn't remember, but not remembering didn't make her crazy any more.

'And you remember nothing of those days?'

'Almost nothing ... some bits ... there *were* some directions. I remember being given them, but not what they were.'

His touch was so gentle, so delicate. She began to feel weightless, both physically and inside, in her mind. She was also aroused, she realised to her surprise, lightly horny in a pleasant, floating, spaced-out way. It was like being in a boat, rocking on a stream, waiting dreamily for a lover. It was a peculiar phenomenon but it made her smile and feel more relaxed than ever.

'Just relax ... Be comfortable ... Don't try to remember ...'

It was so easy ... so effortless ...

'Just relax ... You're floating ... Just let go ...'

Rafe gazed down at her. And found himself gnawing at his lip, feeling anxious, and anxious *because* he was anxious. Sometimes the total vulnerability of his subjects excited him. Dark ideas about what he could do when they couldn't stop him made his cock surge and thicken.

He despised himself but that didn't stop him getting hard and entertaining thoughts of uncovering, touching, pressing, entering.

Focus, man, he told himself, releasing Paula's inert hand and placing the back of his fingers against her forehead.

Cool. Perfectly normal.

He took her pulse, and that was slow and steady too.

Where to start?

He'd told her they'd concentrate on the directions to the Priory first, but other questions jostled on the tip of his tongue, demanding answers.

Who was Isidora?

Who were the two-hundred-year-old man and his Japanese sidekick?

How did someone get to be two hundred years old? Could anyone get some of those extra years?

Genetics were against him. Was just a little more life too much to ask for?

The thought chilled him as it always did. He longed for bravery and stoicism, and hated himself because he didn't possess them. He was a coward. He was afraid. He feared death, especially the bad death his father had endured.

Looking down at his hands, he held them out in front of him and scrutinised them.

No shakes? Not yet, at least. But they might come soon.

Setting them on his knees, he looked at Paula's hands instead. They looked slim and pale against the sheet, but also latent with power. His cock leapt again, hard, as if remembering the way she'd touched him. He found himself smiling again, reassured by his own perkiness.

While he could get a hard-on, there was always hope.

Always life ... Loss of potency would be one of the first signs of the beginning of the end.

'Get on with it, man,' he breathed to himself. He wasn't going to find out the answers to anything if he just sat around ogling Paula and getting the horn again.

'Paula, can you hear me?'

As she said 'yes' in a soft, feathery voice, he took her hand again.

It was like being there.

She was in a beer garden, outside a country pub. The smell of flowers, mixed with the faint yeasty smell of ale, filled the air. It was hot, but she was cool in the shade of a parasol.

She was speaking in her mobile phone, to Jonathan, listening to directions.

'Can you repeat them?' a soft voice asked.

It was a familiar voice, yet disembodied as if she were in Wonderland and the Cheshire Cat was speaking to her from a tree. She felt only mildly surprised to be hearing it and, in obedience, she repeated the list of directions. The turnings and the road numbers and signage that would lead her to somewhere called Sedgewick Priory.

'What else to do you remember, Paula?' coaxed the voice. 'Is there someone there with you? A woman? Can I speak to her?'

She frowned, shook her head. She'd felt relaxed and comfortable until now, loving the warmth on her skin and the light breeze floating. The garden was golden but suddenly a dark shadow crept across it, dense and foreboding.

A beautiful woman was sitting only a few feet away.

Paula only vaguely remembered asking her if it was OK to share the table, but now she couldn't look away from the elegantly dressed figure who was so smiling and attractive to the eye, but possessed of a strange, unsettling aura.

The woman's skin was milky white, her lips were red and her hair jet black. Her eyes were green but seemed to burn with excitement, and a glitter that was both frightening and hypnotic.

'Isn't it a beautiful day?' The exotic stranger's voice was low and sultry, her smile inviting. 'I do so love this part of the country, don't you?'

Paula's lips felt strange. She couldn't speak. But this didn't seem to bother her new companion, who slid gracefully along the bench and deep into her personal space.

'By the way, my name is Isidora. What's yours?'

Rafe set aside the notepad and pencil on which he'd written the directions. He'd snatched it up quickly when Paula had begun to intone them in an odd, sing-song voice, as if she'd been repeating a recording.

Glancing back at her, he got a shock.

What had changed?

She'd been lying relaxed, her hands resting lightly on the sheet, eyes closed, expression tranquil, but now there was a pall of energy around her, a field so tangible it made the back of his neck prickle. And she was twisting where she lay, tossing her head from side to side.

Gooseflesh popped up all over Rafe's skin. He felt a jolt as if he'd been zapped by a defibrillator. He shivered, even while sweat poured off his body.

'What else do you remember, Paula?' he asked. 'Is there someone there with you? A woman? Can I speak to her?'

Eyes still closed, Paula turned away from him, but he could see she was smiling, her mouth a lush, arrogant line, utterly sensual, profoundly manipulative.

'Isidora? Is that you? Will you come out and talk to me?'

He waited for what seemed like minutes, watching the line of her lips, the quirk of that amused, confident smile.

'Do you invite me?'

The voice was Paula's yet not hers. Another woman was using her vocal cords.

Rafe breathed deeply, almost panting. Dear God Almighty, it was true! It was all true! Part of him had just been playing along and humouring her, even now.

'Do you invite me?'

Imperious now. This was someone accustomed to getting her own way.

'Yes . . . yes, I invite you.'

Again, silence. He sensed he was being toyed with.

Reaching out, intending to check Paula's pulse again, he nearly fell off the bed when she grabbed his hand in a grip of iron – and her eyes flew open.

'Did I say you could touch me?'

Rafe swallowed. He couldn't speak. He felt as if his ears were ringing, even though the voice was soft and harmonious and deeply seductive.

He was looking into eyes of deep yet brilliant green.

'Paula?'

Paula – or what had been Paula – drew his hand towards her face and studied his fingers speculatively.

'You have beautiful hands,' she purred, 'very skilful.' Still holding him, she sat up, letting the sheet fall to reveal her breasts and belly. 'Would you like to touch me now?' She drew his hand to her breast, closing it around the soft resilient orb and pressing his fingers down over a nipple that was erect and puckered. As his grip tightened reflexively, a man's natural response to a lush breast against his hand, she made a low sound in her throat and tipped her head back, closing her eyes and moaning and pressing herself more closely into his hold.

For a moment or two, she held his hand there, undulating against him, merely using him as she rubbed herself against him. Her red lips parted and she licked them slowly as she sighed and made more earthy noises.

It was like being drugged. Rafe was entranced, burning with a lust he was reluctant to accept. This was all wrong but the physical sensations were so right.

'Paula?' he queried again as she began to shift her hips against the bed, bearing down and rocking on her sex.

Her green eyes flew open and flashed almost black for an instant, then she smiled slowly, still moving and swaying lewdly.

'No, not your dreary little Paula,' she said, licking her lips and leaning towards him. Before he could react, she kissed him, hard, making his mouth tingle as if her lips were painted with some peppery spice that both seared and frosted them.

The kiss was delicious but terrifying. He felt his blood run cold and yet at the same time feel as if it were boiling. Her tongue dominated him utterly and his cock was a bar of iron. He blushed, furiously, for the first time in years, aware that he was naked and his erection was jutting up angrily from his groin.

His new companion, however, did not yet seem to have noticed it or, if she had, she didn't find it interesting.

When she released his mouth, he gasped for air, his chest heaving. God, when had he last taken a breath?

The entire universe was a pair of green eyes.

He fought for another breath, his chest tight as if banded with wire. Oh, shit, was this it? Cold fear doused him, despite the fire in his cock. Was this the beginning of the disease? Breathlessness, disorientation, inability to think? Those were all early signs. How fucking ironic that it should show up now of all times!

But as the cold hand of his own long-time nemesis struck him like a slap, he was able to break free, think more clearly. He narrowed his eyes and stared back into the cool green gaze of the woman he knew was no longer Paula. Her expression was shrewd, almost crafty, as if she'd sensed his sudden personal fear.

'You're Isidora, aren't you?' he said as levelly as he could, withdrawing his hand. She let him go, but he got the distinct impression that, if she hadn't allowed it, he certainly wouldn't have been able to.

'Isidora? Who is Isidora?'

The woman smiled. Her eyes were narrowed, almost jeering at him, yet at the same time utterly sultry. She shook back her hair and smoothed it off her face. Rafe was puzzled. Did the thick silky strands look blacker than before too?

'You know, the demon or whatever who's got inside Paula.'

'But I'm not a demon. Far from it.' She shifted position and knelt up, facing him. Rafe couldn't take his eyes off her as she ran her hands over her borrowed body, as if really exploring it for the first time. 'I'm . . . well, I suppose you could call me a displaced person. I'm the victim of an evil spell, dear Rafe.' Her face – Paula's – crumpled a little. Was she sad? Angry? Afraid? It was hard to tell, the moment was over so quickly. 'A wicked spell that banished me to a place you don't want to know about, and from which I'd rather like to escape on a permanent basis.' Her hands settled on her belly, cradling its soft curve as she smiled again, slowly and calculatingly.

'And do what?' He shuddered, wondering just exactly what she *could* do. This all still seemed like a crazy dream. He'd listened to Paula and tried to help her, because he liked her and he liked having sex with her. But while his own subconscious had leapt at certain possibilities, he'd still, at heart, believed that what she needed was a psychiatrist.

But now he didn't know what to do or say to this manifestation. Especially as his cock was still rigid and aching. He didn't know what the hell was going on, but he did desperately want to fuck this creature who was Paula, yet not her.

'Countess Isidora Katori, at your service.' Her voice was low and sweet like honey. It oozed over him, delicious and tempting. Her dark head tilted on one side, that calculating glitter flashing in her eyes again. 'And I do mean that, my friend. I have a feeling that there are ways I can help you, if you'd care to help me?'

A new rush of chills rushed up Rafe's spine.

A laugh like pagan music rang in the small room. 'Ah

ha, you're wondering what I can do, aren't you? You're wondering if I can read your mind? If I can control you?'

'Can you?'

She laughed again, more softly. Her eyes grew mellow. Was it a trick? Was it Paula back all of a sudden?

'No. But I've spent hundreds of years watching the faces of men, and I know when I have something a man needs.'

'Hundreds of years?' Was this the source of the two-hundred-year-old man's longevity? And perhaps the answer to his own fears?

'Now that does interest you, doesn't it? Would you like longer life?' Her tongue swept across her lips like that of a snake detecting pheromones – and the scent of fear. 'Foolish question. All men want longer life. Years of vigour and potency. Especially if they live in the shadow of death.'

Isidora was closer now, laying a hand on his thigh, quite gently. Rafe pursed his lips, biting down on his fears. Maybe she couldn't control him but her seductiveness was befuddling.

'So, do *you* want to live long? As I have?' Her fingers moved gently on his skin, cold-hot, inducing exquisite pleasure. 'If you help me, I could reward you with more life.'

Rafe grabbed at the bed sheets when she reached for his erection.

'She's chosen well.' Her fingers curved around his hot flesh, like chills and fever against his hypersensitive penile skin. His hips bucked, thrusting into her delicate, precision grip. 'I always did prefer a lover with a large member. I think we could live well together. Do great things.' Her eyes narrowed dismissively. 'All this modern talk about size not mattering ... Silly young women. They're only making themselves feel better because they're with men the size of a thimble.'

Rafe's head spun and lust roiled in his loins like molten lava, all the hotter for the tincture of blended shame. He was giving in to this thing within moments of its appearance. In the same bed where he'd so recently made love to Paula.

But she is Paula, he thought, drowning. He was sinking under a spell, even as his cock hardened into an agonising symbol of life. With Isidora, his worries could be over. He could have sex, a full, vital life, all the years that his father had been denied.

Even so, he found the strength to fight. There was darkness surging around. In him. He tried to edge away but her fingers closed more tightly, a delicious threat that only stirred him even more.

'How are you doing this? How did you get here? Where's Paula?'

'Questions, questions, questions...' Her chuckle was low, utterly confident, utterly seductive. Her finger began to move again, pumping, pumping.

Rafe groaned as his balls tightened and his spunk began to rise.

His head almost bursting, he made one last effort, grabbing her by the hair, making her look at him.

'Tell me, you bitch! Where is Paula!'

She laughed out loud, doing something with her thumb that made him yelp and nearly climax.

'Forget her. We don't need her. She's just sleeping.' Still holding him, she swooped low and ran the tip of her tongue over his crest in a fast, flickering motion. Rafe's hand locked tighter in her hair, the autonomous compulsion to come making his cock surge to get further into her mouth. 'Where you sent her, my dear young man.' She paused, then flicked him again, before sitting up and running her tongue around her lips as if savouring his saltiness. 'Where *you* sent her, with your skills, when you summoned me. Remember that. *You have summoned me.*'

Rafe moaned again, his loins pounding, his mind in turmoil. He'd never felt as confused in his life. Everything in him screamed that this woman, this thing, was the worst evil and cared nothing for him, and even less for the vessel she was inhabiting. And yet at the same time the need to know gnawed at him. Know who she was. What she was. Where she'd come from. And what she could do.

He was desperate for knowledge, but his spine was melting and his brain was a howling beast shouting, 'Fuck! Fuck! Fuck!'

His mouth opened, to ask a question, but what came out was a bull-like roar as Isidora/Paula's hand moved like a blur and his climax barrelled through him like a blinding white wave. Swaying, he watched, as if from a distance, while his cock leapt and disgorged a white ribbon of semen and Isidora released him to catch his essence in her fingers. As he collapsed sideways, almost falling off the bed, she smeared the silky substance across her own belly, rubbing it into skin that seemed to sizzle. Smiling, she slid her hand between her legs and began to rub herself furiously. A second later, she shouted a curse, in a guttural, unknown language, and her hips jerked in a rapid blur of orgasm.

Spent, but still ravenous for more, Rafe reached for her, but she kicked him hard on the shin and rolled away to writhe feverishly against the sheets, selfishly hoarding her pleasure. Her legs were thrown wide, her sex fragrant where she stirred it, and the rich odour of woman was a drug melting Rafe's brain and his ability to reason.

'Not unless I will it!' Her voice was icy cold, despite her heat.

When he tried again to move towards her, drawn like some primordial organism towards heat or nourishment, she growled with unearthly fury and lashed out with shocking power, to strike his cheek.

White light exploded and Rafe fell back, dazed and winded.

6 **Trust Issues**

As his wits came back to him, Rafe sat up with a jerk, clutching his face.

The woman in bed with him was lying back peacefully against the pillows now, her face tranquil, even though her hand was still at her crotch, her fingers curved to cup her mound.

Paula!

Isidora was gone. He could feel it. She'd disappeared as suddenly as she'd arrived, leaving her vessel in the same hypnotic trance she'd been in all along.

Rafe nearly fell off the bed. He still felt giddy from the blow, but disorientated from much more than that. His gut still glowed from the sex, yet he felt heartsick and disgusted at his own weakness.

What the hell have I done? he thought, his innards churning. What did she mean by 'summoned'? Has something changed?

The sight of Paula, so vulnerable, twisted him with guilt. Yet a part of him still wanted to summon the sorceress again. Her dark enchantment was like delicious, dangerous, addictive alcohol, and he mustn't let it snare him.

She offered power, lush eroticism and possibly the antidote to his greatest terror. She'd lived hundreds of years, she claimed, and she could save him from squalid death at 42.

'What the fuck are you thinking, man?' he hissed at himself. Bringing forth Isidora meant oblivion for Paula, he knew it in his gut. How could he do that to her? She'd come to him for help, and yet he could still hear Isidora whispering eternity in his brain.

He reached out to touch Paula's hand, to stir awakening in her palm, then snatched back his fingers. She looked peaceful and sexually untouched despite the fact she had her hand between her legs. His heart heavy, he slid off the bed and padded from the room, unwilling to shatter her peace and explain the unexplainable. Not the fact that Isidora existed, but the fact that he'd consorted with her, almost fucked her. In Paula's body.

He could still see the sheen of his own semen on her belly, drying in what looked like a lacquered pattern. Moving from side to side, he seemed to see characters and stylised swirls and curlicues for a moment. But then it was gone, and it just looked like spunk on skin again, the depressing evidence of his own weakness. While Paula still slept, he would have to clean it off, but first, and most of all, he needed a drink.

A cupboard in her kitchen yielded a bottle of gin. A supermarket brand, and he didn't even like the stuff, but he poured several inches into a teacup and gulped it down.

The spirit was clean and balsamic and made his eyes water, but he took another big measure and swigged it down too.

With the alcohol hit came a moment of clarity.

As he went to the bathroom to search for a face cloth with which to cleanse her body, he knew he couldn't tell Paula what had just happened.

* * *

I don't think I trust him.

Paula glanced sideways at Rafe, watching his hands and his profile as he drove. They'd been on the road for a while now, following directions she'd apparently given him whilst in her hypnotic trance. An edgy silence had settled between bouts of navigation.

He's keeping something from me, she thought.

Since he'd hypnotised her, Rafe's eyes had been full of shadows. Not that he was looking her in the eye much any more. He seemed to be making every effort to avoid looking directly at her.

'It says turn left after a mile here,' she said, consulting Rafe's notes, 'but according to the map there's no road going that way for forty miles, not even a track. This just doesn't make sense. It's as if the directions include roads that aren't there.'

'Well, we'll soon see, won't we?' said Rafe lightly. 'If there's a turn-off in a mile, we take it. If not, we pull over, go through everything again and backtrack.'

'OK. If you're sure this thing isn't going to break down any minute.'

She wished they'd brought her car, not his. Now she'd put herself at his mercy somehow, not to mention the fact that he'd showed up outside her building this morning in the oldest and most decaying Jaguar she'd even seen.

'Don't worry. Unlike me, even though it looks decrepit, this bus is actually reasonably sound in wind and limb.' He turned to her quickly and, though he was smiling and superficially relaxed, Paula could still see he was tense.

'You're not decrepit.'

Far from it. After he'd woken her from the trance, he'd

made love to her with a strange and tender ferocity. He'd
kissed her everywhere, and repeated her name again and
again, 'Paula, Paula, Paula...' Almost as if he were
reassuring himself who she was, even as he'd fucked her.

He'd also tasted of gin. And afterwards, when she'd left
him sleeping and padded to the kitchen, she'd checked
the bottle and discovered he'd drunk quite a bit of it.

What the hell's going on, Rafe? she asked him silently,
wondering why in God's name she couldn't seem to voice
her doubts. She'd opened her mouth to do it a dozen
times. Then suddenly, somehow, lost the impetus.

Yet more to suspect him for.

'Why do you say that?' she sniped at him. 'You're fit
and you obviously take care of yourself, apart from the
smoking. OK, you've got a bit of grey in your hair but
what difference does that make?'

There was a long silence, during which Rafe put his
foot down, sending them hurtling along the narrow
country lane as if they were rallying. Careering round
blind corners and passing within a whisker of very hard-
looking dry stone walls, Paula found herself gripping the
frayed edge of her car seat.

'Appearances are deceptive.' Rafe's voice was grim as
he wrenched the wheel and flung them round a particularly hairy bend.

'What's that supposed to mean? That ... that...' The
questions, about last night, just wouldn't come. She
couldn't even ask him what he'd done to her.

'Look, can you please slow down a bit? What if we run
into another car or some sheep or cows or something?
There's no point to this trip if we end up mangled in
wreckage!'

Rafe took his foot off the accelerator immediately but a second later he glanced quickly to his right, then shoved his hand out of the window.

'It's going to piss it down any minute. The sky's looking dark as sin and the window seals aren't all that tight.'

'Great,' muttered Paula, but the word was eclipsed by a sudden, booming roll of thunder. Within the space of a few moments, a pleasant summer's day seemed to be heading towards a high-category tropical storm. Humid air pressed down on them and, right on cue, rain burst from the heavens as if someone had opened a giant water cooler in the sky. It lashed the car, the lane, the walls and the greenery with relentless fury where just a minute or two ago all had been dry and basking in the baking afternoon heat.

Up above them, heavy with looming clouds, the sky had gone black. And as the thunder rolled again, two things happened simultaneously.

Water started to drip onto Paula's head through the leaky sunroof and, with a dramatic spit, cough and splutter, the Jaguar's engine died.

'You fucking cunt!' roared Rafe, smashing the flat of his hand down on the steering wheel. Then a stream of similar cursing was drowned out by a more elemental roar. A second crack of thunder, far louder than the last and almost on top of them. Gothic blue lightning ripped across the sky and the rising wind made the trees at the side of the road whip and lash like ghastly claws reaching out to smash the ailing car.

The Jaguar coasted to a stop, with Rafe just managing to coax it to a patch of grass verge in front of a rusted gate. Ironically, just ahead of them and appearing almost out of the torrential downpour itself was the left-hand turning that didn't appear on the map.

'Now what do we do?' Paula reached up to see if she could adjust the sunroof, but her efforts only made the water teem down on her even faster.

Looking to Rafe for help, she saw that he'd pitched forwards and was resting his head on his arms, against the wheel, muttering, 'Fuck! Fuck! Fuck!'

'Well, I suppose we could do that,' Paula shot at him, her temper flaring. 'The back seat seems to be relatively dry, if you want me to oblige?'

The minute she'd said it, she wanted it. Don't be ridiculous, Paula, she told herself. Now is not the time!

Why not? murmured the voice inside her, with shocking clarity. It was almost as if Isidora were in the car with them. Paula shook her head, trying to rattle the dark bitch loose.

But as Rafe straightened up and turned to her and frowned, the sudden, unwanted arousal coiled and stirred.

He looked vexed, weary, troubled and water was running down his face too. But still she wanted him, and wanted him furiously, right now. The seam of her jeans had ridden up into her crotch and it was pressing like a knot of fire against her clitoris. Invading rain was wetting her hair and her T-shirt, but between her legs a different moisture was welling.

'Look, I'm sorry...' Twisting the ignition key, he attempted to rouse the dead vehicle. 'I know you won't believe me, but this old bus never breaks down. I've been in worse downpours than this and she's just sailed on with never a cough.' He twisted the key again, but nothing happened, not even a splutter. 'And she was serviced only last week.' A thick trickle of water landed on his head and he sighed and shrugged.

And you could do with a servicing too, couldn't you, you little slut, murmured Isidora.

'Oh, shut the fuck up!'

Abandoning the ignition as a null issue, Rafe twisted towards her, looking puzzled.

'Not you, Rafe, *her*,' she said, reaching out to touch his bare forearm. His skin was hot and damp, the feel of it evocative of sweat in the bedroom. 'She's muttering again.'

'Do you want me to see if I can banish her for you?'

Now there was a thing. Why hadn't that occurred to her? Maybe it was just as simple as that? Rafe could hypnotise her into not being able to hear her inner intruder.

Low laughter, audible only to her, seemed to suggest otherwise.

'Thanks. I don't think she'd listen though.' She squeezed his arm to reinforce her words. 'But she doesn't seem to be able to hang around for more than very short periods. So if I just ignore her, she'll be gone again soon.'

'Are you sure?' Rafe covered her hand with his, then seemed about to try the engine again when a new leak sprang above him and a steady drenching stream poured down on his head. Paula saw him open his mouth to curse – but it came out as a bellow of laughter. A second later they were both howling as they sat beneath the steady downpour of invading water.

'Look, I don't think we can stay in here.' He shook his head, spraying more water around. 'You're supposed to be safest in your car in a thunderstorm, but I don't think that applies when the vehicle in question has turned into an indoor swimming pool.'

Paula looked down at the list of directions, which had run into a smudged blue blur, and the map, which seemed on the point of disintegration.

'Maybe we can set off and walk? It's only half a mile or so down that lane.' She pointed to the turning ahead. 'We can't get any wetter out in the open than in here.'

'Makes sense. Let's do it!' Rafe reached over the back of the seat for his leather jacket, then popped the driver's side door.

Paula puffed out her lips. Her own jacket was a thin, summer cotton affair. It'd be worse than useless in this rain. She flung it back into the car, grabbed her shoulder bag and leapt out to join Rafe.

Rafe swept his water off his face and studied her wryly. Then with a flourish, he held out his leather jacket for her to slip into.

'I'll be OK.'

'No, you won't. Put it on.' He shook the coat at her. 'I don't need it.'

Paula set her jaw, then capitulated, sliding her arms into the oversized garment. It was heavy but strangely comforting and even in the teeming rain she could still smell the delicious odour of Rafe, herbal and spicy and yet underpinned with the foxy scent of man.

The fragrance only heightened her arousal, especially when he caught her by the hand, his fingers warm and protective around hers.

'Come on, love. The faster we walk, the sooner we get there and the less wet we get.'

'We're wet already,' Paula observed, but smiled as they began to trudge along the lane.

It was hard to believe it was still afternoon. The sky was as dark and glowering as the dead of night, except when it was split by titanic flashes of lightning. Great jagged cracks of electric blue-white arched across the entire sky, illuminating the rain-gleaming stone walls and the twisted trunks of the scrubby trees that hugged the side of the road.

When they reached the left-hand turn, the narrow lane was even less prepossessing. It was rutted and potholed, even though it followed the line of a high stone wall that seemed in fairly good repair.

Paula shuddered, then started wildly at a movement in the undergrowth. Instantly Rafe enfolded her with a protective arm around her shoulder.

'OK?' he enquired, having to shout over the torrential rain, the high wind and the low grumbling precursor of another crack of thunder. As the lightning flashed again, Paula looked up at him, his face stark and strange in the angry lighting, despite the kindness of his smile.

'Yes, I think so.' She grimaced back at him as the hot summer rain lashed her face and her eyes. 'I love this sort of challenging weather, don't you?'

Rafe laughed, his arm tightening around her. 'Come on, love, let's hustle. The sooner we get there, the sooner we'll be inside and hopefully dry again.'

Their strides were of different lengths but somehow they managed. Being forced to trot to keep up helped Paula focus and avoid thoughts about the journey's purpose. Just putting one foot in front of the other without sliding in mud and water took all her concentration, even though her arousal still simmered.

Rafe looked like some wild god of the rain as he strode along, his profile fierce against the blackness of sky. Diamonds of moisture glittered on his close-cropped hair and his dark, water-logged T-shirt clung like a second skin to the muscles of his chest and shoulders.

'Jesus! Just look at this!' he shouted suddenly over a particularly deafening thunderclap. He drew her to a halt and Paula looked around them, realising they'd reached their destination.

Before them stood a pair of tall, rusty wrought-iron gates that had seen better days and were hanging partially off their hinges like some giant malformed mouth. This ominous impression was enhanced by the statuary atop the crumbling, moss-adorned posts on either side of them. Two bizarre Gothic creatures snarled and pranced in frozen menace. They looked like cats who'd been to hell and returned in a furious rage to get their own back on someone.

Something about the creepy feline gargoyles made Paula tremble, and it was on the tip of her tongue to suggest they just go back to the car, wait the storm out there, and then get as far away as they could when the engine dried out.

'Yep, this is it.' Rafe drew her forwards to the nearest gatepost.

Encrusted with grime and discoloration, the words 'Sedgewick Priory' were cut deep into the stone.

'Right,' Paula muttered, then nearly jumped out of her skin when another huge lightning flash illuminated the inscribed words with electric silver. The accompanying elemental snarl seemed to come from the giant cats themselves, a thundering cry of fury.

'Shall we go through?' Rafe nodded at a gap formed by the sagging of the giant gates.

Go?

Retreat?

In a moment of silence, she waited for the voice of Isidora from within, as if the decision depended on her. But there was no answer and inside her jeans the strange marker on her belly remained cold against the sodden clinging denim.

'Yeah, let's do it. We're here now. We might as well see what's up there.' She gestured to the narrow uninviting gravel drive that stretched and twisted away between a gloomy colonnade of wet trees.

Rafe nodded, his face indecipherable. Paula wondered what he was really thinking and what he might be hiding. Her senses prickled at the thought of her hypnotic trance. It had provided them with the means to get here but she still felt there'd been more. Something Rafe was unwilling to tell her, whether to save her feelings or for some darker purpose.

Fuck, I don't trust *you* now! She sighed in the rain, knowing he wouldn't be able to hear it. But what choice had she? She couldn't spend the rest of her life with Isidora lurking inside her, ready to pop out at any moment. And whatever lay at the end of that unprepossessing driveway could well hold the key to banishing her.

Grabbing hold of the slimy-wet gate, Rafe wrenched the gap a little wider for her, and she stepped through, only to feel an electric tingle as if she'd just crossed a charged field. She could almost imagine miniature versions of the blue bolts arcing above dancing between her skin and the iron of the gate.

And then she was through, with Rafe right behind her. He slid his arm around her again as they began to crunch along the sodden gravel of the path.

'It's like Manderley gone bad, isn't it?' She forced a smile, wondering if he'd felt the electric-fence effect too.

'You can say that again. If they ever remake *Rebecca*, they've got a prime location here.'

The path seemed to wind and wind, but the prospect of being struck by the increasingly ferocious lightning as it aimed for the adjacent trees hurried their feet. Within a couple of minutes, they broke out into a wide, open park that matched the gateway and the drive in desolation, but which sheltered a large, dark and ornately semi-fortified house at its centre.

'I thought this was a priory?' Rafe rubbed rain out of his eyes and peered at the structure. 'It looks more like a baronial castle than a religious institution. Love the kitsch Gothic style.' He pointed towards the elaborate building that seemed to sit and sneer at them from among seven circles of hellishly overgrown formal garden. 'Shit, it's even got a Rapunzel tower!'

'It doesn't look as if it wants visitors, does it?' Paula followed Rafe's pointing fingertip to a peculiar tower, perched atop one corner of the rambling, black-windowed Priory. She'd never seen a less welcoming place in her life, and a tumbling festering structure that might have been a chapel, set to one side, didn't help matters. Flickers from the lightning seemed to suggest blue wraiths drifting in and out of its broken stones.

'It doesn't look as if anyone's been here in decades.' Rafe blinked more water out of his eyes as it began to teem even more ferociously from the sky. 'Are you sure your friends are here?'

'No, not exactly *sure*. But I can't think of anywhere else. They've disappeared from their workplace and their flat, and I can't raise them on their mobiles.'

Indeed, it was just her assumption that Belinda and Jonathan had come back here. That, and an inkling she suspected she was getting from Isidora.

Within the chill from her sodden clothing, a deeper, older chill gripped her innards, making her sway. Is this all a trick, you bitch? she demanded silently of her 'guest'. Is there something here you want?

A lightning bolt crashed somewhere right over her head, and she shrieked with fear, tripping as eldritch laughter filled her head. But instead of hitting the sharp, wet gravel, Paula experienced a moment of total disorientation as she seemed to fly up into the air. Grabbing wildly for purchase, she realised that Rafe had whisked her up off her feet and was holding her cradled in his arms, leather jacket and all.

'I'm all right! Put me down!' She wriggled, but his gentle hold didn't yield.

'No you're not. You've hardly been sleeping and you're worn out.' Adjusting his grip on her, Rafe started off down the path that led to the house, carrying her effortlessly. 'We need to get in there.' He nodded towards the dark, Gothic building with its glaring blank windows that glittered blackly. 'Even if it is a ruin, at least it'll give us some shelter until this lot dies down.'

'I'm not sure. I've got a bad feeling about this place.' God, how clichéd did that sound? Like something out of a low-budget horror movie. 'What if there's something even worse than Isidora in there?' Her arms tightened around Rafe's neck as formless fears floated through her imagination and she imagined that low voice saying, *There isn't anything worse than me, you little ninny.*

'Don't worry, I'll protect you from the ghosts and ghoulies.' Rafe sounded almost cheerful, as if being half drowned by a rainstorm amused him rather than pissed him off. 'I'm a big guy. I can handle myself.'

'Oh, I'm sure everything will be just fine,' Paula shot back at him.

Inside, though, she felt a slow, honeyed thrill. There was something primal about being carried in a big man's arms, and the heat of Rafe's body was both reassuring and exciting. He was strong, she had no doubt about it, and her desire, which had been doused by the relentless rain, came storming back. A swift, raw scenario unfolded behind her eyes as her body rocked to the rhythm of his long stride. She saw him kicking down the door of the crumbling Priory, laying her down right there in the entrance hall then ripping off her jeans and her panties and thrusting straight into her.

Pressed against the hard-stitched denim ridge of her jeans seam, her clitoris throbbed and twitched like a little heart. She pressed her face against his short wet hair, breathing in the herbal scent of his shampoo. Even in the sheets of rains, the rich fragrance was still evocative. She snuggled closer to him, seeking the heat of his body.

'Are you OK?' He paused momentarily in his yomp towards dubious shelter and Paula found herself looking up almost shyly into his eyes, convinced he could sense her fresh desire for him.

'Yes. But you're right. We need to get inside.'

He nodded and resumed his march towards the Priory.

Paula closed her eyes, huddling close again, trying not to think about anything other than the sensations of being held and of desiring the man who held her. If she didn't think about Isidora, maybe the bitch would remain dormant. It was only a hope, but she clung to it as tightly as she clung to Rafe.

As the footing changed, her eyes snapped open and she looked around them. Rafe had long legs and a stride that ate up yards, and they were already through the bedraggled flowerbeds and approaching the heavy slab of panelled oak that was clearly Sedgewick Priory's grand entrance. Just as the rain-streaked windows had looked like menacing eyes before, now the door itself looked like a giant hostile face hewn from wood, sulking in the shadows of an overhanging portico.

Well, at least they were out of the firing line of the rain now.

The misshapen nose was a great brass door knocker that she half expected to be in the form of an ogre or a griffin or even the rampant cats from the gateposts. But it was simply a plain heavy ring, heavily discoloured and as menacing in its own way as a death's head or a gargoyle.

Dipping down, Rafe set her gently on her feet and, as her jeans' seam chafed her clit again, Paula gasped.

'Are you sure you're OK?' He touched a finger to her

chin, making her look up at him. Cocking his head, he studied her, his brown eyes inquisitive. 'Just you in there? No visitors?'

'Yep, just me. And we're all fine.' She gave a shrug, amazed that she could suddenly find a joke. Maybe the strange old house wasn't the Arkham Asylum that it appeared to be? Maybe it was having a benevolent rather than malevolent effect?

Rafe laughed softly. 'Good!' The word was barely audible beneath another clap of thunder. 'Best knock then, hadn't we?'

Grabbing the enormous doorknocker, he gave it a heavy, repeated rap. The solid slab of wood reverberated with a disproportionate bang at each stroke, and suddenly the pair of them were laughing.

'What happens if Lurch comes to the door?' Despite her mirth Paula felt a twinge of fear. She slipped her hand into Rafe's and held it tightly.

7 **Across the Rubicon**

For a few moments, the only sounds were the raging wind and the rumble of suddenly receding thunder. But just as Paula was about to urge Rafe to knock again, there was a metallic rattle and the doorknob started to turn.

A second later, the door swung open smoothly on surprisingly well-oiled hinges, to reveal a huge figure smiling benignly out at them.

Looking like a cross between a Norse god and a WWF wrestler taking a country holiday, the newcomer was tall, massively built and clad in blue jeans and a white muscle vest. His broad face was handsome, his expression mild. Welcome shone in his clear, guileless eyes, and his blond hair was closely cropped to his scalp. Without hesitation, he threw the door open to its widest extent, then stepped back, ushering them inside with an expansive gesture.

Paula hesitated, sensing a Rubicon yawning in front of her. Behind was the dark and storm, and the chance to make a run for it back to what passed for her normality. Ahead was a new unknown, a place she'd been told was the realm of baroque, alchemic magic if her estranged friends were to be believed. She spun around, seeking guidance from Rafe.

For a moment, his expression was guarded, then he smiled.

'Well, let's go in.' He took her hand, urging her forwards.

'We don't want to disappoint our friend, do we?' He nodded towards the giant who was still holding the door open, apparently unperturbed by her indecision.

Paula stepped over the threshold and gasped at the tingle of electricity that zapped her as she moved from stone porch to black and white tiling. It was akin to the hit they'd taken at the gate, but more intense, shooting from her fingertips to her belly where Isidora's mark was sleeping, and thence to the quick of her sex.

When Rafe crossed over behind her, she glanced round and saw his eyebrows shoot up as if he'd felt it too.

'Weird,' he mimed, giving her hand a reassuring squeeze. 'Keeps giving me the horn.' His mouth quirked as he glanced down towards his groin.

Shaken, Paula returned her attention to their 'host'. His expression seemed innocent enough, but was there just a twinkle of sly amusement in there too? He was obviously aware of the effect that entering the great house had on people.

The hall they found themselves in was spacious and softly lit. It was also far from the dingy decrepitude she'd been expecting. Mellow lanterns in ornate sconces revealed a haven of calm luxury that was at odds with the ancient festering exterior. The long room smelt of lavender polish, and the few pieces of furniture, all rather heavy and Gothic, had a rich, well-cared-for gleam. At the end of the long expanse, a huge double staircase with a gilded balustrade led to the upper floors, and the sombre wood-panelled walls were interrupted by several doors to other rooms.

The bronzed giant made another of his strangely

elegant 'come this way' gestures, and began walking towards a nearby door that stood open.

Paula felt that someone really ought to say something.

'Er, I'm Paula Beckett and this is my friend Rafe Hathaway. We're looking for Belinda Seward and Jonathan Sumner. I believe they stayed here a few weeks ago, and I was wondering if they'd come back.'

Their host nodded.

Was that a 'yes'? Or just an acknowledgement? Or was he just humouring them?

'Well, are they here?' She stayed put, aware she'd sounded a bit stroppy but getting fed up of his mysterious silence.

'Excuse me, but the lady asked you a question.'

Rafe's voice was cool, but his expression and body language were pure alpha male. If the situation hadn't been so weird, Paula would have found this juxtaposition of two splendid and impressive men deliciously exciting.

For the first time since they'd first set eyes on him, the blond man looked discomfited. He shrugged his enormous shoulders and with a slightly wistful expression on his face, made a curious chopping gesture against his throat.

What did he mean? Was it a threat?

'I'm sorry, mate.' Rafe stepped forwards, comprehension on his face. 'We didn't realise you couldn't speak. That's rough.'

The silent giant shrugged again, and repeated his indication that they should follow.

The room they entered was a library. Warm opulence reached out to envelop them, generated by the tall stacks of hide-bound volumes that covered the walls, the rich carpeting beneath their feet, and the pair of leather chesterfields that flanked the big carved fireplace. Unusually for summer, there was a cheerful fire burning but, after the drenching rain, its golden glow was so welcome that Paula sighed and hurried towards it.

'Thank God for that.' Shrugging off Rafe's leather jacket as she approached the flames she could almost imagine her jeans and T-shirt beginning to steam. As she held out her hands towards the glow, her eye was caught by a portrait that hung above the fireplace. It depicted a breathtakingly handsome man with the most startling blue eyes. He was dressed in old-fashioned clothing but his expression was timeless and challenging.

When Rafe said, 'Cool. Thanks,' she tore her eyes away from the oil painting and turned round to see their blond companion pointing to a well-stocked drinks tray set up on the antique sideboard. He seemed to be suggesting that a brandy might be in order and Paula couldn't think of anything that she'd like better right at that moment.

Well, she could, actually.

Looking at the two tall, disparately handsome specimens of manhood, she could almost see the mists of testosterone. The silent blond giant was an enigma, but Rafe's feelings were pretty manifest. The caveman in his forebrain was intent on defending his claim on his woman.

For the first time in a while, the voice in Paula's own forebrain – or wherever – suddenly stirred.

See them. You could make them fight over you, she whispered creamily. *Or you could have them both. Two men pleasuring you at once, how would that feel?*

Paula shook her head, trying to dislodge her intruder or

at least shut her up. Both Rafe and the blond alongside him turned sharply as her wet hair swished through the air.

'Water in my eyes.' She shrugged and squeezed at a hank of her hair for effect. 'Er, what about that brandy, eh? I could really use one.'

Utilising more of his strangely expressive gestures, their host indicated that they should help themselves – and wait. Following a hand-sign that could have meant five minutes or five hours, he nodded and left the room, striding purposefully.

'Well, we've met Lurch. Who's next?' Rafe grinned as he sat down on one of the chesterfields beside Paula, handing her a brandy balloon containing a huge measure.

'Don't be awful. He seems nice.' She took a sip and, though the fiery spirit packed a hit worthy of the lightning bolts outside, it was exceptionally smooth. It warmed her throat as it slid down, making her shudder.

Rafe shrugged and seemed grudgingly to concede. 'Well, I can't fault his hospitality. A roaring fire, Napoleon brandy, no questions asked. I wonder where he's gone now? To fetch your friends? He seemed to know their names.'

'Yes, I guess they are here.'

They sat in silence. The transition from the wild lashing storm to the calm, luxurious tranquillity was a shock to the system. Paula felt stunned and she sensed Rafe felt much the same. She hadn't the energy to hold a conversation but, at the sound of running footsteps in the hall beyond, she felt disappointed that their tiny interlude of peace and quiet was over.

Jonathan Sumner almost fell into the room.

It was several weeks since she'd last seen her old friend and their parting hadn't been comfortable, but the sight of him now was so welcome that she sprang up and rushed over to him. Without speaking, they gave each other a hug.

'What are you doing here? Are you OK? I guessed it must be you when Oren let me know we had visitors.'

Jonathan's dark eyes were worried and he looked dishevelled. It was obvious he'd come straight from his bed because his dark curly hair was standing up in tufts and he was wearing a silk dressing gown, and what she suspected was very little else. His wiry legs were bare and he had nothing on his feet.

'Sorry, I ... I was taking an afternoon nap.' Hot pink flushed into his smooth cheeks and he twisted at the cord of his gown. 'But, seriously, why *are* you here? Is something wrong? I mean, well, I know we had a row and all but we *have* been worried about you and hoping you were OK. We were thinking we might...' His eyes suddenly darted over her shoulder and his voice petered out as Paula sensed that Rafe had moved quietly to stand behind her.

She turned to him, and found him watching and wary.

'God, I don't know where to start.' She took a step to the side. 'Jonathan Sumner, this is Rafe Hathaway. He's, um, helping me.' The two men continued to eyeball each other. 'Rafe, this is Jonathan, who I told you about.'

There was a terse handshake and inwardly Paula sighed. Her relationship with Rafe was so brief and had sprung up in such turmoil that she didn't really have the measure of it yet. The last thing she needed right now was another show of macho possessiveness and dick-waving.

'Where's Belinda?' she asked, to move things along.

Jonathan's face crumpled. 'She's sleeping. She does that a lot of the time these days.'

'What's the matter with her?' Alarm raced through Paula. Not Belinda too? She wracked her brain, trying to remember how her friend had seemed when they'd visited her in hospital.

'Nothing. Well, not really. It's just something happened during the ritual we told you about, and we're sort of waiting to see if the effects are going to wear off.' He pursed his lips, his fresh young face troubled. As if whatever it was wasn't wearing off as fast as he'd hoped.

'Do you want a brandy, mate?' said Rafe suddenly. 'Let's all have a drink and you and Paula can bring each other up to speed, eh?' As his hand settled lightly on her shoulder, Paula sensed the combative vibe was gone. She turned and smiled at him gratefully, and he smiled back with a wry little shrug.

'Right, you first,' she suggested to Jonathan when they were all settled in front of the fire. Jonathan sat alone, leaning forwards, cradling his brandy, while she and Rafe shared a sofa. His arm felt warm and comforting around her shoulders.

Jonathan's tale was wild and strange. A fuller and more lucid account of what she'd dismissed as a cock and bull story in hospital. Knowing what she knew now, she believed every mad, unlikely word.

The silent Oren returned with a groaning tray laden with sandwiches, cold cuts, pastries and coffee, but nobody seemed to have much appetite, and neither she nor Rafe interrupted the story of how Jonathan and Belinda had fetched up at this strange priory during another thunderstorm and gradually been drawn into the web of Count André Von Kastel, its mysterious yet benign owner.

'That's him.' Jonathan gestured to the handsome oil painting. The striking blue-eyed aristocrat in eighteenth-century dress who seemed to stare down at them as if he were a living, breathing entity.

Paula glanced at Rafe and then at the count. Though the hair was different, there was actually a superficial likeness between the two men. Some quality in the elegant cheekbones and the jaw, and the set of the shoulders.

'And he was ... is ... two hundred years old.' Jonathan was continuing the story, and suddenly Paula felt Rafe's arm tense around her. It was momentary but quite distinct and it puzzled her as she listened to her friend's fantastical account. A yarn that made her head reel and Rafe hold her tighter, for comfort now rather any reason of his own.

Isidora, the bitch! What she'd done to Count André and his beloved was horrific. Condemning them to an eternity apart, with Arabelle confined as just a spirit in a bottle and André compelled to seek sustenance from the sexual energy of human lovers.

Paula turned to Rafe again. What was he making of all this? Did he believe it? He'd certainly seemed to believe her own story.

Finally, Jonathan came to the solution. The arcane ritual – presided over by Michiko, the Japanese white sorceress – that had freed André and Arabelle from their separate state and sent them onwards to another plane of existence. Or whatever. And Jonathan's own part in the event, running interference by having sex with Isidora while the rite was taking place.

At this, Paula's jaw dropped.

'Er, run that by me again? You fucked her, knowing it was her, even though she looked like me?'

He nodded sheepishly.

'I ... I don't know what to say, Jon. That's crazy and creepy on so many levels. I don't know whether to be flattered or furious. I notice you conveniently left that bit out when you visited me in the hospital.'

Jonathan took a long swallow of brandy. 'I don't know what to say, Paula. You just had to be there at the time.'

'But apparently, I was ... *without* my knowledge!'

'But it wasn't you, it was *her*! And ... and ... even though I knew it was her, she still turned me on. She's evil, Paula, but she's irresistible. Believe me.'

'You don't have to fucking well tell me that!' Paula flew to her feet in turmoil. Her anger boiled but she hardly knew how to direct it. If Isidora had been outside her, she would have gone for her, claws out.

Images ... hot sexual mind-pictures flooded in like the surging waters that raged down from the sky outside. She saw – and felt – the touches and the caresses of a beautiful but deadly black-haired woman. And her flesh rebelled and thrilled to them, both at the same time.

The image of a pointed red tongue flicking at her sex seemed to burn into her retinas, while between her legs that same sex fluttered and clenched hard in unwanted desire. Green eyes laughed at her. Then she tumbled to the floor.

'Paula, are you OK, love?'

The voice was soft and gentle, but the sorceress heard a strangely compelling note in it, a beat just beneath the surface. It was interesting and rather clever. She smiled inside.

Stirring, Isidora found herself in a bed. A soft bed, made up with fine, fragrant linens. Her inner smile widened. At last, the kind of comfort and luxury she was accustomed to.

'Yes, I'm fine ... just a little sleepy ...' She turned over, snuggling into the pillows, careful not to open her eyes. 'I'll be all right when I've had a little nap.'

It wasn't sleep she wanted. She'd had enough of its black tormenting dreams. But she did need time alone, to assess her situation and her capabilities. Moments of complete control were as precious as they were brief.

'Are you sure? You just keeled over down there.'

Again that hint of manipulation. He was clever, this delicious man, as well as desirable. But he wasn't André Von Kastel, even though in certain senses he resembled him. He might be able to trick that silly little bitch Paula into doing what he wanted, but he had no idea who he was up against right now.

'Sure, I just need some rest. Why don't you go and chat with Jonathan and have some of that food? Tell him a little more about what's going on.'

Masked by the bed linen, she smirked, calculating. Best not to lay all her cards on the table. Not just yet. 'But not everything, eh? There are some things he and Belinda need to hear from me. Just say I've been having dreams and that we think they're to do with what happened during that ritual.'

'OK then, you have a sleep. I'll come back in a bit. Can I bring you anything?'

'No thanks ... I'm not hungry.' She felt soft lips brush her hair, and ground her teeth at the sudden surge of dark anger they induced.

Now this was the affection and devotion she should have been receiving for decades, nay centuries, from that accursed bastard André Von Kastel! But instead he'd escaped her and lived a life of secrecy and seclusion whining for that milksop Arabelle.

Her fury raged. All those years she'd sought him, and now he was beyond her reach for ever. She couldn't entirely read her vessel's thoughts and memories but she'd pieced together the story from her fragments of consciousness during the toothsome young Jonathan's account. André Von Kastel had escaped via the same spell that had condemned her to pain and blackness. If he'd stood before her now, she would have gouged his blue eyes from his head.

Enough! Suddenly her anger settled like a pond flattening when last remnants of a breeze blew itself out. She would not brood on the past. There was the future ahead and, despite her current disadvantages, she was clever enough to secure it.

Quiet footsteps padded away and, as the door closed behind Rafe Hathaway, Isidora Katori sat up, threw back the covers and stretched luxuriantly.

The pleasure of being corporeal again, even for only a short while, bordered on the orgasmic. She looked down at her hands, imagining the patterns of energy that compelled her fingers to slide between her legs and touch herself. This body was responsive, highly sexual when properly directed, and it would serve her well if she could retrieve the correct enchantments to possess it permanently.

Exhilarated, she leapt from the bed and looked around.

The room was beautifully appointed, done out in greens and gold, with sumptuous furnishings and a thick, soft carpet. She thought momentarily of her fine apartment in the metropolis. She hoped it was being kept in good order for her return.

Against the wall stood a pier glass and, shedding her clothing, she went to it. Paula's dress sense left much, much to be desired, but soon enough it would no longer be an issue.

Enjoying the simple delight of being able to see through physical eyes again, Isidora appraised her host body. Not too bad. Not as smooth and exquisite as the one she'd been so foully ousted from but, once it was hers permanently and she had her powers back, she would make it over.

Magic and pampering would enhance the magnificence of her opulent breasts and the lush grove of her pubis. Likewise the pert high curves of her bottom and the sleekness of her thighs.

The face? Well, there was promise in the superficial similarity between Paula Beckett and the Countess Katori. It would be child's play to remake her into something greater than she had been.

Tilting her head this way and that, Isidora cupped her breasts, assessing their weight and firmness. A frisson of reaction tingled through her, shooting from the sensitive tips right to her clitoris, where it throbbed between her legs. Without a second thought she slid a hand down and began to rub herself.

Oh yes! Oh yes! Serendipity had been kind to her.

Groaning, she thanked mighty Astarte that the very person she'd needed to meet back in that public-house garden had been this responsive and toothsome woman. Facing a mighty clash with a powerful creature like André Von Kastel, she'd had to leave a Thousand Hour Marker on someone for safety's sake. But swirling her fingertips around in her sex, then settling them almost savagely on her clitoris, she was glad that it had been Paula Beckett, who was so juicy and full of erotic potential.

'Oh, Paula, dear Paula,' she chanted, pounding on the delicate seat of her pleasure and jerking her hips like a sleazy brothel dancer, 'I'm going to enjoy this earthly shell of yours. And take much pleasure in stealing it away from you.' Throwing back her head and snarling, Isidora surrendered to the juddering sensations of her climax.

How sweet physical life was after these last weeks of drifting around its edges, snatching at tempting morsels of consciousness between dark and painful sojourns in the other place.

The scent of Paula Beckett's arousal rose up into her nostrils and she breathed it in like a revivifying gas. 'Not long now, my dear,' announced Isidora Katori, smiling archly into the mirror at the other woman's face. 'All I need is to find my grimoire and to persuade that handsome man of yours to help me. Then you'll be gone and I'll live for ever in your body!'

8 Duplicity

The bedroom was empty when Rafe returned but a lovely scent, drifting from the open door to the bathroom, told him that Paula was up and about and feeling better. As he shut the door behind him, she came walking through, towelling her hair and singing softly.

'Feeling better now?'

God, she certainly looked better! Even though her hair was still wet, she was no longer the half-drowned creature he'd carried in from the storm. Her skin glowed and her smile was impish. And she looked a treat in a skimpy T-shirt and what looked like a pair of men's boxer shorts.

'Yes, I'm fine. I think I was just knackered from the storm and everything.' She tossed the towel on a chair back, heedless of the fine antique upholstery, picked up a comb from the dressing table and began carefully teasing the tangles from her hair.

'I told Sumner a bit about what's happened to you. Just the dreams and the fact that you hear voices sometimes. I managed to prise a bit more out of him too.' He tried to focus and remember what he'd said, and what Sumner had said, but somehow it was difficult to concentrate when she was standing in front of the pier glass, slowly working on her shiny black hair and swaying gently as if dancing to some sensuous unheard melody.

'Sounds like this Isidora was supposed to disappear,

poof, out of existence but somehow she's latched on to you and is clinging on by the skin of her teeth. He reckons –'

'Oh, please, let's not talk about her now.' Paula's body stilled for a moment, then she turned to him, smiling as she abandoned her comb and smoothed her hair with her fingers. 'We're in a gorgeous bedroom. We're out of the rain. We're together. Can't we just take a little time out from all this doom and gloom and relax?'

Her hips swayed as she walked towards him and Rafe's cock jerked hard in his jeans. He wanted her, and wanted her badly. He'd been subliminally turned on for hours, he supposed. Catching glimpses of her nipples pressing against her wet T-shirt, remembering the feel of her under him, above him, around him. They'd struggled together through perhaps the crappiest weather he could ever remember and now, in the calm after it, his body craved solace, peace and sensuality. A time out from wild tales of magic and possession.

Yes, just plain simple sex. Comfort sex, basic but fabulous.

His cock leapt again, agreeing with him as Paula wound her arms around his neck and drew his mouth down to hers for a sweet kiss.

Her lips were soft and enticing, pliant at first then demanding as she pressed her tongue inside his mouth and sought his. The way she flicked and probed with it made his cock thicken and harden, almost to the degree of pain, as it seemed to develop an imagination of its own and feel that nimble caress along its length and around its crown. Without thinking, he jerked his hips, seeking friction.

Paula responded with a slow, suggestive undulation, tilting her pelvis and grinding herself against him so closely that he almost imagined he could actually feel her cleft, the tempting divide of her sex lips. He growled in his throat, his hands sinking to cup her bottom. Grabbing, he lifted her off her feet and jammed her hard against him. With the flexibility of a gymnast, she clung on tight, drew up her knees and locked her ankles at the small of his back, pressing her sex against his.

Paula wasn't heavy, yet she wasn't a sylph either. Somehow, the tension of bearing her entire weight only added to the spiralling excitement. He swung her round, loving the savage way she rocked and humped against him. His hunger soaring, he carried her easily to the bed, but, when he tried to set her down, she dragged him bodily over her, not breaking her hold.

Furious heat flared between them, making Rafe's head go light and seem to whirl. Had it always been this intense with Paula? He supposed so. Maybe the novelty and strangeness and the unashamed luxury of their sur-roundings was making the experience extra-spicy and erotic.

'God, you smell good,' he whispered, when at last she allowed him his mouth.

And it was true. During her toilette, she'd anointed herself with some deliciously floral eau de cologne, and the glorious vapours filled his brain like an aphrodisiac.

But that wasn't all. Beneath the flowers he could smell the hot musk of her sex. Even through her shorts, it tickled his nostrils, fierce and strong.

'So do you,' she breathed against his neck, her tongue

moving in a long, sampling stroke as she reached down to cup his crotch, her fingers delicately digging into him.

'I don't!' He laughed. It'd been a long day and he'd sweated hard, carrying her through the Priory grounds against the force of a howling gale. His body was grungy and unfresh and desperately in need of a shower if he could tear himself away long enough to take one. 'I probably smell like a wild dog.'

'I've always been rather fond of wild dogs.' Her voice was a soft growl, and her tongue lapped him again and again, licking his throat, then moving up the side of his face until she was kissing, then biting his ear.

What the hell was she on about? He could feel himself capsizing under the surface of a teeming sea of lust.

Jeez, Paula, I thought I was the hypnotist, he told her silently. But he didn't care. All he wanted was to fuck her, to be inside her, as deep as possible.

With the lobe of his ear still caught between her sharp white teeth, she began negotiating his jeans. Deftly, she unshipped his belt, then flicked open the button and seized the tag of his zipper. A second later, she had him out, hot and rampant in her hand.

Her teeth closed tighter on his ear as her fingertips closed neatly on the swollen crown of his cock. Alternating the pressure, she pinched first on one, then the other, in a delicate and precisely threatening dance. After the rough and tumble of getting on to the bed, it was torturingly surgical.

'Please,' he moaned, astounded by the sound of his own voice begging. He shifted against her, agonisingly tethered by his own swollen cock.

'Please what? What do you want? Tell me immediately or I won't give you anything.'

'I want to fuck you, Paula. I want to fuck you hard. I want to come inside you.'

'Admirable ... That's what I want too.' With a last squeeze she released him, both ear and penis, and then rolled over beneath him as sinuously as an eel. Flexing her body, she pushed upwards, and he found himself coming up on his hands and knees behind her.

As she scooted forwards, she looked back at him over her shoulder and wiggled her bottom. Her eyes were narrow and glittering with a lust that matched his own.

Caught in the act of reaching for the waistband of her boxer shorts, he paused when she suddenly shook her head and murmured, 'Tut tut! Not until I say so.'

Rafe nearly shouted with frustration but then laughed when she twisted round, caught hold of the loose leg of the shorts and revealed to him her pink and pouting sex. The soft folds were vivid and peachy, the lush flesh all a-shine with lubrication.

So it was to be like this again? Doing it with her pants on? He remembered that first night in the alley and the delicious friction as he'd fucked her through the tight gap of her pulled-aside knickers.

He moved towards her, his cock swinging and eager.

'What are you waiting for?' she enquired, touching her own sticky cleft with her fingers as if she simply couldn't wait for him to get in her. Rafe was hypnotised by the lewd, rhythmic action.

'Yeah, just a minute ... Need a condom.' His voice was tight. He could hardly speak. He wasn't sure he'd even been this turned on in his life before.

He almost ripped the rubber getting it out of its packet. Eventually he was enrobed and, unable to wait or indulge in the niceties, he pushed forwards, his cock homing in blindly on her rosy wet channel.

Crying out, he drove home. His head seemed to spin again as if he were diving into a vortex. He almost passed out when she gripped and clasped at him with hot inner muscles. With his hands on her hips, he bore down and down while she pressed back at him with equal and opposite force.

For what seemed like an age, they heaved and jerked against each other, gasping and grunting as if they were in a pitched battle rather than a sensual act of love. Paula was squashed face-down into the mattress, jammed against the bedding, but irrationally somehow Rafe felt she was in charge of him. The way she rubbed herself and circled her hips was mesmerising.

And when he came, she seemed to wrench his soul right out of him.

And when she came, she keened aloud and laughed in triumph.

Rafe drifted, bordering consciousness, feeling as if he'd been wrung out like a soiled rag and beaten on rocks. His strength seemed to have been sapped out of him and into the woman beneath him. He couldn't even lift his body up off hers. He just lay there.

And so did she. Silent at first, then all of a sudden she seemed to gurgle and shake. After a few moments, it dawned on him she was laughing again and, with a great effort, he hauled himself up off her, stripped away the sticky wilted condom and disposed of it, and stuffed his still tingling cock back into his jeans. Strange, black foreboding gathered in his belly but he still felt powerless to speak or move away from where he stood, looking down at his inert, but still chuckling paramour.

Oh, dear God, what have I done?

As the thought surged through his mind, she rolled over onto her back. Her hand was still between her legs, just as before, and she was smiling in supreme, exultant triumph.

A pair of brilliant-green eyes looked back up at him, smug and sultry.

'And now it dawns on him,' she said softly, fingers flexing. 'Now he knows who it is he fucked.'

'Isidora?'

'Who else, delicious man? You don't think your milksop Paula could screw you the way I do, do you?' Abandoning her crotch, she sat up, her emerald eyes locked on him. Rafe felt vertigo again and clenched his fist, digging his nails into his palm. He wasn't sure whether he wanted to smack her across the face or whether he was just inflicting pain to keep himself focused. She was trying to hypnotise him in a way that rendered his own efforts amateurish. What the hell had happened to his so-called empathic gifts? He'd just been so completely taken in that he'd fucked the 'enemy' without even realising it.

'What do you want? Where's Paula?'

'Questions, questions. Can't we just have a pleasant conversation?' She edged along the bed, then patted the space beside her that she'd created. 'A little civilised discourse before we go at it again?'

Rafe felt a tugging sensation that was both psychic and physical. He imagined himself moving towards her, slipping into a deep luxurious ease and lack of conflict, and at the same time his cock throbbed as if her luscious sex were somehow drawing it back towards oblivion. Gouging his palms with his nails, he remembered a classic spy film, one of his favourites, and wished for a rusty nail to drive into his flesh to fight her programming.

'What's wrong, Rafe? What are you afraid of?' In a swift, economical, purely animal manoeuvre, she whipped off her T-shirt over her head and bared her breasts. It hardly seemed like a seductive gesture at all, just a natural movement as if she were simply more at home with her body exposed. She cocked her head on one side, making her silky hair swing like a curtain. 'You *are* afraid of something. I can tell.' She shrugged and her breasts lifted in a beautiful soft jiggle. 'And for once I don't think it's anything to do with me, is it? What are you afraid of, Rafe? You can tell me. I can help you.'

She could. He knew she could. She could take away the constant spectre of his father's agony. All he had to do was help her, and she could more than help him. He felt himself floating, and suddenly he was sitting on the bed just inches from her perfumed body.

No!

Blood trickled in his palms but it didn't seem to make any difference. He looked into her eyes and, though they were still green as jewels, they seemed softer, more sympathetic and the touch of her fingers was light and soothing on his arm.

She didn't speak, but everything about her gently invited the confessional.

'I'm afraid of death.'

The pressure of her fingertips increased a little, but still she didn't say anything. The void of silence seemed to coax him to fill it.

'My father died painfully of a genetic disease when he was only forty-two. It was agonising, and there was nothing we could do to ease his suffering. He couldn't speak and he was losing his faculties, but I could tell he was going through hell ... and I'm afraid of that.' He looked away, still seeing his father's contorted and almost fleshless face. 'I'm not cowardly about anything else, but that I hardly dare think about.'

A cool, smooth hand touched his cheek and turned it until he was looking into green eyes again. Was he imagining things, or did excitement and low scheming shine among the façade of feminine sympathy?

'How old are you now, Rafe?'

Decades of fear churned in his chest, and the wild primeval panic that compelled him to do anything to avoid his fate.

'Almost forty. I've never been tested though. I don't know if I've got the same thing.'

She stroked his cheek and his brow, smoothing her fingertips against his skin. 'Poor Rafe. How cruel life is. You were powerless to help your father, and now you're powerless to help yourself.' Her fingers slid to his throat, hovered there with a tiny hint of threat. And then she was caressing him again, pulling him against her body, her cool hands stroking his back in a coaxing rhythm. The action was so seductive, so easy to accept. He began to drift again, listening to soft, encouraging murmurings.

'It needn't happen, Rafe. Not even if this thing is in your blood. There are ways to cheat the cruel games fate plays. You help me, and I can help you. You can live. We can both live . . . maybe for ever.'

His head full of perfume and sex, and the prospect of life and lots of it, he slid his arms around her, seeking her mouth with his in a natural slide back to intimacy.

Why fight? It was what he wanted. He wanted her.

Her kiss was hot. Cool. Intoxicating. His cock kicked hard in his jeans again and his grip on her tightened, his hands roving her back, her buttocks, her thighs. He could feel the hard points of her nipples pressing against her chest, and suddenly he wanted to feel all of her, naked, against all of him. With a quick twist, he snagged the waistband of her shorts and wrenched at them, and this time she didn't protest but even helped him by shimmying out of them.

Then it was his turn and he pulled at the cotton hem of his T-shirt while she – Isidora, he supposed he must think of her – reclined back on the bed like some naked exotic queen. Her black hair almost seemed to have a life of its own against the white linen.

He shuffled out of the T-shirt and balled it up, ready to throw it, but, just on the point of flinging it on the floor, an anomaly in its colour seemed to strike him right between the eyes.

It was smeared with a darker patch. Blood. For a moment he was puzzled as to its origins, but then opening his hand and glancing down at the scored marks where his fingernails had gouged the skin, knowledge and remembrance and fear and horror came barrelling back to him.

The stigmata of his battle with her began the fight again.

'What's wrong?'

Bare and sultry, Isidora sat up. Her eyes were nearly black with desire but they were also wary. He wasn't sure whether she could read his mind or not, but she could certainly sense the aura of emotion. And she'd tasted the sea change he'd just gone through.

'Second thoughts, Rafe? Why is that?' Reaching up, she touched his face in a possessive action. But just as she seemed on the point of pulling him to her, he snatched at her wrist and brought her arm down.

'If we both live for ever, what happens to Paula?'

The dark eyes narrowed but the pale beautiful face remained a mask as if she were calculating, assessing. She drew in a breath, her chest lifting, and suddenly and inexplicably, she shook her head slightly as if to clear it.

'Why, she lives forever too.' She paused, frowned, as if having difficulty with her thoughts. 'She and I, we share this body.' Putting up a slender hand, she masked an obvious yawn. 'With all those years ahead, there'll be plenty of time for us both. And you'll have the pleasure and variety of two eternal lovers, rather than just one. How does that sound? It must be many a man's dream.'

The provocative voice slurred a little and, with another little frown, Isidora lay back against the pillows, her wrist still held in his grip. For a moment, she seemed to make another effort to allure him, shifting her body in a serpentine undulation against the coverlet, but then she yawned again.

And promptly fell asleep.

The feeling of a gentle caress woke her up. A fingertip slowly circling against her palm.

As she rose from the depths of sleep, Paula became aware of a bedroom around her and the presence of a warm body beside her in bed. It was naked and so was she, the crisp fresh sheets smooth and deliciously cool against skin that was heated, almost feverish.

'Where are we? What happened?'

Hazy memories swirled about in her semi-sleepy brain, and she snatched at them. The big thing, her predicament, made her wince.

'*She's* been here, hasn't she?' The horror was like a cold, biting wind that dissipated the soporific comfort of the soft, fragrant bed.

Trying to shoot up straight, she felt herself restrained by Rafe's strong arm.

'No. No, she hasn't.' His voice was firm, intent, precise, and as he spoke he guided her hand to her bare belly. The skin there was cool and smooth and completely normal. No burning yet invisible sigil indicating the presence of Isidora. 'No need to worry.'

Despite the lack of the incriminating mark, something still bugged her.

'But I'm naked. Did you undress me and put me to bed?'

He laughed, his breath fluttering against her neck. 'You helped, don't you remember? We undressed ... and showered...' His fingers settled over the back of her hand, gently, slowly and rhythmically stroking. 'Then we made love. Surely you remember that or am I so unmemorable?'

Bits and pieces of scenes and actions floated to the surface. Yes, there had been a mutual shower, hadn't there? And gentle lovemaking in this bed. Or was that somewhere else?

'Of course I remember!' She tried to quell the niggles of doubt and suspicion. She was so exhausted that every cell in her body felt as if it were yawning and, yes, the sex had been very nice. And the shower blissful after all that trudging through the rain. 'You were sensational, but that shower was better.'

'Cheeky mare!'

'Sorry, I'm still half asleep. But you *are* good, and I expect you know that, don't you? I bet you have droves of fans at Inner Light. Big handsome man like you massaging them. They must be putty in your hands, to put not too fine a cliché on it.'

There was a silence and suddenly her nerves prickled. Had she insulted him?

'You must think I'm a terrible low bastard.' His voice was light, yet there was an edge to it. She'd hit a sore point.

'No, I didn't mean that ... I didn't mean that you'd actually do anything unethical.'

'You're too trusting, Paula.' The words were suddenly weary, and a little sad.

Bitterness washed through her as other memories roiled and bubbled from the depths. Re-emerging vignettes from her 'lost time'. Fucking hell, she *was* too trusting. At least she had been. She'd been taken in so, so easily. That bitch-cow had even managed to convince her she was a lesbian! When she wasn't, not really.

'You don't have to tell me that!' she flung at him, twisting to almost spit the words over her shoulder, stung to the core by her own stupidity and vulnerability. She began to struggle again, but he held her effortlessly.

'Hey! Relax.' His arms held her firm, but suddenly they

were calming and soothing. 'I didn't mean it that way. What you were up against was beyond the ability of anybody to resist. You weren't weak, love. Just unlucky. Relax...'

Paula slumped, went limp. What was the point of struggling? Especially now, with the approach of night when everything was likely to look even worse than it was? At least she wasn't alone. There was a warm human body in the bed with her, even if it was one of slightly dubious moral compass. Rafe had chosen to try to help her. Why fall out with him?

Especially when there were better things to do.

With one arm still slung around her waist, Rafe began to massage her, his fingers working lightly but with purpose on her upper back and the soft juncture between her neck and her shoulder. He was simply exercising his craft to calm her, she supposed. But it felt so good. Oh God, it felt so good. And not just in her shoulders and her back. Against the odds, she felt arousal coil and stir.

As if he'd read her hormones, Rafe's massaging hand slid down over her shoulder-blade, along her back and around to her breast, where it curved sweetly to cradle her naked flesh. She felt his lips brush her hair and his breath ruffle it.

Sex. Again. It already felt so familiar, even though they were still virtual strangers. But familiarity itself was a sweet weapon, armoury in the fight against her inner darkness.

Rolling over, opening her legs, she welcomed her fellow warrior and offered him pleasure.

9 Cry Havoc

After Paula had gone to sleep, Rafe lay in the gathering darkness.

'You fuck, you sick fuck,' he ground out silently, between his teeth.

In all his life, even when he'd sunk so low as to hypnotise gullible older women into giving him access to their bank accounts, then paid the price for it, he'd never hated himself as much or felt as confused as he did lying naked in this bed.

He could have life, if Isidora were to be believed. A life beyond the constant black spectre of his father's fate. He didn't care about immortality, but forty more years, that would be enough, that would be a dream. He couldn't remember what it felt like not to have a death sentence hanging over him.

Yes, man, you can have all that, but at what cost?

Sitting up in bed, he looked down at the shadowed shape of the woman who'd just given her body to him. He'd offered to help her, but in his bitter heart he accepted he was only helping himself.

Watching her, he seemed to see the other woman. The other woman he'd fucked not so long ago. The one who was beautiful, sinuous, and latently powerful – and who also needed his help if she was to survive.

Sumner had told him that Isidora was a black-hearted

bitch, virtually a demon, the quintessence of evil. But who was to say that was the truth? He sensed she was as selfish as they came, but he'd been in lust with selfish women before, and life had been good with them, especially the sex. His thoughts whirled, spinning through his head like a mad carousel, making him feel sick.

What the hell is the matter with me? I should be able to deal with this!

Relaxation techniques, self-hypnosis, self-healing, the very idea of any of them just made him laugh. His fingers twitched, as if automatically reaching for a cigarette, the weak man's answer.

Sliding silently out of bed, he padded across to where he'd thrown his jeans and slipped into them, and his boots and T-shirt. The night was hot and close, the super-abundance of moisture in the air like a blanket pressing down on him. Suddenly the idea of getting outside was irresistible.

Tiptoeing to the bed, he looked down.

Yes, it was Paula asleep there. Her face tranquil, her arms hooked around the pillow, her hair soft and mussed, she looked as if she hadn't a care in the world. He suddenly wondered whether he would have been inter-ested in her if he'd met her at the Raven under more normal circumstances. She was just an ordinary, average girl. Would he still have wanted to fuck her? Suddenly, he wanted to know. He wanted to go back, to try out want-ing her without all this insane, unbelievable baggage.

Out on the landing, he backtracked as best he could, and eventually found himself in the lofty, echoing hall. The bolts on the front door were heavy but, like the lock, they were well oiled. A moment or two later, he was out on the gravel of the drive and turning back to look at the house.

The Priory looked back at him, its tall windows like long mournful eyes in the night. It didn't have quite the savage air of drama it'd projected while the storm was raging, but it still reeked of mystery and secrets.

He turned his back on it and set off across the grass at a trot.

If he took a run, he might sleep when he got back.

Isidora sat up.

Again? So quickly? Now this was opportune. And no man by her side either.

The thought of sex flitted briefly through her mind but she banished it. There would be all the time in the world for erotic games, centuries and centuries of it when her most pressing of all goals was achieved.

Her powers were depressingly dim while she was in this transient state but she could still taste the magic in this house. It was like a miasma floating in the air, and it was familiar. She knew this flavour, this colour.

Somewhere in this accursed pile of André's was her grimoire. Her own first, great primer of spells – a treasure which had been stolen from her two centuries ago by her lover and nemesis.

Of course she had other books, more comprehensive books. But none was in this accursed country. Only the stolen book was close at hand, and she knew that it at least contained the enchantments that she needed. Not only that, here in a place where a sorcerer had dwelt only a few weeks ago, there would be the raw materials. The placing of the Thousand Hour Marker had been a laughably simple task, executed in moments on the sleeping Paula. But fully purloining the marked body was a far more complex procedure. She knew she could cast it herself – it was designed that way – but, with only relatively short periods of control over this body and the thousand hours rapidly diminishing, she knew she would need some practical assistance. And for that she needed a lover on her side.

The bed was empty. Where *was* Rafe? She'd sensed his diffidence and his uncertainty. But by the same token, he was drawn to her. It was too delicious an irony that he should need her as much as she needed him. Fate had been beneficent, offering into her clutches this man whose doomed future made him capable of manipulation. Yes, he was tough and stubborn and no easy meat for her. But that would only make the game all the more pleasurable. She'd anticipated a sumptuous triumph when she'd finally tracked down André Von Kastel – but this lesser morsel would go some way to assuaging her bitter disappointment for a while.

After rising naked from the sheets, she walked to the window. The night was dark, thick clouds still obscuring the moon but a flash of movement attracted her attention.

There he was, her chosen man, first walking swiftly, then jogging away from the building. What was he doing? Running away from her? She sensed not. It was probably some kind of strangely human kind of constitutional, just a night walk to clear his head or his thoughts.

So clear them, sweetheart. I'll soon muddle them up again when you return to me and I fuck you.

And in the meantime, she had a mission and time was of the essence. Who knew how long she would remain in control of 'her' body and the grimoire contained far more than the spell that would assure her triumph. There was a cleansing spell in it that would have to be destroyed. In the moments before her banishment, when she'd been here before, she'd sensed the presence not only of André and his whey-faced paramour, but the Japanese bitch, Michiko too. If the paint-faced Miko was monitoring this place still, she would no doubt detect disturbances and arrive sooner or later.

And not many hours of the critical thousand still remained.

The wardrobe yielded a suitable robe. Heavy figured silk with a sash and embroidered pockets. She would have set about her search naked. The hot night air was like velvet against her skin but there was always a chance she might run into someone. Maybe that handsome, huge but doltish blond servant she'd glimpsed in a fleeting moment of consciousness earlier, or even Jonathan Sumner or his paramour Belinda.

She felt a surge of cleansing rage at the thought of them. Ah, they would be dealt with when she was restored! She would use them, wring the juice out of them and abandon them as desiccated husks when she was done.

The anger was rich and motivating. Swathing her bare body in the silk robe, she strode to the door, then out onto the landing. The magic in the house was like the circulation in a human body, surging around it through invisible vessels. And somewhere there was a heart. She could sense it pumping and beating somewhere above her. An image of a tower room formed and, within it, an oaken table, bearing her grimoire.

Turning instinctively to the left, she began to hurry along the corridor.

Paula Beckett's feet seemed to know which direction to take and, as she entered a long gallery hung with picture after picture of the accursed André, she espied a door, slightly ajar, right at the far end.

My book! There's my book ... the first step ...

The beautiful robe fluttered like a banner, streaming behind her as she ran on silent feet towards the narrow opening.

Paper. Flames. Smoke. Something indefinable yet precious, utterly destroyed. Black panic, rare and shocking, woke Michiko.

She sat bolt upright in bed, shaking off the quilt and the soft, embracing arms of Hiro. For a few seconds, wonder ameliorated the shocking apprehension that had awakened her. How long was it since she'd allowed herself the luxury of sleeping in a lover's embrace, at peace and vulnerable?

She almost lay down again and snuggled back into his body heat, but the vision of distant fire seemed to strengthen.

A book? No, just pages ... Someone was burning precious, arcane writings. Sleep fuddled her powers, so she shook her dark head furiously to clear it.

'What's wrong, mistress?' enquired Hiro gently in their own language. Sitting up beside her, he placed his hand lightly on her arm, offering reassurance. Given the disparity in their powers, it was fundamentally an ineffectual gesture, but that he'd made it at all touched Michiko's heart and gave her a boost of strength and clarity.

No! Amida, no!

A vision of Lord André's tower room at Sedgewick formed in her mind and at the centre of it, on the oaken table there, lay the great grimoire, damaged and wounded. Ragged edges of the fine parchment proclaimed its rape.

The lost pages were already incandescent ashes in the hearth.

Who? For a moment, she wondered about Balthazar Davenheim, but surely he would cherish such a book rather than destroy it?

Gripping Hiro's hand fiercely, Michiko summoned every ounce of her concentration to illuminate the vision. There was a blank spot, right at the centre, dark and menacing. She frowned and bared her teeth, crushing her lover's hand. Exquisite stoic that he was, he uttered not a single word of protest as if he sensed the critical nature of her struggle.

Again, the support of this most unlikely of sorcerer's apprentices strengthened her.

The blank spot cleared, and the image of a familiar and gloating face sprang into her mind.

Isidora! But how?

Michiko bounced up onto her knees on the futon, shaking her head again, unable to believe what she was seeing. The black sorceress was gone, banished to hell in André's freeing ritual. How could she still be alive?

Clawing at comprehension, Michiko focused her gift as she'd never done before, and the image shifted strangely.

Isidora? But not Isidora ... someone like her?

She sensed the black heart of hers and André's great enemy, but it seemed to be in a different shell entirely.

Who was this person? This woman who smiled so glee-fully with Isidora's smile?

Michiko didn't know for certain, but as the vision began to fade, too distant to maintain in detail for more than a few moments, she had a shrewd idea whose face she'd fleetingly seen.

Back in the shadowed whiteness of the bedroom, Michiko blinked, shaken, and drew in a great breath. She had to return to Sedgewick. As soon as possible. This very night. This very minute.

Turning to Hiro, she saw his face, his suddenly very dear face, crumpled with concern. 'What is it, mistress? What is it? Can I help?'

Michiko had not yet told her eager and pliant new lover anything about her true nature, but, as she stared into his soft brown eyes, she saw more intelligence there than she'd credited him with. He *did* know she was special, but not quite how. And he had sufficient wisdom to wait for the answers in her own good time.

'I have to leave, my sweet,' she said to him, taking the time to lay her hand on his smooth cheek, when every instinct compelled her to spring from the bed, pull on her leathers and dash down and leap astride her motorcycle without further delay. He deserved just a moment of explanation. And farewell. 'Something has happened and I've got to go, this minute. There's no time to delay.'

His skin was so flawless, so tempting, the feel of it revivified her. The strength she drew from it enabled her to relinquish him and rise from the bed.

'You can stay here. Relax. Enjoy ... Treat it as your home.' His large eyes looked puzzled, wounded. 'I don't know how long I'll be, but I'll be back as soon as I can.'

With the grace of a dancer, he bounded up too, and stood in front of her, naked and perfect save for a few lingering pinkish weals from his earlier punishment. Already they were fading, his flesh so wholesome, young and resilient.

'Take me with you, mistress. Allow me to help. I'll do anything, no matter how lowly. Just let me assist you.'

The decision took no making whatsoever. 'Very well. Get dressed right now. We leave this instant. Can you drive?'

There was a luxurious limousine down in the garage. If Hiro were to chauffer her, she could conserve her energies. She had an ominous feeling that she would need every reserve she'd ever had when she reached the Priory.

When he nodded sweetly and dipped in a bow, she almost loved him.

'What the fuck!'

Jonathan Sumner shot up from sleep, clutching his cheek where it stung from a sharp blow. Immediately he turned to Belinda who was thrashing in her sleep, her face twisted in fear and wild distress as she flailed and fought some invisible foe. Swooping down, he scooped her into his arms, holding her tightly against him, trying to calm her half-waking panic.

She struggled, still muttering and gasping and tossing her head.

'What is it, sweetheart? What's wrong? Tell me.' He took her by the shoulders, gently compelling her to look at him, dark foreboding stirring in his gut at the terrified look in her staring, skittering eyes.

'She's here! She's here! We've got to stop her!'

Even as he tried to hold her, she struggled, scuttling across the bed and trying to launch herself towards the door.

'Whoah, baby! Slowly ... Calm down.' Jonathan gripped her, stopping her flight. 'Yes, Paula's here, but there's no need to worry. She's a bit upset. She's having nightmares about Isidora, but she'll be OK. When Michiko returns, we'll be able to sort everything out.'

Not apparently listening to him, Belinda struggled even harder, like a wildcat, almost shaking him off. 'No! No! No!' she shouted. 'Not Paula!'

Jonathan held on, but a dark pall of dread fell over him and a panic to match Belinda's.

Oh no, not again? Surely, she hadn't fooled them? He'd been able to detect her before, because he'd been primed and waiting.

'Who then?' His voice shook. 'Who then, baby?'

Belinda stilled, as if deflated, the fight in her dying. 'Isidora is here.'

It was still a shock. And it was impossible.

How?

'But she's gone, love. She's gone. The ritual banished her.'

Belinda sagged, calm now. She shrugged and looked back at him resignedly.

'She *is* here. I don't know how but she's here and I think we're too late to stop her.'

Jonathan released his love and she shot off the bed. When she swayed, he leapt after her and held her up.

'I think we're too late. We've got to hurry.' Sliding her hand down his arm, she took him by the hand.

'Where are we going, love?' he asked, following her

lead as she drew him towards the door, her nightdress billowing.

'To André's tower. That's where she is.' Her hand on the doorknob, she slumped, her slender shoulders heavy with resignation. 'But I think she's already done what she was going to.'

Paula awoke to the sensation of being carried again. As her eyes fluttered open, she looked into Rafe's concerned face and felt herself being set down on a soft bed. There was an unfamiliar perfume in the air, strong and exotic, but it didn't mask a pungent aroma of burning.

'What's the matter? Where am I?'

Struggling into a sitting position, her head still carouselling, she looked around.

She hadn't the slightest idea where she was. The four-poster bed she was lying on and the dark stone walls of the room it stood in offered no points of reference. Her body was wrapped in a gorgeous silk dressing gown, but she hadn't the faintest recollection of putting it on.

But she did recognise the woman who stood just behind Rafe.

'Belinda!'

Her friend came forwards and sat on the bed beside her as Rafe stepped back. Even as she was wrapped in a warm feminine hug, she couldn't help but notice a stark look on her lover's shadowed face.

'Are you OK, love?'

Still befuddled, Paula pondered her friend's question. She assumed she was still somewhere within the Priory, but she hadn't the first idea how she'd got here.

'Here' was a poorly lit circular space. Odd shadows

crept across the bare stone walls, driven by candle-light and a small fire burning in a sooty grate. The bed she was sitting upon was enormous, swathed in both heavy velvet curtains and voluminous gauze ones, partially tied back. It was luxurious, but it had a forlorn, deserted air.

'I don't know ... not really.' She drew in a deep breath, then almost coughed at the heavy fragrance of the room. 'Actually, I think I'm mostly wrong at the moment, Lindi. How about you?' She stared at her friend, taking in the Victorian nightgown and the slightly haunted look. The pallor of Belinda's skin was readily apparent, even at the most cursory glance. But there was something else, something that made Paula blink and gasp with astonishment.

When Belinda had visited her in the hospital, one of the things that had really irritated Paula most had been the fact that her friend hadn't even done her the courtesy of taking her sunglasses off. Now she could see why. And remembering what Jonathan had said about 'side effects', she immediately understood.

'What happened to your eyes, love? They've turned bright blue.'

'It's a side effect. Well, that's what Michiko says. I'm hoping they'll go back to normal soon.'

Blue or not, her friend's eyes were beautiful – but they were also full of shadows.

Oh, sweetheart, you too?

She grabbed Belinda and gave her another, harder hug.

A discreet cough interrupted their feminine bonding and, with a synchronised sigh that made both of them smile despite everything, Paula and Belinda turned towards it.

Jonathan was standing over an oaken table with carved

legs. At its centre lay a weighty, antique book with thick pages covered in dense black writing and what looked like indecipherable symbols. Paula rose from the bed with Belinda at her side, and walked across the room to look at it.

One thing was very apparent, apart from the alien nature of the book's contents.

A clump of torn edges indicated that several pages had been ripped out. And from the evidence of the damage itself, a silver cigarette lighter on the table and a small pile of curling ashes still smouldering in the huge hearth, it didn't take a genius to work out what had happened.

'What happened to the book? Who burnt the pages?'

Even as she spoke, a slow shiver made Paula clutch at her throat and then her belly. She felt no unusual heat through the silk of the robe but she had no doubt it had been there not too long ago.

No! Oh, God, no! She's taking over!

The enormity of what her physical form had done made her knees buckle, but with a supreme effort and whitened knuckles, she grabbed at the table and kept herself upright. She felt Rafe's hand settle supportively at her waist, but she shook him off, not really knowing why she didn't want his touch right now.

Jonathan broke silence, his usually cheerful voice heavy and serious.

'I think you set fire to them, Paula love. Well, not actually you ... but, well, someone else ... who's sort of inside you.' He ran his fingers down the torn edges, seemingly oblivious to the danger of paper cuts. 'I can't read all this crap. Nobody but Michiko can. But I've a feeling that something pretty serious just went up in flames.'

A chill settled over Paula, making her shudder. She turned from the table and walked over to the four-poster and flopped down, the effort of keeping herself standing up suddenly too great. The thing she'd most feared had happened, the thing she'd been expecting, if she was honest with herself.

Isidora could take over completely now, not just encourage, influence, mock, cajole and goad from the sidelines. I'm just her puppet. What the hell else have I done?

The mattress depressed as Rafe sat down beside her.

'Paula, love . . .' He hesitated, as if choosing words carefully, then laid his hand over hers. His brown eyes were as troubled as the stormy skies outside. 'I can put you under and talk to her . . . to Isidora . . . and ask her what this is all about.' He made a sweeping gesture towards the book, his eyes not leaving hers.

For a moment the words didn't make much sense. All Paula could seem to hear was the ring of sorrow and regret, a silent anguish that burnt in Rafe's eyes.

You've done something, she thought. What the hell have you done? I thought you cared.

The words were silent, but Rafe winced as if he'd heard them, clear as day.

Jonathan lunged forwards. 'What the fuck do you mean "talk to her"?' His normally gentle eyes were blazing. 'You never said anything about this? Talk to her . . . Do you mean to tell us you knew Isidora had . . . had "infected" Paula and you brought her here and didn't tell anybody?'

Jonathan was a slight man of middling height while Rafe was tall and broad, but he still threw himself at his adversary like an avenging angel. Only Belinda's timely intervention forestalled actual fisticuffs. She grabbed her boyfriend by the shoulders and hauled him away.

'Johnny! Fighting isn't going to solve anything. We don't even quite know what's happened yet.' She turned to Paula, her brilliant-sapphire eyes pleading. 'Do you know, Paula?'

Paula closed her eyes for a moment, trying to listen. She didn't want to hear Isidora's voice, but they had to know what was going on.

But all was silence. Perverse silence. Isidora was either deliberately lying low or simply elsewhere.

Paula squared her shoulders, looked around at the faces. Belinda, confused and alarmed. Jonathan still seething and casting black looks at Rafe. Rafe ... oh, Rafe ... confused, guilty, remorseful and at the same time full of a grim determination.

'Well, it seems that this "possession" or whatever has happened to me has taken a quantum leap that I wasn't aware of.' She drew in a huge breath as if the very air might hold some answers. 'I thought this bitch Isidora was just lurking around inside me, murmuring stuff and cajoling me into being a bad girl and whatnot.' She looked narrowly at Rafe. He held her gaze, his expression hard to read. He looked subtle, handsome and complex, and strangely glorious for it. If she hadn't been so angry with him, she would have been turned on. Maybe she even *was* still turned on? 'But it seems she's taken on an autonomous life of her own for part of the time.' She smiled bitterly. 'Apparently, when Paula leaves the building, Isidora is in the house ... And you –' She slid to her feet, reached out and prodded Rafe's chest. 'You've been aware of that fact and didn't see fit to tell me!' He didn't wince and remained rock solid, staring back at her. But there was guilt in his eyes. 'When were you going to put me in the picture, Rafe? Or have you entered into some kind of pact with her? Some secret deal to further your own ends?'

10 True Confessions

She expected him to look away, to the left, to the right, at his feet. Men were like that, they could never meet your eye when they had something to hide. But Rafe kept looking straight at her. His eyes were pained and she knew the answer even before he gave it, but he didn't evade her. Instead, he rubbed his hand over his short hair, thinking.

'No deal as such.' He paused, his mouth twisted. 'But I was offered one, and it was tempting, very tempting ... I was still thinking about it. That was why I'd been out running, trying to decide.'

The words were stark and Paula had difficulty absorbing them, although they were much as she'd suspected.

Jonathan, however, had no difficulty processing Rafe's confession and sprang at him anew, his fists flying. 'You fuck! How could you? You bastard!'

Rafe blocked him easily and Belinda grabbed at Jonathan, manhandling him off with a surprising strength given her pallor and general wan appearance.

'Stop it, Johnny, this will get us nowhere,' she said softly, and immediately the younger man seemed to calm down. Paula suppressed an inner pang of jealousy. They were so close, so attuned, and all she had was this duplicitous but beautiful man who may or may not have been going to sell her down the river.

Rafe was still looking at her, strangely placid given Jonathan's histrionics. He had the face of a death-row prisoner who'd owned up to his crime and had accepted that there would now be just retribution.

The words were difficult to frame, but Paula knew she had to.

'Did you fuck her, Rafe? Did you fuck Isidora in my body?'

Without hesitation, came the stark answer. 'Yes ... yes, I did.'

'You fucking, despicable bastard!' Jonathan's usually witty vocabulary seemed to have deserted him, but this time, at least, he didn't try to land any blows.

Paula spun around to him. 'You're one to talk, Johnny! You did more or less the same thing.'

He looked mulish. 'But that was in a higher cause, Paula. It was necessary.'

She chose to set aside the possible inadvertent insult. 'OK, I believe you. But still ... Don't start judging Rafe until you've heard the whole story.' She turned back to Rafe, her heart twisting, her mind befuddled. Somehow, despite this perfidy she dreaded hearing about, she saw a man she still wanted, desired and illogically cared for. 'And you? When you were with Isidora, did you know it was her? Did you still fuck "me", knowing it was her?'

Rafe's eyes looked hectic and he took a long breath. 'Not at first. At first I thought it was you. That you and I were making love.' The soft way he said the two words was a knife twisting in Paula's heart. 'Then I realised ... but it was too late. I ... I couldn't stop.' He paused again, his face almost a mask. 'And I didn't want to.'

'Why?' was all she could manage. All breath in her

body seemed to have been siphoned away, leaving her empty.

'Because I'm weak. Because I'm a man. What does it matter?' He scowled, showing anger for the first time. She wasn't sure whether it was at himself, at Isidora, or even her, for putting him in this strange moral place to start with. 'Look, I fucked up and I've hurt you. I think it's best I clear off. You should let your friends help you. Maybe this Japanese sorceress woman can exorcise you or whatever ... I've just caused you more problems and I need to get out of your life before I screw it up even further.'

He spoke calmly but there was self-loathing beneath the surface and suddenly, despite everything, especially the revolting act he'd just owned up to, Paula felt sympathy for him, and a ringing sense that there was more to it. More reasons below the surface of weak, macho horniness.

As he started to move away, she caught his arm.

'You talked about a deal. What did she offer you? It must have been something important.'

Rafe glanced from her, to Jonathan and Belinda.

'It was nothing. Not important. I don't want to talk about it.' He started to walk but Paula held on, skittering after him, her silk robe flapping and tangling around her thighs.

'No, Rafe, I want to know. You owe me that.' He stopped in his tracks and looked down on her, the mask gone, his mouth working as if he was squirming on a spot he'd never squirmed on before. 'Let's go to our room, talk this over quietly. We can't all stand around in this chamber of doom or whatever it is, falling out with one another. Let's all go back to bed and then we'll gather in the morning, have some breakfast and thrash out a plan of what to do.'

For a moment, despite the raw peculiarity and awfulness of the situation, Paula suddenly felt proud of herself. God, she sounded like a real grown-up, facing adversity with reason and aplomb. Would wonders never cease?

'You're not going to sleep with him, are you?' Jonathan looked as if he fancied taking a swing at Rafe again.

'Calm down, Johnny. You need to stay out of this for the moment.' Belinda gently restrained her fiery boyfriend and Paula smiled at her friend, recognising that same sudden grown-up wisdom in Belinda too. 'We all need to get some sleep, then in the morning I think we'd better try to contact Michiko. She'll know what to do.' Paula watched Belinda slide an arm around Jonathan, and delicately but with authority begin to manoeuvre him towards the door. 'Don't worry, I know Oren has a way of getting in touch with her. And she's only a couple of hours away in London. She'll be able to understand all this.' About to leave, she turned back to the great book, still open, so obviously ravaged. 'And she'll probably know exactly what it was that Paula ... sorry, Isidora ... burnt.'

After Paula had pushed open the door to their room and almost staggered gratefully inside, it dawned on her that Rafe hadn't followed. When she turned round, he was standing in the corridor, his lips pursed and looking slightly lost.

'Aren't you coming in?'

She knew she should be furious, disappointed, hurt and

repelled by him now, but she couldn't summon any of those emotions. She just felt tired and, despite the fact that she'd known Belinda and Jonathan for donkey's years, it still seemed as if Rafe was her deeper friend, even though he'd put her in danger and betrayed her.

'Maybe it's better if I find somewhere else to sleep? Those chesterfields down in the library are pretty comfy.' In a swift, choppy action, he rubbed his hand across his face and, as he did so, Paula suddenly realised it was wet. As were his clothes, his jeans and T-shirt wringing and stuck to him. 'If I were you, I wouldn't want me anywhere near me at the moment. Especially if Isidora should put in an appearance.'

'Don't be stupid. Come on in.' She made an imperious gesture, which it vaguely occurred to her she might well have picked up from Isidora. 'I'll take my chances. And you're absolutely saturated. You need to dry off.'

Cautiously, as if he were nervous of himself more than her, Rafe followed her inside, then stared around as if he didn't quite know what to do.

'And how come you're all wet anyway?'

'I went for a jog. To think over all this crap and decide whether I was going to be an even more despicable shit than I normally am. I'd just come back inside when I met your friends on the landing, squawking about Isidora and something being wrong in that tower.'

'Well, you'd better get dry, hadn't you, and then we'll talk.'

Still, he just stood there, frowning.

'What's the matter? I've seen it all before ... and so has she.' Paula laughed, against all the odds, seeing the dark and twisted funny side.

Rafe shrugged, his lips quirking too as he kicked off his boots, peeled off his T-shirt and unbuckled his belt. As he started to unzip, despite her bravado Paula suddenly, and ridiculously, felt shy. What the hell was that about? She stomped into the bathroom, plucked a robe from the hook and threw it out to him before bolting the door.

The crying jag was hard but silent. What the hell was she going to do now? The bitch was taking over, commandeering her body, getting more and more powerful. And now she was a fool, a bloody fool, to trust Rafe, even though she wanted to.

Despite all he'd probably done, the thought of his warm body and his enfolding arms still felt like ... like home to her.

Eventually he knocked while she was tidying herself up. The bathroom was astonishingly well appointed, more like a luxury hotel than run-down haunted house.

'Are you all right in there, love?'

Love?

'Yes, I'm OK.' She opened the door. 'But I'm tired. I want to get back to sleep for a while. It must be nearly dawn.'

Clad in his robe, Rafe regarded her worriedly. 'Right ... you're right. You take the bed. I'll take the couch.' He gestured behind him, towards an elegant chaise longue, which he'd already spread with blankets, presumably from the ottoman at the end of the bed. 'I just need a few minutes in the bathroom.'

It was all so awkward. Maybe it would have been better to rant and rave at him and clear the air. Dear God, she had every reason to.

For several moments, she stared at the bathroom door as if the answers were engraved on it. She wanted to trust him. She couldn't trust him. She wanted to trust him. She couldn't trust him. The two concepts swapped places again and again in her head like one of those old clocks where figures popped in and out of niches. Again and again, making her no wiser. The only thing she did know was that she was exhausted. She needed to rest.

After shrugging out of the silk robe, she placed it over the end of the bed but was puzzled when it wouldn't lie flat. Patting the pocket yielded a crackly sound and, when she reached into it, she drew out two old sheets of parchment-like paper with torn edges.

More pages from the book of spells, but not burnt this time. Were they important? They must be. Isidora had stolen these instead of destroying them. They must be critical, but they meant nothing, not a thing, to Paula. The language was foreign and the symbols incomprehensible.

Michiko will know, she thought suddenly. I just hope she bloody well arrives before Isidora takes control again. Folding the pages, she stuffed them under the mattress, hoping against hope that Isidora couldn't read her mind when she wasn't around.

True to his word, Rafe took only four or five minutes, yet he came out with the bloom of a recent shower on his skin. Lifting the towel around his shoulders he began to rub his short hair. Paula stared at the sash of his robe, so firmly and irrevocably knotted.

Why do I still want him, she thought, after he's so comprehensively betrayed me?

'So?' she said, unable to bear the tension any longer as Rafe lowered the towel with a taut expression on his face. 'What has Isidora offered you? What's the deal?' She hesitated, grabbing a hunk of sheet beneath the covers to stop herself from getting in a strop and losing it. It was suddenly about matters so much more tangible and down to earth than supernatural powers and ancient spells and all that shit. 'Or is it that she's just so much more sexy and a better fuck than me?'

Rafe tossed his towel over the back of a chair, and then took the same chair and hauled it around to the side of the bed closest to her. Then he sat down, took a breath and leant forwards, his hands loosely clasped.

'No, actually, she isn't any better in bed than you. She sort of tricks you into thinking she is, but afterwards you realise that what you felt most of all was the fact you were scared as fuck of her.'

It didn't sound plausible, but a tiny seed of thankfulness blossomed, just because he'd said it at all.

'OK, then. What else did she offer you? There must be something.' She stared at him, frowning. She'd been on the point of saying something, but it seemed utterly stupid to her, given that she barely knew him. 'I don't think you're the kind of guy who's into evil for evil's sake.'

Rafe laughed, short, sharp and bitter. 'I'm a low, conniving fuck who's done some pretty shitty things in my time. And taken advantage of a lot of people.'

Distracted from the main thrust of her enquiries, Paula had to ask. 'What things? What have you done?'

'Oh, let me see ... Well, my current speciality is getting paid for my sexual favours by rich middle-aged women at Inner Light. But I guess you knew about that, didn't you?'

'Yes, I put two and two together.'

'Yeah, but you didn't know that I was once an

embezzler, did you?' His voice was flat, cold, full of disgust. Self-disgust. 'I used my ability to hypnotise people to get money out of them and it worked a treat. I'd like to say it was all for my mum, so she'd have a decent life after she was widowed and all the things my father could never give her. But hell, I enjoyed the fruits of my dubious labours for a while too.' His mouth thinned in a hard line. 'Until somebody twigged what I was doing and I was caught. And convicted.'

Paula realised her shock must have shown on her face, because he quickly went on, making a despairing, palms-up gesture as he spoke. 'Yes, I'm a cheat and a liar and an ex-con. Perfect material for Isidora, I'd say. Wouldn't you?'

'Why did you do the things you did? What was it ... just greed?'

He shrugged again, shook his head. Paula noticed there were still a few jewels of water clinging to his hair. 'Yes, I suppose so ... I wanted to live well, while I lived. And I did give some biggish chunks of money to my mother. But fortunately for her, she died before the full truth of what a worthless shit her son turned out to be was revealed.'

I ought to be appalled. I ought to despise him even more.

Yet somehow, she couldn't. There was no bravado in his voice, only self-loathing, and other emotions, buried deeper, that were more painful.

'What about the rest of your family? Your father? What did he think?'

'There was only ever my father, and he's dead. Long dead.'

With that, Rafe pulled in a ragged breath as if he'd suddenly been hit hard, right in the chest. By some great pain that was always there, but never lost its impact.

'I'm sorry about your parents.' She wanted to reach out to him but he'd set his chair cleverly beyond the distance she could get to. Or maybe beyond the distance it took to reach her.

'They're both better off,' he whispered, as if he was still gathering himself. 'Especially in view of my latest heinous behaviour. Consorting with demons or whatever has to be a moral low point in anybody's life.'

'But did you *know* it was her? And not me?'

He looked at her, his brown eyes dark with regret. 'Like I said, no, not at first ... not really.' He lifted his hands in an elegant gesture. 'I mean, who would? It's all so crazy. You'll probably hate me even more, but at first I thought your story was all bullshit, that you were delusional.'

Paula suddenly found herself laughing. 'So, it takes a close encounter with a bodysnatcher to convince you?'

'I suppose so ... I suppose so.' He smiled ruefully, and suddenly looked as young and as out of his depth as Jonathan probably was.

Paula made a decision.

'Look, this is stupid. Just get into bed, will you?' She slid sideways across the mattress, lifting the sheet and making space for him. 'If Isidora turns up, just sock her on the chin and knock her out cold until it's my turn again.'

The tapestry of emotions on Rafe's face grew more complex. His eyes had widened in an instinctive male response as she'd made her invitation. She was naked in bed, and she admitted that it wasn't by accident she'd offered him a glimpse of her body. Despite everything, she still wanted him for his heat and his humanity.

'Are you sure about this?'

She could see he wanted it, and probably her too. His hand was already on the knotted sash of the towelling robe. 'Not dead sure, but who cares?' She flapped the sheet again.

'Shall I keep this on? I mean ... obviously, you won't want to make love with me after what I've done, will you? So it's probably safer if I keep the part of me that *really* can't control itself under wraps.'

'I'll take my chances.' Before he could stop her, she'd reached out, tugged on the sash and the towelling panels of the soft robe had swung free. Rafe's tanned body was a column of gold and firm muscle, beautiful and framed in white. Twisted up in the residue of anger and disappointment, Paula's desire for him roiled anew, clenching low in her belly. Despite her best intentions, she glanced quickly at his cock.

It was nascent, slightly thickened. Definitely perky. But that was a man for you. Ever ready even in the most unpromising circumstances. With a shrug of irritation, Rafe slipped quickly beneath the covers, twisting his body pointedly so as not to allow for any accidental contact. He reached for the bedside light and plunged the room into darkness. The velvet curtains were thick and they lay in the indigo silence for a few moments, as if they were each bedding into their personal space, getting the measure of one another.

'So, spill it,' Paula said eventually. They were going to have to face this, so why drag out the agony any further.

'What did she offer you? And what did you do to allow her to ... to take over?'

'Well, I didn't do much really, and I wasn't thinking straight. She said something like "do you invite me?" and like a stupid bastard I just said "yes", not really thinking about the possible consequences.'

'Great!'

'Well, like I said, I wasn't thinking straight and I wish I hadn't done it now.'

His voice sounded tired and leaden, and Paula was inclined to believe him but there was more she needed to know, and know now.

'And what was the prize? The lure? What did she offer you to help her get rid of me?'

'Life ... she offered me life.'

It came out barely more than a whisper, and even in the still, dark silence Paula had to lean closer to hear it. Their shoulders touched, and his skin was warm and fresh and slightly damp. She expected him to flinch but he didn't, he pressed closer, the contact simple and human rather than sexual.

'You mean immortality? Longevity? Like Belinda's André?'

'Yes, but that's not what I wanted. Not as much as that.'

His voice was still soft, but had an odd hollow quality to it.

Paula frowned in the darkness. His answer wasn't quite what she'd expected. Oh, she'd thought it was something like immortality, the classic lure of a thousand supernatural stories, but it seemed strange that Rafe didn't want it.

'What do you mean, Rafe?' She turned to him,

tentatively placing a hand on his shoulder and getting the shock of her life when she found him trembling.

He turned to her and, though it was difficult to see him in the shadows, his eyes had a telltale fluid gleam.

'I don't want to live for ever. I just want to live.'

11 Lust for Life

He shook. Hard. And it was as if his body was finally surrendering to some enormous stress that it had borne with difficulty for many, many years. Something he'd probably tried not to think about but had struggled to suppress. A great fear. A great sorrow. Some terror that had eaten away at him and probably predicated his life and motivated those acts of his that were less than heroic.

Paula slid her arms around him tightly in a blind attempt to calm, assuage and understand. He buried his head in the crook of her shoulder, and she felt moisture trickle tellingly against her skin. For several minutes, he cried silently, she stroking his hot back. Whatever was troubling him seemed to bring fever in its wake.

'What is it, Rafe?' she said at length, her hand still moving rhythmically over his skin. 'Just tell me.'

She felt him brace himself, drag in a shuddering breath, rub at his face as he rolled onto his side.

'They say men should be able to deal with this stuff . . . be stoic . . . stiff upper lip and all that, but if I allow myself to think about it, really think, I just fall apart like a crybaby.'

'Deal with what? Please, tell me! I need to understand.'

Suddenly, he sat up in the darkness and reached for her hand. The grip he enfolded it in was fierce, desperate.

'My father died young. He was only forty-two and he

died in agony from a genetic disease that's apparently been passed down in our family. One minute he was fine, then the symptoms started and a couple of months later he was gone.' His fingers were cruelly tight around hers, but she stayed silent, barely feeling the effects. 'I'm nearly forty now ... and ... and I seem to spend most of my days waiting for it all to start.' He turned away, his profile a hard shadow in the darkness. 'The beginning of the end.'

Paula's heart turned over, imagining what the burden of such knowledge must feel like. There. Constantly. Colouring everything that you thought, felt and did. She had some inkling of it. Her own mother had died young and been in pain. But it hadn't been anything hereditary, just the luck of the cancer draw.

Shaking off Rafe's hand, she threw her arms around him again and hugged hard and tight. 'Do you know for certain that you've got what your father had?' she asked, pressing her face against his broad chest, listening to his heartbeat. It was strong and true and regular. It sounded healthy. 'Have you ever been tested?'

Rafe hauled in a gusty breath and, to her surprise, laughed wearily.

'In the grand tradition of me being a worthless waste of space, I've never had the courage to take the test.' The laugh turned to a hard, self-mocking chuckle. 'I haven't even got the guts to know the truth.' He drew breath again with an effort as if there were physical weight bearing down on him, compressing his lungs.

Paula was on the point of saying he should take the test, be prepared, then she stopped to consider. Would she do it? She thought of the times she'd put things off in her life, avoided issues. Hell, it had taken her long enough to face up to the current mess she was in.

'You might be OK,' she began. Hell, words were so useless.

She pressed her lips to his chest, relishing the sweet clean flavour of his freshly showered skin as she delicately circled her tongue over it, tasting and exploring. It wasn't meaningless platitudes that either of them needed now, but affirmative action. Against all the odds, and in the face of everything that had happened, suddenly she was the earth mother, the nurturer.

While they both had life, sex was the clearest and sweetest expression of it.

When she found Rafe's nipple, he groaned as she nipped it and flicked the tip of her tongue over it. His hands, which had been light upon her, gripped harder.

'What are you doing, love? I . . . I don't deserve anything from you.' His voice was rough as he began to move uneasily against her. She sensed a war in him, the battle between lust and deeper feelings of guilt and unease.

'Well, you're getting it anyway,' she purred against his skin. Renewing her efforts, she sucked hard on his tiny teat, while at the same time pulling at the bedding and removing the last physical barriers between them. As she pressed closer, she toppled Rafe back against the pillows, following him over using the momentum of her own body, her mouth still at his chest, tasting and kissing.

'Oh, God!' he said as she reached for his cock.

He was thickening, already quite hard, a little satin-textured fluid oozing from the eye. Paula slid her thumb over the tiny aperture, taking up the moisture and beginning to massage him with it. She synchronised her strokes with the action of her mouth and her tongue. Rafe made a low, rumbling sound of appreciation, the vibration of it thrumming through her lips.

How can I be doing this? she thought as she worked him, rubbing her own rousing body against the mattress as she ministered to him. I barely know him. I shouldn't trust him. He's great in bed but, in some ways, I'm not even sure I like him.

And yet all this was meaningless as her body spoke to his.

He was a bastard but, she sensed, deep inside, there was a good man. A man life had screwed over, and who, being human, had fucked up now and again as a result.

Like everyone.

Beneath her, Rafe's body tensed and arched. There was a thump, then another, and straining to look upwards whilst still sucking on his nipple, she saw that he'd grabbed on hard to the brass bed rails above his head.

'Oh, love ... oh, love ...' he groaned, making the whole bed creak as she delicately fondled the groove beneath the head of his cock with her thumb-tip.

As she stroked him, her own sex ached and seem to yawn wide with sudden need. Flexing her thighs, she pressed herself down hard, rotating her hips and rubbing her sensitised clit against the sheet.

Pleasure flared with the friction. Simple, primitive pleasure that rooted her in the moment. God alone knew what lay ahead, for herself and for Rafe. There could be a result for both of them or it could be very, very bad. But for now, she was here, alive, and Isidora wasn't anywhere. And Rafe too had his health and strength and the ability to take joy in sex. Clearing her mind as best she could, she focused on him. After one last kiss, on the tip of his teat, she ventured southwards.

He was sweating now, and his clean skin had acquired a salty flavour. She licked his abdominals, then his tidy indented navel. 'Oh, Christ!' he moaned again, his pelvis lifting. When she thrust in hard, her tongue a point, he jerked again.

With her hand flat on his belly, she probed again, smiling inside at his response. How sensitive he was here. How momentarily helpless he seemed. She had his pride and joy in her hand and she was reducing him to a slave to his senses with her tongue. Feeling wicked, she slid her free hand beneath his bottom and touched a finger to his anus.

'Jesus ... Jesus ...' Craning her neck slightly, she saw him tossing his head, his shadowed face, beautiful and tormented. 'Oh, God, woman, that's sublime ... Don't stop!'

With a flicker of disquiet, she wondered for a second whether he thought she was Isidora. Then realised that, like any man, when so far gone he was probably at the mercy of his senses and beyond caring. She gave a little shrug as she continued to pleasure him. It was a universal truth, a man's response. She couldn't blame him.

'Oh, Paula ... Paula ...' he crooned as she flickered her fingertip rudely in his cleft. 'Oh, Paula, my dear love, you're amazing.'

Love? Love? Did he mean that? She paused infinitesimally, then went on with her ministrations. Men said anything when they were getting their ends away and hoping for more, but there was a raw thread in his voice, a crack of emotion that seemed divorced from flesh and sex.

Exerting pressure with her finger, her tongue and her thumb, she chose to believe him. At least for now. She'd face the truth, mundane and complicated, out of bed. This man was flawed, so very flawed, but she also cared for him. Whether it was love or anything like it, on her part it didn't matter in the capsule of this moment.

Rafe was squirming, murmuring, grunting but, even as he praised her, she began to feel he was resisting. After a few moments, he let go of the bed rails and slid his hands down her body and urged her up and off him with a firm but tender force.

'Didn't you like that?' she asked, knowing it was a nonsense question, yet wondering how a man who'd been enjoying himself so much could call a halt to that enjoyment.

'Bloody hell, Paula, it was fucking amazing but there was nothing in it for *you*. I want us to share. I want to give *you* pleasure too.'

Grasping her by the flanks, he rolled her over, flipping the balance of power as they went. His eyes gleamed in the darkness as he looked down on her. With a strange little frown of regret, he swooped down to kiss her lips.

It was a tender kiss. A sweet kiss that slowly and deliciously gathered fire. His tongue finally dipped between her lips, tasting and probing with gentleness and promise. Making a sound of pleasure beneath his breath, he cupped her breast and strummed his thumb across its crest.

Suddenly so excited that she couldn't stop herself wriggling and moaning, Paula spread her legs in anticipation and an attempt to lure him between them. As if silently answering her, Rafe's hand began to rove, sliding downwards and travelling to her belly.

Where it paused, resting softly ... measuring, testing.

'Sorry, just me. No one's in the house,' she whispered in his ear, lifting her hips again as he settled a small kiss on the edge of her jaw.

'I know. I wouldn't be doing this if there were.' His tongue feathered her skin. 'I'm done fucking demons, love. I only want you.'

Something shivered in the region of Paula's heart, a deep emotion that had nothing to do with what had happened to her recently. This was what she'd always wanted. A man who wanted only her. She'd had a history of falling for men who were interested in other women, her former crush on Jonathan being just the latest instance.

'And I only want you,' she proclaimed softly, sliding her hand down and curving it around his hip, trying to drag him over her. 'So let's have each other, shall we?' She laughed, and Rafe answered with his own chuckle.

'God, I'd love to ... I'd love to ...' He rolled towards her. Then hesitated.

'What is it?' Cold fear gripped Paula. Could he sense something that she couldn't? Was Isidora already bearing down upon her?

'I don't have another condom handy, love.' His voice was low and grave. 'We can't fuck.'

Instantly she saw it. She got his reasons. All of them.

'I've always played safe,' he said falteringly, wracked with emotion, 'but because of my ... my heritage as much as anything.' He reached round and placed his hand over hers where she still held him. 'And there's no way I'd put *you* at risk, in any kind of way.'

She believed him. The cards were on the table now and she knew he spoke the truth. Her fingers tightened, curled around the curve of his bottom cheek, trying to convey complex feelings through the simple skin on skin.

He lay against her, still. And hard. His erection pressed against her thigh, not fading despite their situation. The feel of it made her own sex surge, still wanting him.

'Let's get creative, eh?' he said after a pause, adjusting his position. Lacing his fingers with hers, he drew them to his lips and briefly kissed them. Then he freed his hand and slid it between her thighs, cupping her mound.

Paula's heart thudded. She reached up and touched his face, then kissed his jaw. It was smooth-shaven, and she guessed he'd taken advantage of the toiletries in the well-equipped bathroom. A notion flipped through her mind, and then was lost again as Rafe began to stroke her, his fingers stirring the lubrication between her legs. She smiled as he circled her clit, loving the pleasure and vaguely amused by the idea that he might be trying to hypnotise her by playing with her sex.

'Are you trying to put me under?' she gasped, unable to stop hitching her bottom about. Rafe laughed low in his throat, but he didn't miss a beat.

'No, love, I think I'm putting myself under. Or you are, the way you move and wiggle like that.'

Silky honey welled in her cleft as Rafe continued to fondle her while saturating his fingertips with her moisture. She wriggled harder as she realised his intention. A few moments later she felt those fingers pushing into her, two sliding in while his thumb possessed her clit.

'Oh!' she gasped as he began to fuck her with his fingers. It wasn't quite as good as having his cock inside her, but it was such a close second she was soon rising, spinning upwards towards climax. Grabbing at his body, as he worked her, she arched and flexed, her toes gouging the mattress.

Oh, he was good, so good ... The rhythm, the angle, the degree of delicious penetration, again and again. The steady pressure on her clit of his thumb. There was much to be said for having a masseur as a lover. He knew how to use his hands, God, how he knew! Her sex was flowering with an abundance of fluid. A third finger slid into her easily, making a warm and living dildo, fucking her effortlessly. The repeated stretch and tug of it made her groan, buck ... and come!

Deep ripples drew down heaven and drenched her in it. She shouted Rafe's name and gouged his back and his arm, clenching her fingers to hold on to him, make him hers. As she began to descend again, she was panting like a racehorse.

The temptation to just lie there was like a siren call, the need to float and glow like an irresistible drug. But after a few indulgent moments, she struggled against it.

'You now,' she murmured, turning to kiss first his mouth, then his pleasuring hand as she drew it to her lips. Her taste was unexpectedly savoury and strangely addictive as she sucked his fingers.

'Do you want me to suck you?' she said, in between cleaning each finger.

'I want to fuck you,' he replied raggedly, 'And I'm going to, just trust me. I've an idea.'

Trust. Again. She felt it totally for this man she should

have been a fool to believe in the very smallest degree. Even when he moved over her, in preparation, slotting himself between her thighs.

What?

Then she realised. He was between her thighs. But just that. His cock was a slippery, almost satin-clad bar of heat as he encouraged her to close her legs and grip him tightly.

It was a sweet compromise, the next best thing, close and intimate. She grinned as he began to thrust, then gasped out loud when he bumped and bumped against her still glowing sex. She grabbed his buttocks, urging him on, goading him to ride.

What a wild, strange, funny, tender fuck. She giggled and mewled and whined as they slapped against each other, the sweat – both his and hers – making their bellies and her thighs squelch and slide.

Eventually, the delicious and incessant knocking against her clit was far too much for her. Whooping with mirth as much as pleasure, she climaxed in a hard and juddering rush. A second later, laughing and shouting, Rafe came too, his narrow hips jack-hammering in violent motion.

'Holy shit, that was fun, love, wasn't it?' he grunted as he rolled off her. He sounded shattered and surprised, but his voice was fond. Hooking his arm around her, he pulled her sideways, off the damp spot.

The bed was wide. There was plenty of room, but she snuggled close and tight, despite the heat their sweating bodies generated.

Despite everything, she felt peace and she could finally trust him.

12 The Cavalry

The bedroom door, swinging open wildly, shattered their slumbers.

Blinking and confused, Paula clung to Rafe as the bedroom filled with people and a woman she'd never seen before, a beautiful Oriental clad in leather, strode towards the bed.

'What the hell is going on?' roared Rafe, grabbing back the sheet when the newcomer summarily tried to wrench it clear of them both. 'Who are you?'

The slender dark-haired woman ignored him and demolished Paula's own attempt to scoot backwards and stay covered by ripping the sheet along its length and throwing the torn fragments away from the bed. With a grip like tempered steel, her assailant captured both her hands and forced them over her head in one smooth sweep.

'Michiko, leave her alone! It's Paula! What are you doing?'

Paula swivelled to see Belinda rushing forwards, with Jonathan at her side, and behind them a slim Oriental man with pink-streaked hair who seemed to be just as confused as she was. She tried to struggle but the hold on her wrists was immovable.

'Michiko' stared down at her for a tenth of a second, but, just as the leather-clad woman seemed to make a decision and reach with her free hand towards Paula's body, another shout of anger, right beside them, broke her concentration.

Lunging wildly across the bed, Rafe launched himself at the Japanese woman.

'Get the fuck off her! Leave her alone!'

He grabbed for Michiko's arm and pulled at it but, getting no response, he hurled his entire body, still naked, at her in a rugby tackle. The combined attempt of Paula's own struggles and Rafe's big male height and weight should have dislodged the other woman. But it made not one bit of difference.

Michiko's dark head came up, and her almond-shaped eyes glittered. Not just a sparkle, but a bright, oscillating twinkle like a special effect out of a movie. She uttered four sharp, guttural words in what was presumably her own language, and with her free hand made a swift but complicated pass.

Rafe went hurtling across the room as if he were a scarecrow who'd been snatched up by a twister.

'Rafe!' Paula wrenched at the grip on her and struggled hard, as hard as she could, but another twinkle and another sleight of hand rendered her powerless. She still tried to move but her limbs seemed to have been stapled to the mattress. Only her eyes obeyed her commands and, despite the dark woman looming over her, she strained to see across the room and check on Rafe.

Panting and winded by a resounding impact with the wall, he was already rising again and coming to her aid, but a third spell blocked him in his tracks. Paula got the impression, faint and fugitive, of a shimmering barrier stretching right across the room. Beyond it, Rafe's face contorted in an effort to shout out but despite his efforts not a single word emerged.

The invisible perimeter didn't seem to affect the others in the room, Belinda, Jonathan and the slim dark Oriental guy, but they all just stood there, keeping their distance.

Michiko stared down at her.

'Isidora, are you here?' she said, her tone low and soft, but at the same time bell-like with authority.

Paula tried another struggle, her muscles cracking almost as she fought her unseen bonds. But when she shouted, she found at least she'd not been silenced, like Rafe.

'Look, you mad bitch, she's not here! It's just me. I'm Belinda and Jonathan's friend, Paula.' She put as much force as she could into her voice, even though it felt as if there were strapping around her chest, hampering her breathing. 'That other bitch, Isidora, she's not here now. She was earlier, I think, but she's gone for the moment.'

The Japanese woman narrowed her eyes and seemed to sniff the air for some elusive odour. Her sharp nose crinkled and she glanced from Paula to Rafe, but then she seemed to relax a little, and Paula realised to her embarrassment that all the Japanese sorceress was smelling was fairly recent sex.

'Very well.'

Michiko released Paula's hands but there was still some kind of magic restraint, holding her in place.

'Look, can't you set us free?' She looked to Rafe and saw rage and thwarted protectiveness in every line of his body. He was still straining against his bonds too.

'One moment ... I must check something. It will be more comfortable if you relax.'

The sorceress's face was gentler now, kinder, and something in the line of her exquisitely arched brows and her cherry-pink painted lips seemed to actually suggest deep compassion.

Paula tried to let go and not fight. It was difficult but she immediately felt better. Alas, Rafe wasn't giving in at all, and his face was still furious with the raw effort of fighting the impossible to get to her.

'Perhaps you could leave us?' Michiko turned to the still watching audience. 'Belinda, Jonathan, I'll meet you in the library in a little while.' Her face became almost tender. 'Hiro-*chan*, why not find a room for us and stow away our things? That would be most kind.'

Then the beautiful Japanese turned her attention back to the bed and, as the others filed out, to her astonishment Paula found herself being caressed by this mysterious and martial woman she'd only just set eyes on.

Narrow elegant hands slid over her body, gently tapping her skin as if testing its constituents. It wasn't a sexual contact but, despite herself, Paula started to blush. The touch of the Japanese woman's fingers was pleasurable even though she didn't want it to be. Especially when they cruised across her breasts, carefully examining every inch.

Her cheeks flaming, Paula turned her face to the pillow, hearing only the harsh gasp of Rafe's breathing as he still battled against Michiko's magic.

The touch was so light, the woman's fingers so cool and methodical. It was as if she were reading the surface of Paula's sweaty skin.

Which, of course, she *was* doing, Paula realised.

'It's on my belly, the thing you're looking for. It starts to burn when she's here. Sort of raises like a weal.'

'Thank you, my dear,' said the Japanese, her voice suddenly warm, almost like that of a sister. Her finger slid deftly to the curve of Paula's abdomen, tracking, examining . . . reading.

Still unable to look, Paula was surprised when she felt the mangled sheet being drawn across her hips and settled neatly over her pubis. The area of the sigil was still exposed, but, a second later, Michiko tweaked more folds of the torn sheet across Paula's breasts and upper body.

'I'm sorry I was so peremptory,' she whispered, leaning low and brushing her lips against Paula's temple, 'but I had to be sure . . . I had to know.' Her breath was sweet and perfumed, slightly herbal, not unlike the apothecary -shop scent that Rafe favoured. 'And it's just as I feared.' She paused, her fingers stilling. 'Countess Isidora has left a marker on you.'

'I know that! What kind of marker? What does it do?'

'Hush, I'll explain it in a moment,' said Michiko softly. 'First I need to reveal it so we know what we're dealing with.'

Paula turned from the pillow, glanced at Michiko, whose dark eyes were grave, and then looked towards Rafe. His expression was stormy with anger and worry. He'd stopped actively fighting, but his naked body was still a pillar of tension.

'Look, set us free first,' she told the Japanese woman, finding confidence somehow from the expression in Rafe's eyes. He was here for her in a way that no other person had ever been in her life. Their ambiguous start had only strengthened the sudden bond they had now. 'I won't struggle. Hell, I want to know more than anybody what's going on. And so does Rafe.'

Michiko narrowed her eyes as she looked at Rafe, as if assessing the danger he might present. And when she cocked her dark head on one side, Paula had the distinct impression she was reading his thoughts.

Great, a mind-reader! Just what we need.

But then again, who better than a sorceress who could hear thoughts to detect the arrival of Isidora?

Eventually, and apparently satisfied, Michiko made a tiny, almost imperceptible hand gesture, and all the pressure on Paula's body disappeared. Rafe too visibly relaxed, then shook himself like a dog before heading for the bed. He snatched up their robes from the ottoman and slid onto the mattress beside her, wrapping hers carefully around her shoulders and then adjusting the sheet placed across her pelvis. As he shrugged into his own robe, Paula was aware that not once had he looked directly at Michiko.

'Thank you,' she whispered, reaching for his hand and squeezing it as he hunkered down beside her, like a concerned brother or parent about to support her through a nasty medical procedure. He gave her fingers a firm squeeze, then lifted them to his mouth and kissed them hard, his face frowning.

'Yes, that's good. You must support her,' said Michiko crisply. 'As I uncover the marker there may be some discomfort.'

Apprehension surged in Paula's chest as the other woman inclined over her, fingertips reaching for her belly. She shuddered, then stilled as Rafe's strong arm slid around her shoulders, exerting a steadying force. He still held her hand and she turned her face and buried it in the crook of his shoulder, her rock against this unknown ordeal.

Paula had never had a tattoo, but instantly she was unpleasantly reminded of needles, a thousand needles pricking at one tiny area of skin at once. Something radical was happening to the skin of her abdomen, but the feeling was so intense and uncomfortable that she simply couldn't look. She closed her eyes and pressed closer to Rafe.

She couldn't have said how long the strange, tormenting pain-not pain went on, but trying to ignore it induced a peculiar light stupor. Breathing in Rafe's body fragrance, she floated in a troubled dream of being with him. Blanking out the prick, prick, prick of the phantom needle, she imagined him touching and caressing her, kissing her face and throat and neck while his deft masseur's finger stroked her clit.

Still dimly aware that she had to stay still, she nevertheless felt a bright, kinetic energy building inside her. Bizarre as it seemed, she was aroused again, and her sex seemed to throb softly in time to the ersatz pulses of the psychic tattoo. She moaned against Rafe's throat, wondering if he knew that it wasn't the strange procedure that was bothering her, but a new desire.

Eventually, Michiko, who had been sitting on her heels on the bed, sat back, making the mattress rock. The burning on Paula's belly was already fading to the faintest prickle.

'Just as I thought. A Thousand Hour Marker ... and dangerously few hours still remaining. Look!'

Unwillingly, Paula unwound herself from Rafe, her eyes still closed. He squeezed her hand again and she opened them – and looked down.

In the centre of her belly, an inch or so above her pubes, there was etched an ornate and very complicated design. A collection of symbols and stylised curlicues, interwoven like strange tiny vines, with the suggestion here and there of planets and stars. Its colour was a pale, faintly reddish brown, almost the colour of a freckle or a very light birthmark.

It would have been pretty if it weren't so ominous.

'What does it mean?' Rafe's voice came as a shock. He hadn't spoken since Michiko had bound him, but he sound tense and serious, as if he were fighting hard to suppress his emotions.

He's trying not to frighten me, thought Paula, frightened anyway.

Michiko leapt lightly off the bed, her leather clothing gleaming as she moved.

'I believe we need a council of war. This concerns us all and I will explain everything, to the best of my ability, when I've had a chance to review what I've discovered.' She sounded brisk and businesslike, and the strength and focus she exuded was reassuring. Paula found herself smiling, despite the peculiar ordeal she'd just suffered. It seemed that the cavalry had finally come over the hill.

'Shall we convene in the library in, say, around forty-five minutes?' The sorceress glanced at the rather complicated chronometer strapped to her wrist, then strode to the door. When she turned, she looked intently at Rafe, her dark brows lowered in a frown, her head cocked as if she were reading him. 'A heavy responsibility falls to you now.' Her near-black eyes burnt with power, as if she were compelling him to do her will by sheer force of personality. Paula wondered if this was the way she looked and acted herself when she was under Isidora's sway.

'If the marker begins to darken, even in the slightest,' Michiko went on, 'you must ensure that Paula stays in this room. Bind her, secure her, lock the door . . . but don't allow her to get away from you.' She paused, lifting her hand in a gesture of emphasis, fingers curved into a fist. 'Because if the sigil goes black, the creature you're dealing with will no longer be your lover. She'll be Isidora, who I suspect will try to get away from Sedgewick if there's no one here who'll aid her.' Reaching into her back pocket, she pulled out a glittering metal bundle and tossed it onto the bed. A second later another object, tiny and also metal, landed next to it. 'You'll probably need those.'

With no further glance backwards, the Japanese woman left the room.

Leaving a stunned silence in her wake.

Without pause for thought, Paula coiled her arms around Rafe again, letting out the breath she hadn't realised she'd been holding when his arms folded protectively around her.

'Are you all right, love?' he murmured into her hair, and she was struck again at how completely she trusted him all of a sudden. It had happened somewhere along the line in the beat of a heart, but she couldn't for the life of her pinpoint the moment or explain why she felt so completely sure of him. She only knew that the familiar man-smell of his body meant safety for her.

'Yes, I'm OK. Just a bit stunned. It's not every day a

woman you've never set eyes on before comes stomping into your bedroom, *with* an entourage, and proceeds to rip the covers off you and give you a tattoo or something on your bare belly.'

Rafe laughed, although there was little humour in it. Paula felt his entire body tense up. 'So that's the famous Michiko, the white sorceress?' When she pulled back a little and looked up at him he was scowling at the closed door. 'As they say in the movies, she's a real piece of work.'

'And how!' Paula reached up, touched his face, smoothing her fingertips over his frown lines. 'But at least she seems to be on our side, and she's obviously very powerful.'

Rafe smiled, and some of the taut anger ebbed from him. 'Fucking hell! You can say that again.' He gave Paula a quick hug then scooted away down the bed, picking up the gifts they'd been left. 'Handcuffs, for Christ's sake.' Dangling the shiny metal restraints from one finger, he stared at their key in the palm of his other hand.

They were in peril. She could lose her body, her mind, her life, and Rafe too had a death sentence hanging over him. But still, the sight of the shiny metal cuffs produced a kick of erotic excitement in her belly. And a smile on her lips. Even in the direst straits, the sweet, horny sex urge couldn't be kept down. Even with only 45 minutes left to them before a war council, she suddenly wanted to play again with Rafe.

'I know, I know ...' Rafe chuckled, and she could see the same lights twinkling in his eyes as she knew were in hers. Warmth bubbled in her heart at their closeness.

'But if we get into anything, she'll only come and fetch us, won't she?'

Desire for Rafe and the desire to know what the hell had really happened to her and how to deal with it warred in Paula. He was right though. First things first. A shower, and then the powwow. And then afterwards, who knew? Maybe there'd be time for something sweet and naughty?

As long as the sigil on her belly didn't go black.

'Don't worry, love. If she comes, I'll do my best to hypnotise her. I'll do better now I'm alert to her wiles.' Still clutching the cuffs, Rafe enveloped her in his arms. 'We'll keep her under control until our Japanese friend works out how to get her to fuck off completely.'

Oh, how I want to believe you, love! I really do . . .

But as she clung on to his warmth for a few moments more, the feel of metal against her back was cold warning.

The atmosphere was strange when they walked into the library, edgy and mildly aggressive. At her side, Rafe was tense and watchful, and she seemed to feel his protective instincts billow around her as they moved forwards into the room. Squeezing hard on his fingers, she flashed him a glance, hoping he'd cool it. They needed Michiko. They all had to get on and work together.

The Japanese woman stood in front of the fireplace, still in her leathers. She looked commanding, focused, yet troubled. Which was worrying. The others – Belinda, Jonathan and the young Oriental man – were sitting on the edge of their deep chairs, looking equally uneasy. And sitting at the back of the room, on a row of elegant ladderback chairs against the wall, sat the giant Oren and two very pretty young blonde women who were astonishingly alike. Who were they? Staff? Friends? Lovers?

There was breakfast on the sideboard – coffee, croissants, brioches – but nobody was eating. Was it even dawn yet?

Despite the presence of the commanding portrait of Count André Von Kastel hanging over the fireplace, the focus of all attention in the room was the low coffee table. On which lay open the great damaged book. The ragged edges were a mute accusation. Paula couldn't take her eyes off the wounded pages as she and Rafe took their seats on one of the spacious chesterfields.

'So ... what did I destroy?' Lifting her chin, she met the dark gaze of the sorceress.

'You? You didn't destroy anything,' Michiko said firmly, stepping forwards and staring down at the book. Her smooth brow crumpled and she looked faintly sad. 'But unsurprisingly, as far as I can see, Isidora burnt the pages containing the spell to banish her completely from your body and send her where she deserves to be, for all eternity.' She crouched down and flipped the venerable pages of the grimoire. It fell open at another place, where there also seemed to have been damage. 'There are other pages missing too, containing the enchantment that would allow her to take over your body completely.' She pursed her cherry-tinted lips. 'But I suspect she took that and hid it for her own use later. Although she needs to act quickly. Less than a hundred hours of the thousand still remain ... and she needs to act in that time, just as much as we do.'

'What do you mean?' Panic surged through Paula, but Rafe's hand on her arm steadied her.

'Yes, what *do* you mean? This is Paula's life we're talking about, not some abstract, Harry Potter concept.' He didn't shout, but his voice sounded deadly. The room's fraught atmosphere ramped up a notch. Paula glanced from side to side at the worried faces of her friends, then turned to find the silent but reassuring Oren at her side, offering coffee. She gave him a grateful smile and took it.

'The Thousand Hour limit cuts both ways.' Michiko waved away the cup that Oren offered her. 'If Isidora doesn't banish you from your own body and take it over as her own, she'll never be able to do it. And likewise, if we don't banish her from your body within the allotted time, we'll never get her out.' She fixed Paula with a not unsympathetic look. 'And if neither spell is cast, well, the two of you will be trapped in a turf war for the same mortal shell for the rest of your days. The only way you'll get rid of her is to die. You'll never get any peace from her and she'll only grow stronger. As well as angrier and angrier because she's trapped.'

Paula took a long sip of her coffee then set the cup down by her feet, trying to imagine a life where the bitch kept grabbing chunks of her consciousness. And doing God knows what. How could anyone live like that for any length of time?

'What if I just died anyway?'

'What do you mean, love? What are you talking about?' Rafe's voice was raw and anguished, and when she turned to him his eyes were filled with horror.

'I can't go on the way I am.'

'You can. I'll be with you. I can suppress her. Put her under whenever she appears.'

'It's a solution of sorts, but it's not ideal,' observed Michiko, drawing closer and sitting on the arm of the chesterfield.

'You shut the fuck up,' hissed Rafe to the sorceress. Grabbing Paula's hand, he folded it in his again. 'I'll always be here for you, love. Always.'

A great rush of emotion, of hope, surged up in Paula's heart. Yes, with Rafe at her side, she could do it. They'd fight the bitch together. She smiled at him, loving the dear, determined look in his face and in his eyes. Then suddenly the warm sensation of renewed hope died as quickly as it had been born.

'But Rafe ... what if ...'

Realisation dawned in his face. Agony filled his fine brown eyes. Pain not for himself, she realised, but because he might not be around long to protect her. She surged forwards, enfolding him in her arms, oblivious of the watching eyes of the others.

'Just protect me as long as you can, sweetheart,' she whispered, her hand on his back, feeling the heat of his skin through his T-shirt. He felt so alive, it seemed impossible that in a year he might be gone. 'Then I'll take my chances.'

'What's going on, Paula, love?' asked Belinda, her voice suggesting somehow that she sensed the answer.

Paula drew back from Rafe, still looking into his face, but aware of the others in the room – even Oren and the two pretty girls, and Michiko's Hiro – hanging on her next words. Silently, she asked Rafe's permission to elucidate and he nodded sharply, his lips pursed.

A second later, it seemed he'd changed his mind. He'd tell the sorry tale himself.

'There's a strong possibility that I'll be dead within two years. It's likely I've got an inherited genetic disease. My father lost all his faculties and then died in agony when he was only two years older than I am now.'

His voice was flat, unemotional, but gasps of sympathy rippled around the room.

'I accept it now. Those are the breaks. It's not going to be fun, but I don't care about that. I'm only sorry that I'll not be here to help Paula fight her fight. That's my only concern.'

There was a moment of shocked silence, then Jonathan spoke up.

'I'm sorry, man. I had no idea. I wouldn't have gone for you if I'd known.'

The two men looked at each other. Eyes level, each gauging the other's reaction.

'No, you were right to,' answered Rafe, shrugging. 'I was tempted. I put others at risk from that bitch. You should have kicked my arse.'

'Yeah, like you'd have let me.' Jonathan's voice was rueful, but he smiled and, after a moment, Rafe smiled back.

'But maybe Michiko can help Rafe?' suggested Belinda, leaning forwards. 'Do some magic to banish whatever it is that's wrong with him?'

They all looked towards the white sorceress.

'Alas, it's unlikely I can help. Hermetic magic is problematical in matters of genetics.' Her expression was complex, both exasperated and compassionate. 'The only way would be to cast a longevity spell similar to my own or Isidora's. But it might not work. You might end up living for centuries in the same condition your poor father endured in his last days. So whatever promises Isidora made to you, they are most likely empty.'

The mood in the room was suddenly sombre and horrified. Silence reigned again until Rafe seemed to lose patience and rose to his feet, striding to the fireplace and the place of precedence that Michiko had quit. Paula looked up at him, struck by the accidental resemblance between him and Count André, in the portrait behind him. She glanced quickly at the Japanese woman and saw her brow was puckered as if she too saw the likeness.

'So, assuming I'm not going to be around, what can be done for Paula?' Rafe demanded, cracking his knuckles as if to instigate creative thought. 'Is there another book somewhere? With the same spells?'

Suddenly, Paula remembered and felt like kicking herself. She reached into the deep front pocket of the soft hooded top she was wearing. The torn-out but undamaged pages she'd hidden under the mattress. Dragging out her prize, she held it out to Michiko.

'I found these in my pocket. I think she was going to hide them to use herself. I think it's the spell to banish me, not her.' She paused. 'I mean, she'd only burn the ones to banish her, wouldn't she?'

The Japanese woman scrutinised the yellowing pages.

'Correctly deduced, Paula, and we're lucky that she lost control again before she had the chance to do any more than tear these from the book.' She reached out and pressed her hand reassuringly on Paula's shoulder. 'The kami have smiled on us in this at least.'

Kami? What are kami?

'The powers that be, the gods of my ancestors,' Michiko said kindly.

Paula trembled. Michiko could read her mind then. The idea made her cringe, then a second later came a rush of relief. At least someone here can tell instantly when Isidora's around, she thought. Without me having to take my clothes off.

Across the room, Jonathan suddenly yawned. He suppressed it and muttered, 'Sorry, it's been a strange night. If it is still night?' Looking around their circle, Paula saw tired faces. Even Rafe looked utterly exhausted and, though she had no way of knowing what kind of reserves Michiko had, her young friend, pretty Hiro, looked beat.

The Japanese woman sprang to her feet.

'Yes, we are all weary. And Jonathan is correct, it's been a strange night,' she said firmly. 'I need to lock these pages in a place where they'll be safe. I suggest we all retire to our quarters and get a little rest. Then regroup in a couple of hours.' A frown puckered her smooth brow. 'There are answers to be had but I need to think, to refine them.' She made as if to go to Hiro, but then paused in front of Rafe who was also on his feet.

'I rely on you.' Her voice was intent as she looked up at him. She was almost a foot shorter than him but she still seemed commanding. 'While I'm occupied, you are our first line of defence. You must contain Isidora by any means at your disposal, whether physical or psychic.' Slipping her hand into the pocket of her tight leathers, she drew out a small smooth stone, marked with tiny symbols. 'This talisman will enhance your hypnotic gifts and assist you in subduing her.' She put the magic item into Rafe's open palm. 'But remember, those handcuffs should stop her going anywhere. Her powers and her physical strength are limited without total dominion over a human body.'

She turned to Paula, apology in her dark eyes. 'Your body, alas, my dear. It means you must be restrained. I regret the necessity but it's the only way to be sure she doesn't bolt while your lover sleeps.'

'I won't sleep.' The words were harsh but measured, and there was steel in Rafe's eyes. His hand was still open, the talisman resting there as if he didn't want to accept it.

'I believe you will attempt not to, but we cannot take the risk.'

Paula glanced from Michiko to Rafe and back again. They didn't particularly like each other, or even trust one another, but there was respect there, despite the antagonism.

Rafe took a deep breath. 'Fair enough. You're probably right. I've got feet of clay and I've failed before.' A spasm of guilt twisting his face, he closed his fingers around the small magical stone. 'So it's probably best to take all precautions.' Paula grabbed for his hand and squeezed it lightly where he held the talisman and Michiko gave him a stiff little nod of respect, then turned to the room.

'We'll gather here in two hours then?' She looked from face to face. 'By which time I hope to have more in the way of solutions to offer.'

As if by mutual agreement, they all filed out of the library. Silently at first, but then, as they split into couples, murmurs of conversation began.

'I won't let her get a grip this time.' Rafe's voice was

grim as they moved out of earshot of the others. 'Not this time Not ever again.'

As they ascended the stairs, Paula almost believed him.

Hiro fell asleep quickly and, as soon as his breathing steadied, Michiko flung on her robe and made her way back down to the great library to collect the damaged grimoire. Cradling it to her bosom, as if it were an injured child, she returned to André's tower with it, seeking the centre of the Priory's power. She placed it on the work table that had belonged to her former friend and lover, wracked with guilt that she'd allowed the great book to be sullied.

OK, it had been Isidora's book of spells in the first place, but having spent two hundred years in André's possession it had shed her dark influence and acquired his more benign aura.

'If you were here now, my lord, we could banish her between us.'

She stared up at the fine portrait of her friend, hanging in his most intimate chamber. In the two centuries he'd had the book in his possession, André Von Kastel had learnt by heart most of the spells within its pages. He would have known the form of words for the banishment and the ingredients required to make sure the job was done right. Michiko knew only general principles, outlines, fragments.

There was no way she could safely banish Isidora from the body of Paula Beckett without reviewing the actual spell. To take the risk was to condemn the unfortunate young woman to the same fate as her nemesis. Or worse.

Running her fingers along the torn edges, she opened

her mind, willing the enchantments to form from the echoes still lingering there. She imagined clean blank sheets, gritting her teeth, trying to conjure the details by main force.

Nothing happened.

She blanked her mind again, begging her dear friend to contact her from the Great Beyond, but though she sensed his eternal presence – and his concern – her thoughts remained formless.

But if André was beyond the reach of her requests, who else could help? Someone who had a book such as this? Intact? There was one, of course, someone who'd be happy to help her. For a price.

Michiko frowned.

Balthazar Davenheim. Collector, connoisseur, minor sorcerer – and major pervert. None of which was necessarily a fault, but she knew what he'd want and she wasn't sure she could give it. Especially now, when Hiro was proving so very interesting and coming to mean so much. Still, she felt a frisson of half-troubled excitement at the thought of accepting the latest in a long line of invitations. She'd so often wondered what it would be like with him.

As she pondered, the sound of footsteps alighting the stone staircase made her jump.

But it wasn't Balthazar Davenheim who entered the tower room, only Belinda. In her silk dressing gown and slippers, the younger woman looked fresh considering the broken night but, then again, her sleep cycle was still unusual.

She smiled and rubbed her short reddish hair. 'I'm

awake for a change.' Her mouth quirked with a worried little smile. 'Is there anything I can do?'

'Not really, my dear,' Michiko replied, turning from the book towards her friend. For a moment, memories of lust between them stirred, and she couldn't suppress the urge to search the younger woman's body with her eyes, remembering its delights, its willingness.

Maybe some other time?

'Don't worry, Belinda.' She touched the other woman's arm softly, sampling her disrupted aura. 'You will return to normal. If you want to . . . It's already happening.'

Belinda shrugged, her pretty face lighting in a wry smile. 'Yes, I want to return to normal. Jonathan's normal. We have normal lives to go back to. I think it's better that way.'

Michiko raised her hand, stroked Belinda's face, looking into her eyes. 'They're less blue . . . definitely. It's only a matter of time and you'll be as you were.'

Belinda smiled, but it faded when she glanced down at the book.

'But what about Paula? What can we do for her? I really thought that cow Isidora was gone for good.' By silent mutual consent, the two women moved to the bed, and sat down on its edge, side by side.

'She can be banished, for good this time. There is a spell.' Michiko rubbed her forehead, working at the frown that she knew had reappeared. 'If only I could remember all of it, rather than just scraps.'

'Isn't there another copy of the grimoire?' Belinda glanced at the open book.

'Yes, there are several in existence. And one I know of not all that far away.'

Belinda almost bounced on the bed. 'Can we get access to it? Borrow it or something? I can't bear to think of Paula stuck with that bitch inside her for ever.'

Michiko stared down at her own wrists. They were narrow, but infinitely strong. Could she see them bound and at least feign weakness and submission, in the cause of the greater good? She'd entered into such games before and enjoyed them mightily, but only with trusted friends and lovers that she cared about. The man she had to go to, whose co-operation they required, was largely unknown to her, his motives possibly suspect. Possibly dark.

Could she let Balthazar Davenheim bind and shackle her, and play with her body?

13 The Ties that Bind

Staring up at the elaborately moulded ceiling of their bedroom, Paula tried to remember the last time life had been normal. What was it – a month ago, more? Certainly less than a thousand hours . . .

She'd set out in her little car to meet Belinda and Jonathan. She'd spoken to them on the phone, calling from a pleasant country pub where she'd stopped for lunch. Then a beautiful woman had spoken to her and turned her world inside out.

Her memory was starting to clear now, but she wasn't sure if that was a good thing or bad. Especially in relation to what she'd done with Isidora. She could remember being kissed and touched and given orgasms. But she couldn't remember the state of desire for a woman. Lying here now, it was still men that she wanted.

Correction, man.

In the tense silence she glanced sideways at Rafe, still not sure how or why she'd fallen for him. His profile looked austere in the soft early-morning light. He was tightly wound. Worried about accidentally nodding off, he was sitting up in bed, his back against the pillows piled behind him. In his lap, glittering and silvery against the towelling robe he wore, lay the handcuffs, a silent accusation. His eyes were closed, but she knew sleep was far away, every line in his face and body told her that.

Have him, a voice seemed to murmur, but Paula didn't know if it was Isidora coming or just her own instincts.

Now she knew him, and knew what drove him and what haunted him, there was a special beauty to Rafe that touched and stirred her. She would never have found such a man desirable before, especially in such parlous circumstances as these, but now everything about him turned her on. She loved the way his short hair just curled slightly at his hairline, and she even loved the slight dusting of grey amongst the black. She wanted to look up into his intense brown eyes and see them dark with passion, then bright with pleasure. Life-affirming pleasure that eased the soul and made the impossible to deal with more bearable for a while.

'Rafe ... are you OK?' She touched his arm, feeling the solid muscle and the heat of his skin, even through the fabric of his robe. He was so full of life, and she had to remind him of that. 'Why don't you lie down and relax for a while? Look –' she tugged apart the panels of her robe, to show her belly '– the mark is normal, no darkening. It's just me.'

The sigil made her frown, despite her reassurances to him. One section of it had already changed, and she deduced that it was meant to be a numeral, signifying the number of hours left out of the thousand.

Bloody hell, I've got a countdown on my skin!

She looked up into Rafe's eyes and they were dark and troubled.

'I think I'll just stay awake,' he said, and the cuffs chinked softly as he leant over and kissed her lightly on the forehead. The action was delicately tender, yet it made Paula think of his fierce, raw lovemaking in the alley, just a couple of days ago. Who would have guessed that he'd turn from rampant one-night-stand to noble guardian so quickly?

She reached for him, pulling him down for a better kiss. Or at least one that was different, and less chaste. As she pressed her lips against him, cradling the nape of his neck, his tongue responded. The cuffs jingled again as he moved over her, deepening the contact, taking her mouth.

Paula coiled her arms around him. His back was broad where she held on and he smelt divine. Their bathroom was provisioned with a five-star collection of toiletries and grooming products, and he'd chosen a light and spicy cologne that was not unlike the fragrance he usually wore. The skin of his face and jaw was silky-smooth, as if he'd shaved again.

When he'd been in the bathroom, he'd left her fastened to the brass rails of the bed and the thought of that now, as they kissed, made her body tingle and rouse. Even though she knew the life and death serious reason for her bondage, it still produced a deep and sexy frisson.

Was Rafe thinking about it too?

Suddenly she wished for Michiko's powers of thought reading. The ability to reach inside his mind and touch his emotions. Had Isidora possessed such abilities when she was in her own body? If she had, she certainly wasn't sharing them with her temporary host.

So it's up to me to show you how I feel the old-fashioned way, thought Paula, surging against Rafe, rubbing her body closer to his.

To her delight, as he shifted position, she discovered he was erect. It made her smile, her mouth curving beneath his kiss.

Despite her freakish dilemma, despite the still ambiguous nature of their relationship, despite his kick in the gut fears about his own life expectancy, despite all this against them, the power of sex prevailed.

He wanted her. She wanted him. At least that was simple.

Then he drew back. Looked into her eyes. In his there was a moment of doubt, then he too smiled.

'Yes, it's me,' said Paula firmly, her fingers tangling in his thick hair. 'Can't you tell?'

'Sorry, love, I shouldn't doubt you. I don't doubt you. It's me. I don't want to get so blinded by lust that I'm beyond seeing the difference.' He let out a gusty breath. 'I'm just a man. Whatever happens we're pretty much ruled by our dicks.'

Paula pushed on his chest, making him sit up and face her.

'Look, if we let her stop us making love because we're scared of her, she's won. She's controlling what I do, and what you do, even when she isn't around.' Before Rafe could respond, she slithered out of her robe, leaving herself naked. 'See, nowhere to hide now. I know you'd know if she put in an appearance, but this way you can be doubly sure.'

Rafe's eyes flared with light. A familiar hot light. He touched her thigh, trailing his fingers over her skin almost reverently. But he still hesitated.

'Look, love,' Paula persisted, warming to her theme and to the prospect of savouring his long, fit body. His robe had shifted in their tussle and she could see his cock thickening and growing, dark with vibrant blood. 'If you're worried about her showing up while ... while we're fucking, well, you can always stop, can't you?'

'Knowing what I know now, that's probably a certainty.' He shrugged. 'I don't fancy her. In fact I can safely say I hate her. I'd most likely just wilt the minute she appeared.' His fingertips glided over the surface of her skin, the caress simultaneously erotic but far, far from sex. 'I know it's the same body, but I don't want her. I only want you.'

Paula lurched forwards, pressing her lips hard against his, knowing there were the beginnings of tears oozing down her cheeks, but not caring. How strange and wonderful it was to have found what she'd always been searching for under these most bizarre and unlikely of circumstances.

Rafe's arms folded around her again, and he rolled them over until he was on top of her. The handcuffs were beneath them, digging into her buttocks but she didn't care. The small discomfort seemed to fire her pleasure, especially when Rafe's skilled masseur's hands began to travel, revisiting zones that he already knew well.

He kissed deep. He touched deep. Within seconds he was circling her clit, fondling and patting it as he leant over her, his tongue in her mouth. Naked against the sheets, Paula wriggled, feeling the metal of the cuffs press against her bottom. As he fingered her, she imagined him touching her in the same way, but when she was shackled, chained up to the bedhead. She'd want to touch him in return but be unable to. The idea of being bound and restricted made her sex flutter, and within moments she was gasping and coming lightly.

Rafe pulled away, looking down at her. Was he looking for the intruder? Maybe not. He just smiled and said, 'That was quick. What were you thinking about?'

Paula grabbed him lightly, a hand on each side of his face, grinning back up at him as her flesh continued to shimmer. Men were all the same, even the best of them. Always ridiculously pleased when they'd made a woman orgasm.

'I was thinking about the handcuffs, actually ... about bondage.' She gave him a little wink. 'Now that we've got them, we might as well use them. And then if you do fall spark out asleep when you've come, "she" won't be able to get up and go looking for the door key.' She glanced around momentarily, wondering just where he'd hidden it when she was in the bathroom, but knowing it was best she didn't know. 'Of course, you'll have to put the key to the cuffs out of her reach too.'

Rafe narrowed his eyes at her, in mock suspicion. 'Are you sure she's not here already?' He slid his hand from between her legs and moved it, still moist with her arousal, to her cool belly, examining it by touch as well as sight. The design was still reassuringly pale. 'Either that or you're learning devious tricks from her.'

'Heaven forbid,' murmured Paula, keeping her voice light even though she meant it. Fiddling around beneath herself, she drew out the shiny cuffs. Silently, she held them out to him, keeping her eyes locked on his. Telling him she trusted him.

Rafe took the cuffs, hooking a finger in one, letting the other, on its short chain, dangle. The metal glittered in the soft light like a cipher, and he cocked his head on one side, still questioning.

Paula didn't speak, but with a tiny nod she answered his silent enquiry.

Slowly, Rafe lowered the metal construction until the lower cuff just brushed against her breast tip. The sensation was delicate and silvery yet it made her want to squirm again. He circled the cuff and she wanted to wriggle more, open her legs, reach down. But she fought the urges, imagining she was already secured.

The metal slid against her, bumping and flicking at her nipple, sending little streaks of pleasure straight to her sex. He repositioned the cuff and taunted her other nipple, round and round. Unable to contain herself, Paula whimpered, her hips lifting.

'You're horny this morning, baby,' said Rafe huskily, letting the cuff trail down until it hit the dink of her navel. Paula grabbed the bedding, twisting it in clumps, pulling at it. The stimulation was disproportionate, unexpected even while she was still smiling inside at what he'd said. She imagined him back in his treatment room at Inner Light, speaking much the same way to one of his 'ladies', yet strangely she felt no jealousy or scorn. This was just play, and play-talk was appropriate.

The cool metal slid lower, edging against her bush, and he inclined over her for a closer view.

'Hold yourself open,' he commanded, his voice firm, but not harsh. Even so, Paula shuddered, her heart a-flutter.

Reaching down, she parted her pubic hair, exposing the delicate, glistening anatomy of her sex. She wrinkled her nose as a gust of woman smell rose up. Rafe smelt it too. She could tell from the way he drew in a deep, deep breath.

With slow, infinite precision, he drew the metal of the

cuff down her body and settled it in between her labia. It felt so cold and hard that Paula mewed out loud.

'Shush,' he chided her, working the cold metal up and down, over her clit. The contact was light, almost ethereal, but she felt herself beginning to clench and gather, to rise. She wanted to grab his hand, force the damn thing against herself, rub and rub, crudely and roughly, almost painfully, until she came. But she still felt compelled to resist, as if mentally shackled.

As she fluttered on the edge, Rafe lifted the cuffs away and she moaned like an animal.

'Easy, baby, we've only just started,' he said, leaning and whispering the words right in her ear. Even as she still writhed, he caught her hands and went to work, finally putting the cuffs to their actual purpose. Making her raise her hands over her head, he secured one wrist, then slid the chain through the metal bed railings, before clipping the second cuff around her other wrist.

She was bound.

'How does it feel?' He leant in close, in her face, his eyes shining as if they were polished. He didn't touch her, but just held himself above her, poised. Paula arched her body, reaching for contact, but he slid backwards and knelt up, out of reach.

How did it feel?

Terrifying.

Exciting.

Strangely comforting.

She rattled the cuffs against the rails. They were hard around her wrists and uncomfortable if she fought them. But when she let off the tension and there was slack, they were OK. To ensure she didn't tug involuntarily, she curled her fingers around the rails and clung on.

'Different. I've never done this before.'

'I have.'

'Now why doesn't that surprise me? Do you chain up your massage ladies?'

It just slipped out, and she wondered for a moment if she'd smashed the mood. But he just gave her a wry smile and started tugging at the sash of his robe.

'I never said I was the one doing the chaining up.' He laughed softly as the robe parted and, after slipping the handcuffs key in one of its pockets, he shrugged it off and tossed it away. He was a good shot and it landed across a chair, several feet away.

Which left him kneeling up on the bed but just beyond where she could effectively get to him. And resplendently naked as he leant over and reached into the bedside drawer and pulled out a fistful of condoms. On a hunch, Paula had glanced in there a little while ago and discovered that the Priory was just as well provisioned in contraceptives as it was in everything else.

As she'd done before, she wondered whether he sunbathed naked or used a sunbed. Or maybe his luscious golden skin colour was just natural? Whichever way, his body gleamed in the filtered light, deliciously healthy. There's nothing wrong with you, she thought, trying to convey her conviction to him. I don't believe in that death sentence for a minute, even if you do.

For a moment a tiny frown puckered his brow as if he'd heard her, then he smiled, licked his lips and touched his cock.

Shivers of sexual electricity quivered through her body. She'd expected his tactic would be to touch her and caress her until she was half-mad with just-denied pleasure and wanting him. But it seemed now as if he was taking a different tack.

Slowly, slowly, he caressed himself, carefully stiffening even further an erection that had been mighty in the first place. Licking her own lips, she admired the fullness and the gathering rosiness of his flesh and the way the narrow love-eye cheekily pouted as he pumped himself. Shiny fluid, thin and glassy, quickly coated him.

When he was hard, massive and pointing at her crudely, like a cudgel, he loosened his fingers and seemed to present his erection to her.

Here it is, he seemed to say, look but don't touch.

For a moment, she wondered if he was going to simply ejaculate over her, but a second later it seemed he had other ideas. He began touching himself again, his fingers lightly and leisurely exploring. But not his cock this time, just the rest of his body. Caressing himself as if he loved himself – which he maybe did at this moment. He grinned at her, then blew her a mimed kiss.

Oh, dear God in heaven, how she wanted him! And how perverse and delicious of him to put on such a show.

With leisurely grace, he swept up his hands, ran them over his scalp, ruffling his short hair and tipping his head back as he did so. And with every movement, great or smaller, his heavy cock swayed. Paula clenched her fingers around the metal bed rails, knowing that if she didn't she'd wrench at the handcuffs and hurt her wrists. Rafe's golden skin seemed to call to her and his well-honed muscles purred softly to her fingertips, inviting them to touch and glide and explore.

His majestically rampant cock seemed to shout, You want me, don't you? You want to touch me, you want to hold me. You want me in you!

And Paula's mouth began to water and tingle with the deep yearning to suck him. She was being offered everything beautiful, hard and male, just inches from her reach. He didn't have to touch her or even talk to her. Just the sight of him inflamed her beyond reason, and she cried out incoherently.

Rafe shook his head, then eyed her narrowly. The slow sweet smirk on his sensual lips was a caress in itself. 'What do you want, baby?' he said, his voice a mocking parody of porn-star sleaziness. His eyes were laughing and filled with merriment and, despite her screaming lust for him, Paula couldn't help but laugh right back at him.

'You!' she growled at him, lifting her hips, shimmying at him as enticingly as he'd shimmied at her. 'I fucking well want you! I want you inside me just as much as you want to be inside.' She nodded to his erection, waving slightly, its tip slick with pre-come.

'Patience, baby, patience,' he teased, his hand dropping again to his cock. He plied his fingers over his hardness a moment, then moved towards her. But didn't put it within her reach. Instead he inclined over her and cupped her breasts, fondling them vigorously, his thumbs sliding over her heated skin and flicking her nipples.

Oh, it was so good, but it was also so bad. Between her legs, her sex gnawed at her, demanding contact. She wove her hips trying to press herself against him and secure a bit of ease.

'No, no, no,' he crooned, twisting his body clear of possible contact without faltering a moment in his caresses. His hands and fingers worked cleverly, massaging firmly without ever overstepping the boundary of discomfort.

The delicious teasing went on for just long enough to play havoc with Paula's senses. She was just a ball of unresolved hunger, craving more, more, more . . .

Then Rafe kissed her, his tongue sliding in and possessing just as his hand proceeded deftly to her sex. As he as good as fucked her mouth, his fingertip danced upon her clitoris. And as the inevitable occurred and she climaxed hard, he held her to him, sliding his free hand around her waist and lifting her up as he pressed against her.

The orgasm was light and clean and intense. Paula gripped the bed rails hard, rattling them on their fixings as her sex fluttered and clenched repeatedly. She wanted to hold him, desperately, but not holding him only intensified her pleasure.

'Oh, God, please . . . please . . . I want you,' she gasped as he released her mouth while his fingertips still devilishly plagued her clit. 'I can't take much more of this. I want you inside me. I want to be fucked!'

Rafe laughed. But it was a warm sound, a verbal caress.

'Anything for you, love.' Still chuckling, he rummaged amongst the condom pile and plucked one out, rolling away to put it on.

Paula's shackled fingertips itched to be able to do the service for him. To be able to enrobe his big thick shaft in superfine rubber and touch and caress him in the process.

He seemed to be taking an inordinate time about things, even though his movements over his erection were smooth and deft.

As she writhed uneasily against the bed, her hips seeming to have an electrical energy of their own that had nothing to do with her conscious thought, Rafe slid over her and then parted her legs, kneeling between them. Paula whimpered, the stretching of her tendons increasing the tension in her sex-flesh.

Coming up on hands and knees, he drew his hard, latex-covered length over her body, sliding the tip against her skin, across her marked belly, up and down her thighs and into the hollows where her legs joined her torso. Slowly, slowly he dragged his hot flesh over her skin. Teasing, taunting, promising, acquainting her with what would soon be inside her. And as he did, he kissed her face, her throat, her shoulders.

Paula groaned, almost wanting to weep with frustration as her sex wept with it too. She could feel silky fluid sliding out of her as it welled in welcome, making ready for Rafe's sweet cock.

Finally, he stilled, his erection resting lightly against her cleft, simply the heat of it a caress to her burning sex. Looking down into her eyes, his expression was complicated, a chiaroscuro of emotion. She saw playfulness, desire, yearning – but more, so much more. He caught his breath as he reached down and positioned himself, and caught the minted scent of toothpaste in his gasp.

He didn't ask her to beg for him. The teasing was over now. Guiding his penis with his fingers, he pushed right in. In his eyes, emotion flared, and they sighed as one.

Paula longed to hold him, but felt, somehow, that she

was holding him with her heart, if not her arms. He felt huge inside her, and right and good. His flesh belonged there, it was his natural home – she felt complete.

With tenderness, with care, but still with huge passion, he began to thrust, whispering sweet, loving nonsense in her ear. As he moved inside her, pleasure bloomed, reborn anew.

And suddenly, it was all so simple. The pleasure. As her body gathered itself, everything was clear and pure, untrammelled. Genetic death sentences and unspeakable supernatural threats couldn't touch them when they were like this. All that mattered was the pleasure and their sudden, unlikely and completely unlooked-for love.

As orgasm bloomed, their cries were mutual, their fates entwined.

A set of bonds far greater than metal joined them now.

Afterwards, without speaking, Rafe released her and, like a long-married couple, they settled down for their much delayed hour or so of sleep. The only unusual part of the process were the cuffs and Paula's bondage.

Rafe still insisted he could stay awake, but they both knew his claim was probably bravado. It fell to Paula, who felt wise beyond her previous limits, to convince him that it was still necessary to keep her bound. The release of pleasure had made her sleepy, but not too relaxed to ignore the same effects in him.

'OK then,' he said, a soft masterful smile playing around his lips, 'but we do this my way.'

When Paula returned from the bathroom, she found

the pillows and the bedding radically rearranged and sideways on to the bedhead.

'This way you can lie more comfortably,' Rafe explained, as he moved her into position with her hands in front of her rather than above. Then with infinite tenderness, he wrapped her wrists with strips of cotton from a torn T-shirt, lightly padding them so the metal cuffs wouldn't bite and chafe.

'How's that?' he whispered in her ear as he adjusted the pillows again. Then he slid his warm naked body beneath the sheets behind hers and curved his arm protectively over her, cupping her belly, his fingers curving over the sigil as if to keep Isidora's darkness out.

'Wonderful. Thanks, love.' Paula nestled against him, loving the feel of his soft cock against the back of her thighs. It was quiescent now, but she couldn't help but smile, remembering the power latent in it.

Whatever might happen, she was safe, with him.

Rafe shivered and opened his eyes, not sure whether he'd slept an hour or a minute.

The previous night had been warm, but the morning seemed cold. There was gooseflesh all over his body, despite the thick, luxurious quilt that covered himself and Paula. Even though sunlight was streaming into the room through the slightly open curtains, the air seemed strangely icy and heavy and not quite right.

With a horrible surge of knowledge, he shot up in the rearranged bed and scooted towards the foot of it, his eyes on his still curled-up partner.

She was motionless, her back smooth, soft, normal. He

should have felt a surge of love and affection and rich memories of their joining and their sweet sex games.

But all he felt was antipathy and a shuddering revulsion.

Slowly, and with a sleek, sinuous grace despite her shackles, Isidora turned over.

'Handcuffs, Rafe?' she enquired creamily, her green eyes glittering, her smile lascivious. 'I'm sorry I missed that game. What a shame you wasted it on Paula. I'm sure she doesn't appreciate erotic bondage and the exchange of power as much as I do.'

How could I have contemplated co-operating with this creature, thought Rafe, wrapping a sheet around his body. Isidora's form was Paula's, the shape that he loved now, and his blind, unthinking penis couldn't tell the difference and was thickening beneath the bedding that covered his groin.

He wanted to kill her, destroy her, annihilate her for invading the woman he loved. But the fact that they inhabited the same body was agonising. The fury within him locked up his throat and tongue. He couldn't speak.

'Nothing to say, Rafe?' Her voice – Paula's – was utterly seductive, but it left his heart cold.

She tipped her head on one side, her hair swinging like a curtain of blue-black silk. 'Perhaps actions speak louder than words then?'

Twisting towards him, she exhibited the body he adored. Her nipples were dark and erect, exquisitely tempting and, as she parted her thighs, the pungent, complex odour of her femininity wafted towards him. Even the black sigil on her belly exerted an exotic and deeply menacing appeal, almost pulsating against the pale, silky gleam of her skin.

His cock twitched, increasing his horror. In that moment he would have given anything to be a eunuch, sexually unfeeling, yet still capable of devotion and sacrifice for the woman he loved. He would forsake sex for the rest of what remained of his life if it meant he could rid Paula of this evil, evil thing.

'Rafe ... oh, Rafe ... why not give in to it? You know you want me. You can have both of us. For all eternity ... Let's make love now, and then afterwards we can make our plans for the future.' Her lush lips curved, red and tempting. 'For the three of us, Rafe, remember that. You can be the lover of two women, in the best of all worlds.'

He couldn't succumb to her but he mustn't alert her to the plans of Michiko. He couldn't even let her know that her perfidy with the grimoire had been discovered. With difficulty, he manufactured a smile.

'I'd dearly love to accommodate you,' he said, forcing his body to relax and suggest repletion, 'but Paula is a sexier girl than you realise, Countess. We've been making love all night while you've been sleeping.' He moved a little closer, even though his flesh was crawling. Even though this creature couldn't read his mind and, according to Michiko, her powers were limited in this half and half condition, she was still sharply clever and intuitive. 'I'm beat. I won't be able to get it up for a while.'

Isidora eyed him, her tongue sneaking out to moisten her rosy lips. 'Let me help you, lover.' She shimmied her hips again, proffering dark delights, twisted pleasures.

'That's one of my talents, the rousing of men. I'll have you hard again in a matter of moments.'

The horror of it was that she probably could. If he let her touch him. He had to think fast. As she kicked at the covers, to facilitate her seductive writhing, the answer came.

Rafe forced himself to slide forwards, holding her gaze, making his own a sultry, salacious mirror of her own. Controlling himself strictly, he reached for her narrow foot and began to massage it, thumbs pressing in a circling motion that had often had his Inner Light ladies cooing. With a supreme act of self-discipline, he bent down and kissed her instep.

Isidora cooed too, just as he'd hoped she would. She was devious, evil and determined to get her own way. But at heart she was a greedy sensualist and, trapped in an alien body, she was hungry for sensation. Arching and moaning, she allowed him to nibble and suck her toes.

In between kissing, in between viciously suppressing his nausea and self-disgust, he began to murmur to her. She was clever and evil, but he was clever in his own way too. And he'd done less than admirable things using the power of his voice coupled with the caressing skills of his hands and fingers.

Isidora was a woman, and beguiling women for his own ends was his speciality.

He barely knew what he was saying. He spoke softly and cajolingly, just as he'd done, years ago, when he'd used hypnotism to persuade rich widows to gift him sizeable amounts of cash. He'd got caught and prison had been the richly deserved price he'd paid but at the time the ruse had worked, and worked a treat. Now, fighting for Paula, and for their love, the stakes he was gambling for were infinitely higher.

At first, he could feel Isidora resisting him. He could almost taste her suspicion and she was strong. But his inner anger drove him on, lifting his skills to a new level of guile and subtlety, aided by the talisman. When he described their future, mirroring the very situation with which she'd tempted him, he felt her mellow, yielding to temptation and to flattery.

Yet right on the point of slipping under, she murmured, 'Lover . . .'

'Yes?' He kept his fingertips moving on her foot, circling and delicately massaging. The technique, his way of inducing a trance, worked as well there as it did on a subject's hand.

'There were some pieces of old paper in the pocket of a robe I had on. Did you find them? They're important to us. I need to know they're safe.'

Never had subterfuge been more difficult. Every instinct in Rafe's body screamed at him to confront her.

'Yes, I found them and I put them in a secure place. I guessed you might need them.' He held his breath. 'What are they?'

'A spell, delicious man. A spell to prevent those who are jealous of me banishing me for ever. Cruel people would do that even though I have a right to live.'

Lying cunt! howled the raging spirit inside Rafe as he fought the instinct to crush the delicate bones of her foot with his bare hands. The spell she'd preserved was the one to banish Paula, not herself. With a supreme effort, he kept the caresses light and worshipful, knowing that it was his beloved's body he'd injure if he lost control.

'It's safe, dearest ... perfectly safe ... and so are you ... Relax now ... all will be well ... all will be well ...'

His voice was honey while his rage curdled inside and burnt his gut.

She shifted slightly on the bed and sighed with all the feigned innocence of a selfish child lapsing into unconsciousness. Rafe checked her vitals cursorily, then leapt from the bed, hurtling for the bathroom, his innards churning.

Crouched over the toilet, heaving and vomiting, he felt filthy and polluted.

I'll get you, you bitch, he swore inside as he retched. I'll really get you! I'll set Paula free of you and banish you for ever if it kills me.

Slouching against the pedestal, he panted for breath, feeling the chill steel of dark determination grip his heart.

Staring at the shiny black-painted door, and its well-polished knocker, Michiko seemed to see Hiro's face, not her own fuzzy reflection. His soft brown eyes had been a picture as she'd left him, the pain and acceptance in them only making her care even more for him.

She'd deliberately spoken to Balthazar Davenheim on the phone with Hiro in the room. It had seemed important that he knew exactly what she was planning and what she'd have to give in order to receive what Paula needed. Why, she didn't know. She'd never revealed so much of herself to her lovers before, not even André, but somehow the urge to share with Hiro was almost natural.

Share pain, share pleasure, share secrets. She hadn't told any of the others what Davenheim wanted. She'd just taken off while the others were still in their rooms, leaving a written message with Oren saying she'd be back as soon as she could.

Time was of the essence. Even Davenheim accepted that. He'd agreed to take just a little taster on account, and Michiko had driven like a maniac to London, relying on the fact that she could bewitch her way out of any speeding ticket she might incur.

Breathing in deeply, she pressed the bell push and waited. Far inside the elegant house, she heard a chime. The doorstep felt hard beneath the thin soles of her shoes and, looking around the elegant Belgravia square, she focused on its routine activities to calm her unexpected nerves. A courier sped by on his motorcycle, dark leathers and visor making her wish she were dressed for biking. People hurrying to offices, ready to fit themselves into various hierarchies and levels of subservience. A woman in a shiny black mackintosh and high heels, who could just conceivably have been a dominatrix.

Michiko suddenly wished she too was about to assume that role, then felt astonished at herself for feeling fear, because she wasn't.

Why are you so craven, Miko? she quizzed herself, as activity beyond the black-painted barrier made her heart surge. Surely you can take what you dish out? Don't be a weakling.

The door swung open to reveal a large figure, clad in black and smiling.

Balthazar Davenheim had aged a little since she'd last encountered him. But not as much as a normal man should have. His hair was thickly grizzled with grey, but if he had been a normal man the hair itself would have all but disappeared by now. If he'd been a normal man, he'd have been rotting in a box.

'Do come in, Madame Michiko,' the tall, broad man said softly, stepping back into his spacious hall to let her pass. As she moved into the cool, airy space, Michiko caught a waft of rather delicious men's cologne, green yet spicy, and, despite the seriousness of her mission here, she felt a smoky twist of lust.

'Would you care for a drink first?' His voice was low, even and cultured, the sort that inspired confidence and trust. She supposed he might have trained it to be that way, for the benefit of his patients. Or perhaps for others that he consorted with for pleasure. A pleasant-speaking voice was such an asset in a master.

It crossed Michiko's mind to refuse his hospitality and stress the urgency of getting on with the matter in hand. But suddenly the idea of a social moment with this man she barely knew became appealing. His manner intrigued her. It wasn't at all what she'd expected.

'Of course. That would be lovely. Thank you, Balthazar.'

In the shadowy hall, his dark eyes flared. Had she made a mistake? Were they already playing? But in their hazel depths she saw humour, and a definite hint of respect, and, as he nodded and indicated that she precede him through an open door beyond him, her interest gathered and her heart began to thud.

This is just business, she told herself as they entered an elegant, tall-ceilinged sitting room. Not pleasure, definitely not pleasure. But as her spirits began to rise, she felt a pang of guilt amongst them. Although she'd said nothing to him, she'd made an unspoken promise to Hiro she wouldn't enjoy this. But now, she suspected she would. And that was surprising.

She eyed Balthazar slyly as he made his way to a silver tray on the sideboard and, without consulting her further, poured two glasses of what appeared to be dark rich sherry.

He was a big man, tall and burly, broad of face and chest. A little heavy in the paunch, but just on the right side of the line between stocky and fat. There was an overpowering aura of substance about him that would have been there whether he had powers of magic or not, but as a surgeon she suspected he was capable of pinpoint delicacy too.

Which may or may not be a good thing.

He brought her glass to her and put it in her hand, sipping almost greedily from his own as he did so. Taking it from him, she noticed that his eyes were glittering with a strangely boyish enthusiasm.

She took a sip, and almost grimaced. The sherry was incredibly sweet. And yet after the first shock of its caramel-like flavour, she felt an intense warmth bloom in her throat and then her belly.

Have you dosed me?

Balthazar gazed back at her, his broad face insouciant, as if he'd read her thought and was giving her the 'who, me?' treatment. With a graceful gesture he indicated that she sit down on one of his deeply upholstered sofas.

So it was to be social civility before the dark games, was it?

Balthazar took a seat on a matching sofa across from

her. The cushion sagged as he sank down, his considerable body apparently relaxed as he lounged back and sipped his sherry.

'So?' he enquired lightly. They'd made their deal over the phone. There wasn't really any need for these pleasantries.

'So?' She lifted her chin and met his frank gaze. Why on earth was she so nervous? She'd played a thousand games in her long lifetime, so why be anxious now? It wasn't even as if she'd never taken the sub role before. She'd tried it, and found it diverting, even if she'd secretly not succumbed in the slightest.

But with Balthazar, she suddenly didn't feel as if she wanted to fake anything. For the first time, piquantly, she wanted to be what he wanted of her. Especially now she had these delicate feelings for Hiro bubbling inside her.

She studied her companion as he studied her. Balthazar wore black. A fine-knit turtleneck and jeans, a classic understated master's choice. Especially with the shiny black-leather belt at his waist. Even as her eyes flitted over his broad shoulders, his sturdy thighs and his truly enormous hands where they rested lightly against the creamy-pale upholstery, they kept returning again and again to that belt.

His bright eyes narrowed as he lifted his glass. Apparently savouring the sweet drink, he didn't once look away from her. 'So,' he repeated, setting the glass down again with a soft clump, 'shall we get down to business? I'm anxious to begin.' As he spoke, he ran his fingers over his belt buckle.

Michiko sipped her own sherry, liking the glow it fired in her belly more and more. She couldn't remember the last time she'd ever felt afraid of anything. Her powers made her hyper-confident, maybe as invincible as it was possible to be in the modern world. But here in this quiet room, with this man she'd previously dismissed as inconsequential, she felt anxious. And she realised she'd miscalculated.

Balthazar Davenheim was redolent with consequence, exciting in his palpable machismo and raw strength. In which case she had to hold fast to her mission, her own requirements.

'I need to see the grimoire first. I need to know that I'm going to get what I came for.'

Snagging his full lower lip, Balthazar grinned.

Laughing softly, he steepled his fingers, still watching her.

14 Show Me the Grimoire

'Show me the grimoire, eh?' mocked Balthazar lightly, licking his lower lip as if a drop of sherry lingered there.

'It's why I'm here, Balthazar.'

She had to maintain an equilibrium here. Even though she had to submit to him sexually, she couldn't afford to forget her true purpose in coming to the city.

Moments stretched out, as did Balthazar's long, solid legs in front of him. He seemed to be having a wonderful time already. Deep into his games, although technically the proceedings weren't yet open.

'Very well. Fair enough,' he said with sudden cheerfulness, leaping to his feet, his large form making her jump. 'I'll get it. Why don't you have another sherry while you're waiting? Won't be a mo.'

After moving swiftly across the room, he paused at the door and winked at her, then was gone, presumably to the safe place where he kept the precious grimoire, a book, which like André's, was beyond any estimation of monetary worth.

This man isn't at all what I expected.

Michiko sprang to her feet too, strode to the drinks tray, and refilled her glass as he'd suggested.

And I'm not at all what I expected I'd be around him.

Again, Hiro's sweet face swam into her mind's eye. He and Balthazar were about as unlike as two men could possibly be but, to her surprise, she realised that there was something about their eyes that was similar. Both very beautiful, and full of knowledge and inner character.

As she drank down her sherry, and refilled again, a new image grabbed her imagination.

Herself, with Hiro *and* Balthazar.

Balthazar and Hiro together, as she looked on, touching herself.

Could that work? Could she get these two special men together?

Ideas, dark and deliciously perverted, swam in her mind. When this was over, both tonight and the more serious and difficult task beyond that, she would engineer the fulfilment of her fantasy. She stepped away from the drinks tray. From slightly despising the heavy sweet wine, she'd moved to suddenly having quite a passion for it.

Much like Balthazar himself.

There was a tall mirror on the wall, she noticed, smiling. Part of the games paraphernalia no doubt. Maybe to allow his subs to watch themselves being whipped or fucked or whatever else he liked to do with them. Striking a pose in front of it, Michiko appraised her appearance. She was dressed according to Balthazar's specifications. Part of his price for allowing her access to his priceless book.

How strange she looked to herself in a slim-cut grey business suit, sleek of skirt and sharp of jacket. The fine silk worsted skimmed her body only lightly, without a wrinkle or deviation in its streamlined elegance. Though her physique was slender and athletic, the crafty suit somehow seemed to imply femininity and corporate curves without revealing anything in the way of gross displays. Even its length was conservative and modest, the kick-pleated skirt lovingly skimming the mid point of her knees.

The shoes were also Balthazar's choice, and slightly more sexualised with their high slim heels and classic court shape. They were shiny dark patent, embracing the foot like a lover, their fetish perfection enhanced and augmented by her fine-denier hose the colour and texture of wood-smoke.

She looked serious, professional, hardcore, in total control of herself.

And that was what Balthazar wanted – so he could shatter the image and crumble her composure in his hands.

As a way of reassuring herself, she patted her hair, so smooth and black, part of the real her, not the payment package she'd made herself into. Pursing her lips, she assessed her make-up. Understated as the rest of her, apart from the red-stained lips, but for a moment she seemed to see a layered image in the glass. Her own reflection from this moment, but also the picture of herself from another time – as an exquisite geisha, her face white, her kimono sublime, her hair elaborate.

A manufactured construction to please a man for money, just as she was now, in some ways. Only now it was goods and services for which she would perform.

She sensed his presence approaching long before she heard his heavy steps. Moving soundlessly, she settled on one of the sofas, crossing her legs to show her narrow ankles to advantage.

Balthazar entered, toting his grimoire.

The book was bigger than André's prized volume, and

far shabbier-looking. Much like its owner, thought Michiko with a hidden smile.

'Would you like a quick look-see before we ... um ... get down to business?'

His voice was bland, but there was real excitement in his rich brown-green eyes. For a moment she got an impression of an overgrown schoolboy, jigging about in anticipation of receiving a long-cherished prize. There was a definite aura of enthusiasm about him, and she hoped, she really hoped, that it wouldn't get the better of him during their proceedings.

'Of course,' she said smoothly, rising to join him at the heavy desk where he'd set down the book.

Its appearance, close up, made her frown. There were nicks in the dark stained leather of the cover and she could see that some pages had torn edges. What if the relevant spells were missing from this one too? What the hell could she do? The critical thousand hours were even now speeding by in a dreadful countdown, and she couldn't imagine how she would cope with Isidora on her back for the rest of her days, never mind an ordinary ungifted woman like Paula. It was unthinkable. But if the spell wasn't here, there wasn't sufficient time remaining to seek out yet another copy.

Anxiously, she flicked through the discoloured pages, then gasped with relief when she found a section dealing with markers. Ah, there it was! The banishing spell, as well as the assimilation hex that Isidora had stolen. And yes, other related enchantments too, codicils that weren't even in André's grimoire at all. She licked her lips, leaning over and becoming absorbed in these 'extras'.

Until a soft but pointed cough, right beside her,

wrenched her attention from the arcane world and back into the real world of here and now. And her situation.

'Has it got what you need?' Balthazar's eyes were even brighter now, and his mouth looked shiny as if he'd been licking his lips again. Perhaps he had. She'd been so absorbed in the venerable book that, behind her back, he could well have been admiring her legs and her bottom in the trim skirt of her suit.

'It's perfect. Just what I need.' She hesitated, about to casually call him 'Balthazar' and treat him as an equal. But suddenly she realised it was time to pay the price.

'Thank you, master,' she murmured, bowing her head.

Even though she wasn't looking at him, the great wave of his exultation hit her. Joy. Glee. Sexual excitement. That boyish enthusiasm that rather worried her, but which also seemed strangely appealing in a man of apparent middle age.

'Very good, very good...' There was a smile in his voice, though it was obvious he was trying to sound stern. 'But one thing before we start.' He paused, reached out and cupped her cheek with his large hand, making her look at him. 'No magic, eh? Just us. I don't want any tricks. You have to play fair or no deal.'

He still looked happy, but there was a hint of seriousness, of direct dealing. Touching his mind lightly for what she acknowledged had to be the last time for many hours, she sensed just what she'd expected. He knew she was the greater magician and that, playing by her own rules, she could easily outspell him and make him *believe* he'd received his payment, even if he hadn't had as much as a sniff of her.

'Of course, master. As you wish, master.'

Dropping her gaze to the carpet and the polished toes of her shoes, she threw an invisible psychic switch inside her brain. And suddenly felt utterly naked inside her suit and her carefully chosen underwear. She was just Michiko now, a submissive woman, not an all-powerful Miko.

She could no longer even tell whether Balthazar had sensed the change.

'Good. Now we understand each other.' His voice was low and firm, quite thrilling in a way, and Michiko idly wondered if he had sensed the 'off' switch after all. 'Move to the centre of the rug, slave, if you would. And then stand there, facing the mirror, hands on your head.'

A delicious, shivering sensation sluiced through Michiko's innards. As she walked to the specified spot, and took up her pose, she sent her mind back over the decades to the few occasions when she had played the sexual submissive to a man's mastery. How in great Amida's name could she have forgotten the excitement? How could she have forgotten the delicious, weakening rush of lust?

As she raised her hands and set them on the top of her head, as prescribed, her breasts lifted subtly inside her jacket. The crisp lace of her bra was scratchy against the sensitive tips and sent little flags of sweet dark feeling to her sex. Almost immediately, she felt moisture soaking her thong.

Not having been instructed to look up, she kept her gaze firmly on her shoes and the fine Persian rug beneath them. Balthazar was a successful surgeon in the straight world and he liked nice things. She found it rather endearing that he still liked to earn his living in a non-magical way. Much like she'd done for a while in the Takarazuka.

She felt him come up behind her, his presence huge. He really was one of the biggest men she'd ever been around, and his sheer physical bulk only added to his ability to master. He didn't have to do anything, just to be.

The room was very quiet, apart from the crackle of a small fire burning in the hearth. The day was unseasonably cool, but the cheerful blaze seemed to be more about fostering the ambience of a mentor's study, harking back subtly to schooldays and traditional discipline. She had to bite back a smile, imagining Balthazar in a mortar board and gown.

'What's so funny, slave?'

His big hand under her chin, he made her lift her face and look at herself, and him behind her, in the mirror. She thought she'd contained the grin, but obviously she hadn't. Balthazar had spotted it.

He cupped her face with his long sturdy fingers, almost covering half of it, and Michiko's knees went weak when he pushed two of those fingers into her mouth, pressing down on her lower lip and making her open up. His skin tasted clean and fresh, but there was the faintest hint of citrus as if he'd had an orange for breakfast and peeled it himself. Without thinking she began to suckle on the digits like a baby.

'Good ... that's good,' he whispered in her ear, pushing down harder, making it difficult for her to suck neatly and tidily. Her mouth gaped, and she felt exposed and controlled, utterly vulnerable. As he mastered her mouth, his free hand came up, cupping her crotch through the fine cloth of her skirt.

Her sex trembled as he kneaded her quite roughly, and

she teetered on her high heels, leaning back against his rocklike form for support. Her lashes fluttered down. She was unable to look at herself and face how quickly and completely she'd succumbed to him, but Balthazar said 'No, look!' and adjusted the angle of her face with his huge mitt.

For all the strangeness of the situation, they looked good together. The counterpoint between Balthazar's height and breadth and her more slender, athletic shape was harmonious. And the sight of her mouth open and working as he gripped and released, gripped and released between her legs compelled her to moan as best she could around the obstruction of his fingers.

'You like that, don't you?'

He was smiling, and his voice sounded jolly. Happy. Despite the fact that her sex was throbbing and she was suddenly aching to come, she was struck again by how enthusiastic and boyish he was as a master. He put on no airs and affected no poses. He just enjoyed handling a woman and having her at his mercy. He was strange. He was unexpected. He was refreshing.

She nodded in his hold and his wide face lit with a beaming smile.

'Good. Now let's see your panties. I love panties.' He nodded in satisfaction.

For a moment, Michiko wasn't sure what to do, then Balthazar nodded, indicating she could lower her hands to her task. He stepped back, releasing both her mouth and her groin, and she almost moaned again, bereft of his touch.

Her skirt wasn't overly tight, but it was slim cut and she had to slide it carefully up over her hips to show her underwear. She clutched it in a bunch, around her waist, so he could see.

'Now that's a sight to rouse even a dead man,' observed Balthazar roundly, his hazel eyes gleaming fierily as he perused the sight in the mirror.

Michiko's exquisite lace-encrusted white satin thong looked like an exotic flower against the honeyed tones of her silky skin. The contrast screamed out, enticing and both pure and deeply sluttish.

'Now then, stick your finger in your pussy. Wiggle it about a bit, then pull it out again.'

Clutching awkwardly at the bundle of her skirt, Michiko obeyed him. Her cleft was swimming with juice and, where it had soaked into the thin crotch piece of her thong, she found the cloth was saturated. She had to bite her lip as her fingertip brushed her swollen clit and, embarrassed, she closed her eyes.

'No ... no, you must watch. Come on, slave, forage about a bit, make sure your finger is nice and sticky.'

Gasping involuntarily, Michiko complied, gazing helplessly at the lewd sight of herself fishing about in her underwear and trying not to knock her finger against her clitoris in the process. She was close to the edge and, if she came without permission, she'd let him down.

'Now taste yourself.'

The words made her sex flutter dangerously, and this time she did sway. Balthazar's arm came around her waist, holding her up and embracing her where she was holding up her skirt.

'Go on, slave, have a suck ... You know you'll like it.'

Michiko withdrew her hand from her crotch and slid

her glistening fingertips into her mouth. The taste was quite bland really. Vaguely salty, vaguely oceanic. But she made a show of sucking enthusiastically as if it were primo sushi, spicy, hot and pungent.

'Now do it again. I want a taste.'

If anything, there was even more juice down there when she slid her fingers back beneath the edge of her thong and into her niche. Obediently, she scooped some of it up and drew out her fingers again, lifting them up and offering them silently for Balthazar's approval.

His mouth was like a furnace and he sucked at her essence like a baby with a lollipop, going 'mmm ... mmm ... mmm ...' all the time as he cleaned her off.

'Again!' he commanded, and a moment later he was savouring her again.

'Delicious!' he proclaimed when they'd repeated the process a couple of times more. 'You're a wicked, dirty, horny, juicy girl, aren't you, Madame Michiko,' he said, his voice soft and joyful. And even though he'd used her name, she still felt deeply subservient. If anything, more so, as if his hold over her nullified her status.

Her fingers were clean now, but still he went back again and sucked them, his tongue active, flickering and exploring. It was the most tantalising sensation, as if he were crouched between her legs, licking her clit. Out of her conscious control, her hips bucked and danced.

'Ah, lady sorceress, you want to come, don't you?' he murmured after giving her fingertips a last once-over.

Not speaking, Michiko nodded. Why deny the fact? She'd not expected much of this encounter when they'd first discussed it, but suddenly she realised that Balthazar was turning out to be one of the most exciting men she'd ever played with, dear Hiro and long-beloved André notwithstanding.

'Ah well, my sweet, there are a few things yet to do before that happens, I think.' He grinned, pleased with himself but somehow not unkind. 'This is a payment, after all, isn't it?' His eyes met hers in the mirror, glinting wickedly.

Then, without warning, he whipped open the buttons of her suit jacket and gripped her breast through the wafer-delicate silk of the thin camisole she wore beneath it. His big hands could almost have encompassed both her dainty rounded breasts, but he concentrated on just one, kneading it firmly like baker working dough. The caress was rough, but it was just what she'd been hoping for. Between her legs, her sex throbbed and the juices flowed anew.

Balthazar made a low sound of approval in his throat and pushed aside the camisole, wedging the thin silk awkwardly beneath one of her breasts in a way that pushed it up and seemed to present it. After licking his finger and thumb as if he were about to turn the page of a book, he then took hold of her nipple in a pincer-like grip.

Lust rolled low and hard in Michiko's belly as she both watched and felt him manipulate her teat, twisting it this way and that, hurting her, but not inflicting anything that she couldn't bear or wouldn't have invited. It became harder and harder not to groan out loud and roll her hips like a helpless, horny slut.

And still he tugged, his broad face wreathed in smiles of pleasure, as if touching her was as good as touching himself. Maybe it was? His own powerful hips were thrusting forward, pressing a huge erection into the small of her back.

'Oh, pretty sorceress ... how I do want to spank you,' he whispered, leaning over to speak right into her ear, his breath soft and strangely sweet against the side of her face.

Do it! Do it! she wanted to shout, her bottom almost throbbing in anticipation. Pressing back, she worked it against his great thighs and the rocklike knot of his hard-on.

'Wicked girl ... you're trying to entice me,' he purred, reciprocating, rubbing and still tweaking at her nipple.

She pushed back harder.

And then he was manipulating her, manhandling her. She found herself bent over then swung around, her head dangling so that she could see herself in the mirror upside down, her face to one side of her naked bottom, the cheeks exhibited perfectly bare by the configuration of her thong. Just a single strand of narrow silk bisected the peaches of her backside, sharp white against the golden honey of her smooth skin.

Balthazar positioned himself alongside her, his merry eyes meeting hers in the mirror. He was the cheery, gleeful adolescent again, totally happy in the moment, younger than springtime, despite the grey hair of his apparent years and his true and much greater age. For a moment, she seemed to see Hiro to the other side of her displayed body, and she experienced again the powerful urge to enjoy the two of them together, taste the pleasures of both of her sexy, kinky boys.

Silently, as Balthazar reached down to cup her bottom cheek and assess its resilience, she vowed that, when the serious endeavour ahead of her was dispatched, Paula safe and Isidora banished, she would get her two men into bed together with her as a reward. Whether it was her reward, Balthazar's or even Hiro's she wasn't sure.

Balthazar was almost purring with appreciation again, and as his fingers palpated and tantalised, making her body fill with an energy that compelled her to press herself into his grip, a cool dispassionate part of her assessed him as he assessed her.

He was the strangest sexual dominant. More like a great teddy bear than a strict, forbidding master. He was in charge, but he really liked her and she sensed that all this was as much fun to him as anything. And yet he had enormous personal power and charisma to match his immense physical presence. And he had strength to hit her really, really hard if he wanted to.

One last firm squeeze, then he lifted his hand.

'Oh, you have such a lovely arse, Madame Michiko,' he announced.

Then with no further ado, he let fly the first spank.

Despite the vague idea she'd had that she'd be quiet and stoic, Michiko too let fly. With an enormously loud yelp to match the enormous burst of stinging heat in her buttock.

Great Amida, the man could hit! One strike and her arse felt as if it was in flames – and as more blows fell the fire was stoked.

Both cheeks were soon raging, and all thought of grace under pressure had vanished. She moaned and mewled and clutched at herself, only to have her hands gently dashed away from her own flesh to clear the path for

Balthazar's greater hand and its divine purpose. When her fingers kept stealing back to her bottom cheeks of their own accord, Balthazar tut-tutted like an old-fashioned schoolmaster.

'Now, now, sorceress, that won't do at all. You're interrupting my concentration,' he chided gently, his hand still swinging, still impacting with her reddened cheeks, first one, then the other, matching the radiance. 'If you want something to do with your hands, my dear, why don't you play with yourself and be done with it. You're going to come sooner or later anyway. It might as well be now, might it not?'

Michiko found she'd lost the power of coherent speech, but she sobbed and gasped when her fingertips found their way into her cleft.

She was right on the brink, right on the edge, standing on the cliff. It would barely need anything at all to tip her over.

And when Balthazar slapped her quite softly, the impact of his hand jostling hers, she launched into the void, screaming and jerking in white-hot pleasure.

There was a bird singing outside the bedroom window and it woke Michiko from a brief, light doze. For a moment she lay still, monitoring her body and the aches and pains and twinges in her bottom and thighs, then she drew in a big gasp of air and began to chant silently, her lips moving.

Swiftly and efficiently, the healing spell swept away the lingering burn of pain from her spankings and the impact of Balthazar's belt. There would have been a perverse pleasure in just allowing it all to dissipate naturally, like badges of honourable suffering. But time was passing, the thousand hours were ticking away.

She sat up and looked at the owner of the bed. Balthazar was sprawled every which way, his legs akimbo, his arms hugging his pillow and his sizeable penis resting quietly against his long hairy thigh. The impression of a sexy teddy bear was reinforced, and she felt a twist of fondness in her heart.

What had threatened to be a chore had in the end been a delight. He had punished her severely. With belt and hand and a pair of silver nipple clamps that were now glittering amongst the bedding close by. But afterwards he'd been more than generous with pleasure.

What had touched her most was – when he'd enquired as to her relationship status and she'd described her fondness for Hiro – that he'd declined to penetrate her. Which she could only assume was some weird, old-fashioned chivalric notion of not fucking another man's woman.

He'd done a lot of other things though, using his big strong hands with a surgeon's precision that took her breath away. And not just his hands. She could still picture his grizzled head jammed between her legs as he'd licked her to the point when she could no longer think straight.

In return all he'd asked was that she allow him to ejaculate on her.

Which he'd done several times, exhibiting astonishing powers of recuperation. Great areas of her skin, principally breasts, belly and thighs were tight with dried semen.

First a shower, and then she'd quickly secure the

grimoire and get back to the Priory as fast as she could. There were more preparations to make than she'd initially been aware of. Complications with the enchantment she hadn't foreseen.

'Where are you going, sweetheart?'

A huge paw clasped her arm as she made to rise from the bed. The sleeping giant was actually awake and eyeing her carefully from his place amongst the pillows.

'I have to go now, Balthazar. I have to get your grimoire to Sedgewick Priory and start the rituals tonight or we'll never get rid of Isidora.'

His deceptively sleepy eyes narrowed and his grip remained resolute. Michiko could have shaken him off magically, and possibly even physically, given her martial-arts skills. But even so, she remained where she was, watching him.

'I can't remember saying you could take my book with you. I thought the deal was just for a look at it.' He sat up, letting her go, as if he was sure she wouldn't move.

Michiko gave him a wry look. He was trying it on. He'd definitely agreed on 'borrow'.

Balthazar grinned and shrugged his big shoulders. 'OK, OK, you can take it.' He moved forwards across the bed and took her hand again, but this time his hold was light, almost pleading. 'But let me come with you. I can help. A trained physician will come in very useful.'

As her mind filled with notions and images, Michiko experienced a flush of guilt that made her blush. Despite the danger of Isidora, despite the peril that threatened Paula and her future, the first thing that had occurred to Michiko was the prospect of getting Balthazar and Hiro under one roof.

But he was right. She did need him. And his skills.

She twisted her fingers in his grip, took hold of his big hand and squeezed it hard.

'Thank you, Balthazar. I'd be glad of your help. Your expertise will be invaluable.' She leant forwards, kissed his broad, stubbly cheek. 'Especially if you can lay your hands on a defibrillator unit. At a moment's notice.'

Yes, if they were to kill someone and bring them back to life, they were going to need modern technology as well as ancient magic.

15 Endgames

'No! That's not possible! There must be another way!'

Still in shock from Michiko's explanation, Paula flinched at the anger in Rafe's outburst. He seemed more appalled at what lay ahead than she was.

'I'm afraid it's the only way,' the Japanese sorceress said, her voice gentle and regretful. 'To expel Isidora, or indeed any spirit attached to a Thousand Hour Marker, the physical host has to die.'

'No!' repeated Rafe in a low, angry growl. 'There must be some other option. Some other spell. Paula has to live ... she *has* to.' His face was set and hard but, when she looked at him, his brown eyes were full of pain and confusion. 'If there's anything *I* can do, just name it. I'm here.' Almost choking with emotion, Paula wanted to hug him for caring so much. Dear God, all this, even Isidora, was worth it to finally know a man who loved her so completely. She reached for his hand, squeezing it hard, lost for words.

Sedgewick's spacious conservatory was almost tropical in the early-evening sun; they'd been sitting and talking quietly about inconsequential things. Somehow it had been important to just do something normal for a change, even though Rafe had thought it best to remain around the house where it was easier to keep an eye on her. For changes.

A short while ago, Michiko had joined them, back from her lightning trip to London, bringing with her a new-comer to the Priory. Balthazar Davenheim, who was apparently a famous plastic surgeon as well as a some-time sorcerer and the owner of an undamaged grimoire containing just the spells they needed.

Paula glanced quickly his way. The man was sitting on one of the wrought-iron garden chairs, half swamping it. He was very tall and hugely stocky with grey grizzled hair, yet he had a face that was strangely kind and reassuring. His bedside face, she guessed, though she instinctively sensed he was on their side, or at least prepared to be in order to please Michiko. She wondered fleetingly what Hiro was feeling about the new arrival.

The Japanese sorceress sprang lightly to her feet and began to pace the green dappled space as if being in motion helped her think.

'Actually, there is a way you can help, Rafe.' She spun to face him. 'Balthazar's grimoire contains a variant that wasn't in André's. The Thousand Hour Marker can be transferred to someone else.' She took a deep breath. 'But then, of course, *that* person has to die instead.'

Paula opened her mouth. She wasn't sure what she was going to say but there was no way that she was going to put someone else in danger. She'd take her chances.

But before she could speak, Rafe had pre-empted her.

'Well, that's it then. Job sorted. Transfer it to me.'

'No!'

'Yes!'

Rafe grabbed her by the shoulders, made her look at him.

'Please … Let me do this for you. I need to know I've done just one worthwhile thing with my fucking useless existence.'

'But you're not useless,' Paula insisted, and was about to elaborate when she was interrupted.

'I'd let him, if I were you.' They all swivelled towards Balthazar Davenheim. 'The guy looks as if he's got a pretty strong constitution. He'll be much easier to bring back afterwards.'

'Bring back?' whispered Paula, her hand creeping into Rafe's again as they waited for clarification.

Bring back made *die* seem marginally less frightening, but she realised she was still holding her breath.

'Yes, the marker host only has to die long enough for the spell to shake Isidora free.' Michiko took the floor, standing square, her hands on her hips. She'd returned from the city dressed in the most extraordinary way. In her crisply tailored suit and killer heels she looked like a businesswoman about to give a marketing presentation.

'And once she's gone, I can bring you back,' said Balthazar almost casually, leaning back in his chair. 'I've done it before. More times than I care to remember.' He shrugged his large shoulders. 'I might have sold out and become little more than a high-priced cosmetician nowadays, but I worked my share of A&E when I was a young doctor. I still know my way around resuscitation and we've brought the equipment.'

Paula frowned suddenly. Was the technology even necessary?

'But can't you do it with magic?'

Michiko laughed and sat down in a chair beside her. 'Magic is a fickle thing and it doesn't follow a rationale.

Some things you can do, some things you can't. The "yeses" and the "nos" of it aren't always logical.' She paused, tipping her head on one side. 'What we have ahead of us is what you might call a "hybrid" procedure.'

'I still don't see why it shouldn't be me who goes through it.' Paula frowned, feeling the tension in Rafe's grip and his entire body at her side. She could sense him about to protest again when Michiko held up her hand.

'There's another reason why Rafe would be a better candidate,' the Japanese sorceress said, her voice intent. 'He has powers of his own. He has a more developed sense of mind-control than you, Paula. And Isidora is going to fight tooth and nail not to be banished. Rafe has latent psychic powers, he can hit back against her much better than you can.' Paula felt her other hand taken hold of, the grip soft yet redolent with power. 'If she were to get the better of you during the enchantment, it might be for ever. And you both might end up insane, or worse.' Michiko put both hands around Paula's now, squeezing quickly, then releasing her. 'Let him do this for you. It's safer and the chances for success are immeasurably greater.'

Silence fell in the room. Paula's mind whirled. There was too much to take in. She felt so overwhelmed that all she wanted to do was run, far away, as fast as she could – as if the sheer act of fleeing might leave this completely unreal situation far behind.

Tears welled in her eyes but she bit down hard on her lip, screaming at herself inside for being a wimp and at the horrible thing in residence for even existing. She wanted to shout and rage at life and fate for getting her into this mess. Why the fuck had Belinda and Jonathan pitched up at this stupid priory in the first place? Why the fuck had André Von Kastel dragged them all into his centuries-old conflict without so much as a by your leave? Why couldn't I have met Rafe in some other context without all this stupid baggage? Without all my troubles we could have dealt with *his* troubles better.

As if he'd heard her, Rafe's arm went around her, pulling her close, and she threw her arms around him in return. He was solid. He was real. He was no fantasy or magical apparition, and the heat of his body shored her up and gave her strength.

For a moment, she leant against him, absorbing what he offered, then she straightened, squared her shoulders and dragged in a great breath.

'OK then, let's do it. And the sooner the better so we can all get back to normal. Whatever *that* is.' She slid her hands up to Rafe's face. Looking squarely into his eyes, she hoped that those latent psychic gifts of his were working and that he could read the things she couldn't say in front of Michiko and Balthazar. 'And you,' she said to him, making her voice mock-disciplinarian, 'you'd better make with the primo mind mojo and get shut of that bitch completely. Because I've had sex with her once and I sure as hell don't want to have to do it on a regular basis. I'm sticking to two in a bed from here on in . . . not three!'

Rafe's eyes popped open wide. He looked stunned. Then he started to laugh, shaking his head. Smiling back at him, Paula found herself giggling too. Almost insanely, the whole thing was so absurd.

'So, what do we have to do?' she asked eventually, when they'd both settled down and the hysteria was over.

But it started to bubble again, but not from mirth, as Michiko quietly explained.

The first stage of the preparation was both awkward and slightly hilarious. Paula would have got the giggles again if things hadn't been so serious. As it was, she had to hide her smiles when Rafe complained about being tickled.

'It should really be a tattoo but we haven't got the time,' pronounced Michiko, leaning forwards and staring intently at his naked belly, while Hiro knelt backwards, wiping his brush carefully on a rag. 'This should suffice though.' She inclined in closer, her eyes narrowing as she scrutinised what was displayed between the open flies of his jeans. Then, with a nod, she glanced at Paula and at the faint freckle-coloured lines and whorls of the sigil that were visible above her lowered knickers, reflected in the mirror she'd been holding against her abdomen.

'Well, it looks the same to me,' the Japanese woman said, touching a fingertip very lightly to Rafe's belly, 'and it's dry already.' With a satisfied smile, she turned to her lover and gave him a lingering kiss, full on the lips, her slender hand cradling his cheek. 'Well done, my darling. You're a true artist.'

Hiro smiled, looking far more sure of himself than he had at any time since Balthazar Davenheim had appeared at Sedgewick, and they all took time to study his finely wrought calligraphic handiwork. Rafe now had the mirror image of the Thousand Hour Marker painted on his abdomen, an exact, reversed replica of the hateful image that Paula had on hers.

'Can I zip up now? Or will it rub off? I'm not exactly

enamoured of walking around with my dick almost hanging out, you know?'

Poor Rafe, thought Paula, giving him a hug. Despite the fact that he was a sensualist who was comfortable naked and seemed to enjoy using and displaying his body, he really hadn't liked the experience of having another man draw things on his belly.

Michiko frowned. 'One moment...' Slowly, elegantly, she made a complex pass over the painted sigil and suddenly it rippled as if it were a serpent. A second later, a small section of it morphed.

Another hour counted off the thousand.

'I think it would be safer if you were naked or wore a soft robe. We can't take any chances.' The sorceress's pointed chin came up and she fixed him with a beady look. 'And remember, you will have to be unclothed for the ritual.' She turned to Paula, her eyes steely. 'Both of you. Maybe you should get used to that. There's precious little time to waste, and I'm sure Balthazar has almost completed the preparations in the chapel.'

As if he'd been given his marching orders, Hiro picked up his ink pots and brushes and prepared to leave, but Michiko swept her arms around him and gave him another kiss. 'You've done beautifully well, my sweet boy. We couldn't have done this without you. But now you need to come to our room with me and help me prepare. Then go to the library and wait until this is over. Will you do that?'

Accepting his praise and dismissal with an admirable grace, he nodded, then bowed elegantly and left the bedroom.

Michiko hung back. 'You understand what has to be done?' Her gaze flipped from Paula to Rafe, from Rafe to Paula. 'Very well. I will leave you alone, but in thirty minutes we will all assemble in the chapel.' Her expression softened. 'It will be just Balthazar and me. And Oren too, for his strength and his knowledge of first aid and healing. The others will all wait in the library until it's over.'

Rafe laughed, and Paula squeezed his hand again. At least the audience would be limited. 'Well, that's not so bad, is it?' He flashed her a roguish wink. 'Just two blokes I barely know and a Japanese sorceress watching me while I make love to you. Piece of cake.'

She grinned back at him, but it took a great effort.

And when Michiko had gone, they sat in silence, just holding each other until it was time to meet their fate.

Dark unease stirred in Rafe's gut as they entered the old chapel.

Oren led them down a narrow winding staircase at the back of the house and across a small courtyard towards their destination. Halfway across the cobbled area, they'd been waylaid by Belinda and Jonathan, and the flurry of hugging and tears had only added to his growing sense of foreboding. Especially when they'd looked at him sorrowfully as if he had a death warrant hanging around his neck. Which he still had, he supposed, even if this strange night went well.

When the great studded door of the chapel swung closed behind them, under other circumstances he might have burst out laughing. The place was a cliché, an amalgam of every spooky, haunted crypt he'd seen in a thousand horror movies and television shows. He half expected Count Dracula to come creeping between the pews. The walls were tall and ominously festooned with carvings and gargoyles, and the flickering light came from candles of all different shapes and sizes, set in sconces and candelabra scattered around the room. It was all very kitsch and gothic and medieval except for what looked like some pretty high-tech medical equipment set to one side of a great wooden table that stood in the centre of the nave. He noticed vaguely that there was a weft of electric cabling snaking away from it and out through one of the open windows towards the main house, and digital indicators and tell-tales were flashing reassuringly. The lights and paraphernalia of modern medicine seemed incongruous in the gloomy bygone setting but he was bloody glad to see it all.

Two figures were waiting for them.

Balthazar was hovering by what looked like a resuscitation unit, observing readings and apparently going through a checklist of its functions.

And Michiko looked so different it was hard to recognise her.

The Japanese sorceress was dressed in the full geisha finery of an exquisite, multi-layered kimono, elaborate wig and white painted face. Her lips were a tiny crimson cupid's bow and her eyes finely outlined with a precision line of kohl. She inclined her head as they approached, her hand resting on the grimoire, which lay open in pride of place on a heavy lectern that stood to one side of the table.

'Perhaps you two need a moment?' She gestured gracefully towards the end of the front pew. 'There are still one or two final preparations to make.'

Rafe slid his arm tight around Paula and guided her to the cushioned seat. Once there, he pulled her close, just holding her. There didn't seem to be much more to say that they hadn't already said. He tried not to think, to do nothing but enjoy the closeness and the faint perfume of her body against him. *This* was their last moment of intimacy, this was very possibly their last embrace. Not the joining that lay ahead during the ritual.

A soft cough fractured their silence. Rafe looked up to see Balthazar Davenheim standing in front of them, holding out a porcelain beaker filled with a dark murky-green fluid. It looked like a pretty disgusting concoction, and there was a little frill of bitty froth clinging to the edge of the cup.

'It's not that bad, actually,' said the big man with a quirk of grin.

'What is it?' Paula reached out fearlessly for the weird brew, and Rafe took a grim satisfaction in her courage.

'A potion. Part of the spell,' said Balthazar gravely, then his big face lightened. 'And there's a spot of aphrodisiac in it too. A sort of herbal Viagra, only more controllable. It'll smooth out your inhibitions.' He nodded to the table.

'Do *I* need it?' Paula wrinkled her nose.

'Don't worry, it works for girls too.' Flashing her a wink, the tall man stepped away and returned to his equipment. 'Drink half each,' he added over his shoulder.

Fear surged in Rafe's chest. Fear for Paula. As she lifted the beaker to her lips, he stayed her hand. 'Let me taste it first.' He took hold of the white porcelain container, drew in a deep breath, then drank down half of the contents in one gulp.

The brew was slightly bitter but not really unpleasant. There was a perfumed quality to it, and he recognised rosewater and cinnamon in a muddy, earthy base.

'So?' Paula quirked her eyebrows as she took the cup back from him.

'Well, it'll never be recommended in *What Wine* but it's better than the paint stripper they serve in the Raven. Take a sip.'

As he watched her wrinkle her nose again and pluckily drain the cup, a warm glow started to spread through Rafe's chest, radiating outwards from his throat and his stomach and sinking down through his torso, his belly and then his loins. Astonishingly, his cock twitched suddenly, then thickened, glowing too, just like the rest of him. He felt a sudden, thudding urge to touch himself, or reach out, take Paula's hand and bring it to his body to assuage his growing need.

'Holy shit! It works,' he whispered, unfolding the long dark robe he was wearing and glancing down at the solid erection pushing hard at the thin white cotton trousers he'd found to wear. It was deforming them so much that the light drawstring at the waist was pulled downwards, exposing the painted sigil on his belly.

'Crikey, so it does.' As she put aside the beaker, Paula's face was already flushed, her eyes glittering. The pink glow in her skin had already extended to her neck and throat, almost as if she were fresh from an intense orgasm, and he could see her nipples dark and erect through the thin cotton of the button-through dress she wore. He watched her shimmy, as if in pleasure, then frown suddenly, her soft mouth hardening in a line.

'She feels it too. She's stirring.' She placed her hand over her belly, to the sigil.

'Then the sooner we do this, the better. I want that bitch out of you now, and out of this world for good!' He gave her a quick, hard kiss, then drew back, looking into her eyes. They were still Paula's, but troubled as if a storm were approaching. 'Come on, love.' He drew her to her feet and they approached the table.

Michiko had thrown a thin futon over the hard surface. 'We must begin,' she said, inclining her head elegantly, her neck looking extraordinarily slender beneath the dark bulk of her complicated wig.

Rafe looked around. Davenheim was studying the read-outs of his equipment with a ferocious intensity. Oren was standing by the window, gazing out into the moonlit park. Obviously these were attempts to provide them a modicum of privacy.

Michiko moved to her lectern, her steps tiny in her geisha footwear. She began to chant softly, and suddenly the air in the immediate vicinity became warm, almost steamy.

For their comfort.

Rafe had planned that they would couple still with some clothing on, to preserve Paula's modesty. With his long robe shielding their bodies, at least she was protected.

But now, in the strangely balmy atmosphere, that seemed unnecessary, and Paula was already unbuttoning her dress and slipping out of it. Low on her belly, the sigil was prominent, and even as he watched it seemed to swirl, and she gritted her teeth, fighting for control.

'No, you bitch! No! We do what I want!' He could see her fists clenched, ready to strike out at the thing that was within her, then with no further hesitation, she climbed gracefully onto the table and held her arms out to him.

Shedding his robe and his trousers, he followed her, intensely excited despite the strangeness and the danger. As Michiko softly intoned words in a language he didn't think was even Japanese, it seemed like the simplest thing in the world to move between Paula's warm thighs and enter her. For a few seconds, the old qualms about unprotected sex flitted through his mind, but those considerations seemed a thousand miles away now, and the least of their problems.

Immediately and sweetly, she coiled her arms around him, pressing upwards, moulding her belly to his, matching her sigil to its inverted mate on his skin. For a few moments, they lay joined, still and quiet. Was anything happening? Where was the magic? All seemed normal, or as normal as it was possible to be when you were fucking your lover in an abandoned chapel, before an audience.

But then, simultaneously, the air seemed to crackle and Paula began to moan and thrash, her face twisting in alternating grimaces of anger and distress. Around his penis, she felt like a furnace, hot and volatile, her flesh rippling as if in orgasm.

'No! No! No!' she ground out, struggling in his grip, then letting fly with a stream of foul obscenities and incomprehensible growls of rage. Rafe tried to look into her face, to see who he was lying with – his beloved, or her nemesis – but Paula's eyes were rolled up in her sockets, just the whites visible and shining fluorescently.

Dimly he felt the cool hand of Michiko at the small of his back. She pressed on his spine, grinding some faintly gritty substance into his skin, and yet at the same time drawing upon him, her touch electric and tingling like a magnet.

Astonishingly, and against his conscious will, he felt his body gather for climax, his loins jerking, ready to ejaculate and fling his semen forth.

And then he heard it, not the fierce cries of the woman beneath him, not the oaths, not the strange high hum of some kind of electrical field gathering around their joined bodies and the stinging heat that burnt his painted belly.

No, it was an angry, bitter litany of protest and threat and menace that suddenly seemed to echo right inside his skull. In that instant he understood the horror of what his beloved had been subjected to, and as his body seemed to orgasm at a distance, experiencing a pleasure that was almost pain and nothing holy, he felt her surge and jerk beneath him as that awful presence left her.

Paula reached her peak, then collapsed away beneath him, limp and spent. And inside his mind the scream of fury rose to a crescendo.

Lifting himself clear of the stunned woman beneath him, he flung himself back on the table, hugging his own naked chest, holding the invasion within himself, separating himself from Paula's body and setting her free.

'It's just you and me, bitch,' he growled, closing his eyes tight and seeing a green-eyed vision of hate behind his lids. 'Just you and me, cunt, and you're going down . . . You're going down. You're going *down*!'

Still panting, still sweating, Paula hauled herself upright and turned to Rafe, then blanched in horror.

Even so soon after their hot, furious coupling, he was as white as a sheet, his face working furiously and his teeth clenched as he fought with what had been inside her. Perspiration slid down his cheek and pooled in the hollow of his throat. The battle was titanic, far harder than it had ever been for her. She grabbed his hand, but he shook her off with a rough, frantic jerk.

'No, love! Get away from me now. Please stay clear. Please stay safe!'

This is what it feels like when your heart starts breaking, thought Paula, sliding off the table then staggering back. In a swift movement, Oren enveloped her in a soft blanket, then, looking at her only briefly but worriedly, he surged forwards and joined Michiko and Balthazar around her beloved. Paula clapped her hand over her mouth, holding in a cry of anguish. They had work to do. They couldn't worry about her right now.

Rafe began to writhe and shout, flinging out incoherent blasphemous growls. He jack-knifed upright and whipped back his hand to aim a blow at Michiko. But before he could land it, Oren and Balthazar, enormous men both, had thrown their weight on him and manhandled him back down onto the table. With hands that were swift and deft and far, far stronger than they looked, Michiko secured him with conveniently placed leather straps, almost flying around the table, sure-footed on her towering geisha clogs, even though the stone flags of the chapel floor were uneven.

'I might have known it was you!' bellowed Isidora, deforming Rafe's vocal cords into an approximation of her own shrill angry tones. 'Von Kastel's whore! Treacherous bitch, you were always jealous of me, weren't you, you cunt?'

It's like *The Exorcist*, thought Paula, terrified.

And suddenly it was even more like that famous terrifying film.

Michiko impassively ignored yet another torrent of obscene abuse and, as she returned to the lectern and began another soft, clear chant from the pages of the grimoire, the temperature in the chapel plummeted in an instant. Paula clutched the blanket around herself as gooseflesh rose painfully on her body, and her breath and that of the others grew misty. The only hot things in the entire space were the twin burning green orbs of Rafe/Isidora's eyes, and the marker on his belly that was glowing red now, like a fresh brand.

'No! No! No!'

Paula wasn't sure whether it was she who'd shouted or the evil creature still trapped inside her shackled lover. But Michiko suddenly said 'Yes' in English then returned seamlessly to her arcane and rhythmic chant. Rafe began to struggle even harder, making the table creak and groan, and Paula's eyes widened when she realised the cause of the wildly renewed struggling.

Balthazar was priming a hypodermic, Oren holding a thick black cushion in both hands.

The chill around the table seemed to increase exponentially and the roar of rage that rose from it made what was left of the windows rattle and shatter. Undeterred, Balthazar plunged the needle directly into Rafe's jugular. As he stepped back, Oren moved forwards with his innocuous-looking but still deadly cushion.

Paula did cry out now, but the sounds that echoed in her own ears were distorted and drawn out as if time were running at half speed.

Rafe arched and jerked on the table, kicking and struggling for a few moments until the drug and the denial of oxygen took him. As his body went slack and he lay motionless, Oren still kept the cushion firmly in place.

All was silent. All was strange. Paula felt on the verge of collapse, but still stayed upright, her heart screaming, her higher mental functions almost as blank as Rafe's now were.

For what seemed eternity, the silence stretched on, but then, faintly at first and then gradually louder and louder, an odd, buzzing static roar of a sound gathered in the chapel. As Michiko began to chant again, it seemed to centre on a spot halfway down the aisle and radiate outwards, charging the air. Paula felt a sensation of suction, although there was no physical wind at all, and her hair seemed to be starting out from her head. She gasped as a spot of vague, fuzzy blackness formed at the source of the ever-loudening sound, then seemed to grow, circling and spinning like a vortex.

Then another sound rang out, layering itself over the strange, almost electronic drone. An agonised wail of terror and anger and despair. Paula spun towards Rafe's prone body.

He seemed to be floating up in his restraints, as if caught in a static field, and, as Paula watched, a thick yet misty green light formed about his mouth, his eyes and ears, even his cock. Most of all it hovered over his belly, where the sigil was and, slowly at first, then faster and faster it condensed in a flickering mass.

No! No! No!

The silent scream echoed out and, as it did, the green light narrowed, elongated and shot away from Rafe's abdomen, streaking through the frigid air of the chapel, straight past Paula, and then disappeared into the black whirling void.

The instant it had all passed, there was a loud pop, and Paula felt the same kind of inner-ear equalisation sensation as she would have done in an aeroplane at altitude.

There was one second, perhaps two, of absolute calm, then the watchers around the table swung into instant, frenzied action.

No horror movie now, but a scene from an A&E department, an operating theatre, a major accident. Only with the added extra of a chanting Japanese sorceress.

Totally focused, Balthazar began cardio-pulmonary resuscitation, counting aloud as he pounded on Rafe's chest with the heels of his hands, his arms out straight, while Oren worked around him attaching Rafe to various monitors. Paula knew nothing of the detail of what they were doing, but the hideously flat green line on the small black screen made her want to wail and compel it to jump by pure force of will.

More CPR. More ventilation. More CPR. More ventilation. Paula's own heart felt as if it were being crushed and twisted.

And then . . .

'Got something,' shouted out Balthazar. 'I'm going to shock him.' He slapped the paddles of a cardiac defibrillator flush against Rafe's chest. A moment later, the surgeon cried, 'Clear!' and Rafe's inert body jerked violently on the table. After the shock, Oren slid an oxygen mask over her lover's chalky-pale face.

Mute with horror, Paula watched the procedures repeated again, then again, then again. Injections given, to no apparent effect. Her teeth were chattering with the icy cold, and she could barely think, but on some deep level she registered that the low temperature was beneficial for Rafe. Didn't cooling help slow brain damage in those who were clinically dead? That was why Michiko was chanting – to keep the chapel unnaturally chilly and give Rafe the best possible chance of a full recovery.

'Clear!' intoned Balthazar.

Rafe's body leapt up from the table, then settled back, lifeless.

The surgeon listened with his stethoscope, frowning. Paula's own heart lurched as she saw him lift his shoulders in a helpless shrug and glance at Michiko.

'No! Try again! Give him a chance!'

Almost losing her blanket, Paula flew across the space to where Rafe lay. His skin was waxy and his lips were bluish. He looked gone, lost, extinct. She reached for him but Oren gently held her back while the defibrillator charged, and they went through the whole gruesome process of shocking Rafe all over again.

With the same result. No rhythm. Balthazar looked at her sadly, no hope left in his weary eyes.

Anger, crazy and irrational, boiled in Paula's chest. Forgetting her blanket altogether, she scrambled onto the table, crouched alongside Rafe and pounded wildly on his chest.

'How dare you leave me! How dare you give up! Live, you coward, live! You owe it to me!' She thumped and thumped, barely aware that she'd shouted out loud at him. He was going to be bruised black and blue when she'd finished with him, but he had to live.

All of sudden, Rafe began to cough, gasp, drag in breath. Oren lifted Paula back off the table to give Balthazar room to work.

The next few minutes were agonising as Paula watched the big surgeon give Rafe a couple more injections, listen to his heart repeatedly, take his pulse, peel up his eyelids and check his pupils. She grabbed her blanket and huddled in it, even though the moment Rafe had started coughing the ambient temperature had started to rise again. The chapel was deliciously warm now, thanks to Michiko's spells.

Then Rafe's eyes opened naturally and, as he flexed his hand and arm, reaching, Oren released him from the straps that still held him.

When Rafe's fingers found Paula's, they gripped tight and held on.

'Are you all right, love?' His voice was faint and reedy, but, when he smiled, his eyes were bright and lucid. She leant over him, her tears of thankfulness dropping down onto the bare skin of his chest in between the sticky pads and wires.

'I'm fine, you idiot, how are you?'

'OK, I think,' he wheezed, trying to sit up, not quite achieving it, before having Oren let him gently back down.

Rafe blinked, shook his head, reached up and rubbed

his face. Caught by the action, Paula's eyes widened. Good grief, what had happened?

Rafe no longer had a few grey-haired streaks at his temples. His entire head of hair had turned white in the space of a few minutes. Although no one but she seemed to have noticed yet.

'Yeah, I'm fine . . .' His voice was still thin, but already sounded stronger. 'I think I've got all my marbles still. And no mental lodgers as far as I can tell.'

'Thank God for that!' She flung herself over him, wound her arms around him and buried her face in his neck. He smelt good, warm, real. As his arms came around her, she sobbed with happiness and breathed him in, savouring the simple fact he was alive, and the two of them were just two now.

The soft sound of clapping broke them apart and, as Paula drew back and Rafe sat up shakily, they looked around to see Michiko, Balthazar and Oren applauding, smiles on all of their faces.

'She's gone now. I can't sense her at all,' said the Japanese woman with satisfaction, then she reached over and tweaked down the blanket that Oren had flung over Rafe's hips while he and Balthazar had been working. The ink of his painted sigil had flaked away to a fine dust, and when she blew on it delicately it drifted away to leave his belly quite unmarked. Similarly, when Paula exposed the matching area on her own abdomen, there was nothing there, just her skin, pale and smooth.

'All gone now, love,' whispered Rafe, inclining towards her, resting his forehead against hers. 'Just us now . . . just us . . .' He sagged against her, and she felt him try to fight his weakness.

'Yes, just us,' she confirmed, sliding her arms tight around him and supporting his weight. 'And you need to rest, my love. You need to rest.'

Ah, the inner silence was lovely. Just her now and the man she loved, for as long as they'd got.

16 Aftermath

'How can you possibly want to shag a white-haired old ruin like me?' Rafe gasped, laughing, as he levered himself off Paula and rolled to one side, his arm still possessively across her belly.

'Quite easily,' Paula panted back at him, her body still glowing, her sex still fluttering and alight with after-shocks. 'Because you're not an old ruin, you have the body of a buffed young stud, and your new hair is gorgeous.'

She turned towards him, reached up and swept her fingers across his short pale hair. It was beautiful, a soft creamy white, dusted with gold, like silver-gilt. It was strange and erotic, and it had an almost alien quality that seemed to turn her on all over again.

But that didn't surprise her. In the three days since the expulsion of Isidora, her thoughts and her urges had turned constantly to sex. It was as if the sorceress had left her erotic appetite behind when she'd gone. Except instead of being dark and manipulative, it was sweet, fine, blatantly lustful and a joyous celebration of life.

Rafe had died and come back again, and the way to affirm that seemed to make love over and over again.

I wasn't even all that interested in sex until she moved in, thought Paula. *But now I'm mad for it.*

She wasn't complaining though. She couldn't think of anything better. And if Rafe did have to go again, and sooner rather than later, she was going to give him the best possible time while he was in a fit state to enjoy it.

And yet she still couldn't believe he was doomed. His body was marvellous, fit, full of life. He'd obviously always been a man who took care of his physical condition, and his ordeal didn't seem to have affected him other than the hair thing – and the bruises that still lingered on his chest from the CPR and her fists.

'If you say so, love,' he said easily, watching her as she still stroked his hair compulsively. 'And I suppose this is better than just the grey bits I had before.' He grinned. 'Maybe I could dye it? I could ask Hiro. He's a hairdresser among other things. He could probably give me some advice as to what colour to go.'

'No! I like it like this! It's glorious.'

Rafe's arms snaked around her, pulling her closer. 'In that case it stays.' She felt his cock harden again, and it was her turn to smile. Rafe's libido had taken a revivifying jolt just the way hers had.

Half crawling on top of him, she was reminded of the sight of him prone on that table, and a question she'd been wanting to ask sprang from her lips, finally escaping her qualms about posing it.

'Rafe, when you were, you know, when you were "gone", was there anything there? What did you feel? Did you see a white light to go towards and all that stuff?'

He looked up at her, his eyes clear and brown. Almost tranquil.

'No white lights. Nothing concrete at all, really ... It's hard to describe it.' He blinked, and suddenly his eyes seemed more shiny, as if tears were forming. 'I only know I was OK. And I wasn't scared. Because you were there.'

He rested his hand against her face, the tips of his fingers warm and real and alive. 'It was like a place out of time and you were already there waiting for me. Does that make sense?'

'Yes, perfectly.' She plunged in for a kiss, her own eyes swimming. Everything she believed and wanted and loved beautifully confirmed.

The wild sweet tide of sex was rising again, but it was love that bore her up on it. She'd found her man, and he'd found her, and whether they had months or years or decades, they were together.

Epilogue

Paula watched as Rafe dialled the number.

They were sitting outside a café bar across from the Raven, enjoying a cappuccino in the Indian-summer sunshine. The afternoon was idyllic, they both had a day off work, and they'd spent most of the morning in bed, making love.

But this afternoon, there was a truth to be faced, and somehow it seemed important to be out of the flat to face the news.

It was three weeks since their strange sabbatical at Sedgewick Priory, and to Paula at least it seemed like yesterday, and yet the same time in another world. The whole interlude had been like a dream, sometimes bad, very bad, but sometimes good.

She'd been possessed by what amounted to a demon, but she'd also found the man she loved.

They'd stayed over a week at the Priory, and funnily enough it had turned out to be the holiday that she and Belinda and Jonathan had originally planned, only with a whole lot of delicious, unforeseen extras. An idyll of sun-kissed luxury in a gorgeous house, eating, drinking, laughing, roaming around the gorgeous park and swimming in the river. And of course, when they were alone, having ridiculous amounts of deliciously experimental sex. She still got a hot flutter every time she thought of some of the outrageous things she and Rafe had got up to, but the best thing about it was that, when the bedroom door closed, it was just the two of them. No subversive third party in her mind.

But eventually the party had broken up. Michiko had left for London, with Hiro *and* Balthazar. The mechanics of that particular relationship were intriguing. Especially when it had become apparent they were all sharing the same room. And the same bed.

Belinda and Jonathan left when she and Rafe had finally hit the road. Her friend had finally got back to normal. Belinda's eyes were hazel again and she was keeping the same hours as everyone else. Maybe it was because Isidora was finally completely gone and the natural equilibrium had normalised? Michiko seemed to think so, but Belinda had said she didn't really care as long as she was just an average woman with an average life again.

Only Oren and his two female companions remained at Sedgewick now, holding stewardship of the beautiful house and keeping it ready for any of the party to return for a holiday.

And now, at last, she waited for the final cloud of doubt to be resolved one way or another.

'Time I stopped being a coward,' Rafe had said. 'It's not fair to you, and I can't keep living in limbo, not knowing how long I've got.'

'Whatever happens, don't forget, you're stuck with me,' Paula had replied, as her lover had picked up the phone to make a hospital appointment.

And now, here they were. Waiting for the results.

Rafe's face was set and intent as he listened. The

tension was unbearable, and the sweet balmy, late summer's day seemed to freeze as if not just their lives, but all life was on hold until the answer came. Paula catalogued every detail of his face. His fine brown eyes, his strong jaw, his sensual mouth and his dazzling hair, white gold and shining in the sun.

The moments of waiting went on and on, and still Rafe didn't speak.

But suddenly there were changes, and her heart flew.

His eyes widened, a smile curved his lips, he let out the breath he'd been holding. And suddenly he was saying, 'Thank you, thank you, thank you . . .' into the phone.

Paula threw herself sideways in her seat and flung her arms around him, kissing the side of his face, his cheek and his neck while he was still speaking to the doctor on the other end of the line.

Eventually he snapped the phone shut, threw it down and kissed her. Hard. For at least a minute and laughing at the same time.

'All clear, love! All clear,' he announced, grinning from ear to ear as they broke apart, dimly aware of all eyes in the open-air café being upon them. 'But the bad news is that you really are stuck with me for the duration of my three score and ten now.'

'*That* . . . is good news!' Paula couldn't stop smiling, her lips curving into a silly grin of her own. And that wasn't the only physical phenomena she couldn't control. She glanced quickly across the road to the Raven and the entrance to a certain alley that ran behind it. 'And I think we should celebrate. Immediately. Don't you?'

Rafe followed her glance, and chuckled and shook his head.

'Back where we first *met*, eh?' He slid his hand over the side of her face, his fingertips curving so softly and seductively that Paula seemed to feel the subtle caress of them between her legs. 'I'm all for it. Although I must say I had something else in mind first.'

Paula pulled back a little. Confused, but happy.

'What were you thinking of?'

'Well, I thought we might go in there.' He nodded towards the entrance to the town's main shopping precinct, further up the road. 'And find ourselves a jeweller's maybe? Do you get my drift?'

She got it. 'Oh my God! I didn't think you were so conventional, Rafe.' She laughed and gave him a smacker of a kiss on the cheek. 'Not that I'm complaining.'

'So? What's it to be?' Rafe rose to his feet, drawing her up too and sliding his arm around her waist. 'Ring?' Eyes twinkling, he put his lips to her ear. 'Or wild sex against a wall in an alley?'

'*Both*,' replied Paula firmly, turning her face to his and stealing another searing kiss.

But as her heart swelled with happiness and the heat of desire pooled low and heavy in her belly, it was towards the Raven that she led her beloved first.

Visit the Black Lace website at
www.black-lace-books.com

LOOK OUT FOR THE ALL-NEW BLACK LACE BOOKS – AVAILABLE NOW!

All books priced £7.99 in the UK. Please note publication dates apply to the UK only. For other territories, please contact your retailer.

GEMINI HEAT
Portia Da Costa
ISBN 978 0 352 34187 7

As the metropolis sizzles in the freak early summer temperatures, identical twin sisters Deana and Delia Ferraro are cooking up a heat wave of their own. Surrounded by an atmosphere of relentless humidity, Deana and Delia find themselves rivals for the attentions of Jackson de Guile, an exotic, wealthy entrepreneur and master of power dynamics who draws them both into a web of luxurious debauchery. The erotic encounters become increasingly bizarre as the twins vie for the rewards that pleasuring him brings them – tainted rewards which only serve to confuse their perceptions of the limits of sexual experience.

THE NEW BLACK LACE BOOK OF WOMEN'S SEXUAL FANTASIES
Edited and compiled by Mitzi Szereto
ISBN 978 0 352 34172 3

The second anthology of detailed sexual fantasies contributed by women from all over the world. The book is a result of a year's research by an expert on erotic writing and gives a fascinating insight into the rich diversity of the female sexual imagination.

To be published in May 2008

BLACK ORCHID
Roxanne Carr
ISBN 978 0 352 34188 4

At the Black Orchid Club, adventurous women who yearn for the pleasures of exotic, even kinky sex can quench their desires in discreet and luxurious surroundings. Having tasted the fulfilment of unique and powerful lusts, one such adventurous woman learns what happens when the need for limitless indulgence becomes an addiction.

CHILLI HEAT
Carrie Williams
ISBN 978 0 352 34178 5

Let down by her travelling companion at short notice, Nadia Kapur reluctantly agrees to take her recently divorced mother, Valerie, on her gap-year trip to India. However, her mother turns out to be anything but the conservative presence she had feared. As the two women explore India's most exotic locations, it is Valerie who experiences a sexual reawakening with a succession of lovers and Nadia who is forced to wrestle with her own inhibitions and repressed desires. The landscape and the people ultimately work their transforming magic on both mother and daughter, causing Valerie to think again about her ex-husband and tempting Nadia with the possibility of true love.

MAGIC AND DESIRE
Portia Da Costa, Janine Ashbless, Olivia Knight
ISBN 978 0 352 34183 9

The third BL paranormal novella collection. Three top authors writing three otherwordly short novels of fantasy and sorcery.

Ill Met By Moonlight: Can it be possible that a handsome stranger met by moonlight is a mischievous fairy set out to sample a taste of human love and passion? But what will happen when the magic witching month of May is over? When he loses his human form will he lose his memories of her as well?

The House Of Dust: The king is dead. But the queen cannot grieve until she's had vengeance. Ishara must descend into the Underworld and brave its challenges in order to bring her lover back from the dead.

The Dragon Lord: In the misty marshlands of Navarone, the princess is being married. Her parents desperately hope this will cure her 'problem', which they have fought to keep secret for years. Her 'problem' has always been her tendency to play with fire – she lights fires in the grate with her eyes when no one is looking and she is lustful in a land of rigid morality.

To be published in June 2008

SOUTHERN SPIRITS
Edie Bingham
ISBN 978 0 352 34180 8

When hot-tempered Federal agent Catalina 'Cat' Montoya is partnered with her former lover Nathan Ames on her first undercover investigation, she is determined not to let feelings get in the way of work. But the investigation into charismatic criminal Jack Wheeler's latest enterprise – Southern Spirits Tours, an exclusive members club on a supposedly haunted luxury train, the Silver Belle – soon envelops her in a passionate love triangle. As she travels through the most haunted areas of the Deep South, where sex mixes with the supernatural, Cat surrenders to the extremes of erotic experience and is finally forced to solve a fifty-year-old murder mystery.

FORBIDDEN FRUIT
Susie Raymond
ISBN 978 0 352 34189 1

The last thing sexy thirty-something Beth expected was to get involved with a sixteen-year-old. But when she finds him spying on her in the dressing room at work she embarks on an erotic journey with the straining youth, teaching him and teasing him as she leads him through myriad sensuous exercises at her stylish modern home. As their lascivious games become more and more intense, Beth soon begins to realise that she is the one being awakened to a new world of desire – and that hers is the mind quickly becoming consumed with lust.

Black Lace Booklist

Information is correct at time of printing. To avoid disappointment, check availability before ordering. Go to www.black-lace-books.com.
All books are priced £7.99 unless another price is given.

BLACK LACE BOOKS WITH A CONTEMPORARY SETTING

❏ THE ANGELS' SHARE Maya Hess	ISBN 978 0 352 34043 6
❏ ASKING FOR TROUBLE Kristina Lloyd	ISBN 978 0 352 33362 9
❏ THE BLUE GUIDE Carrie Williams	ISBN 978 0 352 34132 7
❏ THE BOSS Monica Belle	ISBN 978 0 352 34088 7
❏ BOUND IN BLUE Monica Belle	ISBN 978 0 352 34012 2
❏ CAMPAIGN HEAT Gabrielle Marcola	ISBN 978 0 352 33941 6
❏ CAT SCRATCH FEVER Sophie Mouette	ISBN 978 0 352 34021 4
❏ CIRCUS EXCITE Nikki Magennis	ISBN 978 0 352 34033 7
❏ CONFESSIONAL Judith Roycroft	ISBN 978 0 352 33421 3
❏ CONTINUUM Portia Da Costa	ISBN 978 0 352 33120 5
❏ DANGEROUS CONSEQUENCES Pamela Rochford	ISBN 978 0 352 33185 4
❏ DARK DESIGNS Madelynne Ellis	ISBN 978 0 352 34075 7
❏ THE DEVIL INSIDE Portia Da Costa	ISBN 978 0 352 32993 6
❏ EQUAL OPPORTUNITIES Mathilde Madden	ISBN 978 0 352 34070 2
❏ FIRE AND ICE Laura Hamilton	ISBN 978 0 352 33486 2
❏ GONE WILD Maria Eppie	ISBN 978 0 352 33670 5
❏ HOTBED Portia Da Costa	ISBN 978 0 352 33614 9
❏ IN PURSUIT OF ANNA Natasha Rostova	ISBN 978 0 352 34060 3
❏ IN THE FLESH Emma Holly	ISBN 978 0 352 34117 4
❏ LEARNING TO LOVE IT Alison Tyler	ISBN 978 0 352 33535 7
❏ MAD ABOUT THE BOY Mathilde Madden	ISBN 978 0 352 34001 6
❏ MAKE YOU A MAN Anna Clare	ISBN 978 0 352 34006 1
❏ MAN HUNT Cathleen Ross	ISBN 978 0 352 33583 8
❏ THE MASTER OF SHILDEN Lucinda Carrington	ISBN 978 0 352 33140 3
❏ MS BEHAVIOUR Mini Lee	ISBN 978 0 352 33962 1
❏ PAGAN HEAT Monica Belle	ISBN 978 0 352 33974 4
❏ PEEP SHOW Mathilde Madden	ISBN 978 0 352 33924 9

- THE POWER GAME Carrera Devonshire — ISBN 978 0 352 33990 4
- THE PRIVATE UNDOING OF A PUBLIC SERVANT Leonie Martel — ISBN 978 0 352 34066 5
- RUDE AWAKENING Pamela Kyle — ISBN 978 0 352 33036 9
- SAUCE FOR THE GOOSE Mary Rose Maxwell — ISBN 978 0 352 33492 3
- SPLIT Kristina Lloyd — ISBN 978 0 352 34154 9
- STELLA DOES HOLLYWOOD Stella Black — ISBN 978 0 352 33588 3
- THE STRANGER Portia Da Costa — ISBN 978 0 352 33211 0
- SUITE SEVENTEEN Portia Da Costa — ISBN 978 0 352 34109 9
- TONGUE IN CHEEK Tabitha Flyte — ISBN 978 0 352 33484 8
- THE TOP OF HER GAME Emma Holly — ISBN 978 0 352 34116 7
- UNNATURAL SELECTION Alaine Hood — ISBN 978 0 352 33963 8
- VELVET GLOVE Emma Holly — ISBN 978 0 352 34115 0
- VILLAGE OF SECRETS Mercedes Kelly — ISBN 978 0 352 33344 5
- WILD CARD Madeline Moore — ISBN 978 0 352 34038 2
- WING OF MADNESS Mae Nixon — ISBN 978 0 352 34099 3

BLACK LACE BOOKS WITH AN HISTORICAL SETTING

- THE BARBARIAN GEISHA Charlotte Royal — ISBN 978 0 352 33267 7
- BARBARIAN PRIZE Deanna Ashford — ISBN 978 0 352 34017 7
- THE CAPTIVATION Natasha Rostova — ISBN 978 0 352 33234 9
- DARKER THAN LOVE Kristina Lloyd — ISBN 978 0 352 33279 0
- WILD KINGDOM Deanna Ashford — ISBN 978 0 352 33549 4
- DIVINE TORMENT Janine Ashbless — ISBN 978 0 352 33719 1
- FRENCH MANNERS Olivia Christie — ISBN 978 0 352 33214 1
- LORD WRAXALL'S FANCY Anna Lieff Saxby — ISBN 978 0 352 33080 2
- NICOLE'S REVENGE Lisette Allen — ISBN 978 0 352 29984 4
- THE SOCIETY OF SIN Sian Lacey Taylder — ISBN 978 0 352 34080 1
- TEMPLAR PRIZE Deanna Ashford — ISBN 978 0 352 34137 2
- UNDRESSING THE DEVIL Angel Strand — ISBN 978 0 352 33938 6

BLACK LACE BOOKS WITH A PARANORMAL THEME

- BRIGHT FIRE Maya Hess — ISBN 978 0 352 34104 4
- BURNING BRIGHT Janine Ashbless — ISBN 978 0 352 34085 6
- CRUEL ENCHANTMENT Janine Ashbless — ISBN 978 0 352 33483 1

☐ FLOOD Anna Clare ISBN 978 0 352 34094 8
☐ GOTHIC BLUE Portia Da Costa ISBN 978 0 352 33075 8
☐ THE PRIDE Edie Bingham ISBN 978 0 352 33997 3
☐ THE SILVER COLLAR Mathilde Madden ISBN 978 0 352 34141 9
☐ THE TEN VISIONS Olivia Knight ISBN 978 0 352 34119 8

BLACK LACE ANTHOLOGIES

☐ BLACK LACE QUICKIES 1 Various ISBN 978 0 352 34126 6 £2.99
☐ BLACK LACE QUICKIES 2 Various ISBN 978 0 352 34127 3 £2.99
☐ BLACK LACE QUICKIES 3 Various ISBN 978 0 352 34128 0 £2.99
☐ BLACK LACE QUICKIES 4 Various ISBN 978 0 352 34129 7 £2.99
☐ BLACK LACE QUICKIES 5 Various ISBN 978 0 352 34130 3 £2.99
☐ BLACK LACE QUICKIES 6 Various ISBN 978 0 352 34133 4 £2.99
☐ BLACK LACE QUICKIES 7 Various ISBN 978 0 352 34146 4 £2.99
☐ BLACK LACE QUICKIES 8 Various ISBN 978 0 352 34147 1 £2.99
☐ BLACK LACE QUICKIES 9 Various ISBN 978 0 352 34155 6 £2.99
☐ MORE WICKED WORDS Various ISBN 978 0 352 33487 9 £6.99
☐ WICKED WORDS 3 Various ISBN 978 0 352 33522 7 £6.99
☐ WICKED WORDS 4 Various ISBN 978 0 352 33603 3 £6.99
☐ WICKED WORDS 5 Various ISBN 978 0 352 33642 2 £6.99
☐ WICKED WORDS 6 Various ISBN 978 0 352 33690 3 £6.99
☐ WICKED WORDS 7 Various ISBN 978 0 352 33743 6 £6.99
☐ WICKED WORDS 8 Various ISBN 978 0 352 33787 0 £6.99
☐ WICKED WORDS 9 Various ISBN 978 0 352 33860 0
☐ WICKED WORDS 10 Various ISBN 978 0 352 33893 8
☐ THE BEST OF BLACK LACE 2 Various ISBN 978 0 352 33718 4
☐ WICKED WORDS: SEX IN THE OFFICE Various ISBN 978 0 352 33944 7
☐ WICKED WORDS: SEX AT THE SPORTS CLUB Various ISBN 978 0 352 33991 1
☐ WICKED WORDS: SEX ON HOLIDAY Various ISBN 978 0 352 33961 4
☐ WICKED WORDS: SEX IN UNIFORM Various ISBN 978 0 352 34002 3
☐ WICKED WORDS: SEX IN THE KITCHEN Various ISBN 978 0 352 34018 4
☐ WICKED WORDS: SEX ON THE MOVE Various ISBN 978 0 352 34034 4
☐ WICKED WORDS: SEX AND MUSIC Various ISBN 978 0 352 34061 0
☐ WICKED WORDS: SEX AND SHOPPING Various ISBN 978 0 352 34076 4
☐ SEX IN PUBLIC Various ISBN 978 0 352 34089 4

☐ SEX WITH STRANGERS Various   ISBN 978 0 352 34105 1
☐ LOVE ON THE DARK SIDE Various   ISBN 978 0 352 34132 7
☐ LUST BITES Various   ISBN 978 0 352 34153 2

BLACK LACE NON-FICTION

☐ THE BLACK LACE BOOK OF WOMEN'S SEXUAL   ISBN 978 0 352 33793 1   £6.99
     FANTASIES Edited by Kerri Sharp

To find out the latest information about Black Lace titles, check out the website: www.black-lace-books.com or send for a booklist with complete synopses by writing to:

     Black Lace Booklist, Virgin Books Ltd
     Thames Wharf Studios
     Rainville Road
     London W6 9HA

Please include an SAE of decent size. Please note only British stamps are valid.

Our privacy policy
We will not disclose information you supply us to any other parties. We will not disclose any information which identifies you personally to any person without your express consent.

From time to time we may send out information about Black Lace books and special offers. Please tick here if you do <u>not</u> wish to receive Black Lace information.   ☐